And it All Falls Down

Martina M. Lanier

Title: And it All Falls Down

Writers Kornered Publishing The Healing Woman023 LLC

ISBN: 978-1-7372257-2-0

Books can be purchased in bulk by emailing

WritersKornered@gmail.com

Synopsis

36-year-old Jason Walsh is handsome, witty, and one of his town's top criminal defense lawyers. Jason has the wife of his dreams and couldn't be happier, that is until the skeletons he buried deep in his closet start crawling out to be seen. With his secrets on the front line, he has to figure out how to keep it all together before it all falls down. Just how far is he willing to go to maintain his perfect image and keep his family together?

From the outside looking in, Tamera Walsh has it all. She has a fine, successful husband, the most brilliant set of twin boys, and a lifestyle others envy. But that's not enough. Tired of supporting everybody else and their dreams, Tamera decides that she's ready to get back out in the world and shake it up. The only problem is her husband prefers her at home raising their children. Choosing to go against his wishes, she has to decide if her dreams and goals are worth losing the only family she has.

Growing up with a praying family and feeling loss after loss, Lynn gave up on God and decided to live life the way she wanted instead. If God didn't give her what she wanted, she would take it and not care who got hurt in the process. Just when Lynn thinks she has it all, something happens, bringing her to her knees, and she wonders if it's too late to finally start leaning on God.

A WORD FROM THE AUTHOR.

I want to thank everyone in advance for reading this book. I pray every night that my book is not only used for personal enjoyment but that some of the things my characters endure can be used as therapy for someone else. I don't create any characters who I look at as the bad person. Every character of mine has a story, a trauma, one that they had to grow from. Being an advocate of therapy, I aim for growth in all of my stories. So you will always see everyone elevate and become better than how they started.

I want to thank my babies, my three daughters, for sticking with mommy when mommy worked all morning and then got off of work and then had to work on her books. You guys are so loving and patient, and I thank God for blessing me with the most perfect beings.

Thank you to all my family who served as a voting tool for me and helping me to decide on things like a title, to my cover for my book. You are appreciated.

Thank you to my beta readers and my friend who bought an editing program for me without me having to ask, and everyone who has supported me through this whole ordeal, and I hope that you all stay on this journey with me until the wheels fall off!

TRIGGER WARNING*

A trigger warning is a statement made before sharing potentially disturbing content.

In this book, there will be moments where these topics are mentioned: ex, Drug overdose, Mental disorders, rape, miscarriage, religion, suicide

This book is fiction and is not based on any person(s). Any name or instance that may relate to you or anyone is just purely coincidental.

TABLE OF CONTENTS

CHAPTER 1
TAMARA

I rolled my eyes and sat back on the bed in disgust, reading a text; another night, my husband had to work late at the office. I understand lawyers have many cases, but damn, what's the point of the paralegal if you're still there all night and can never spend time with your family? This situation was getting old, and I was more fed up than I wasn't. I was bored with being a stay-at-home mom. I had no friends, and I missed my husband. I was missing his kisses, his touching, and his loving.

Ok, wake me up when you get in. I love you. I sent a text back before sitting the phone on the nightstand.

I never thought I'd get a doctorate in psychology just for me to stay at home and not use it. Don't get me wrong, I love my boys, but I want more out of my life. I want to come home and discuss my day with my husband, too. Have my late nights at work, or be able to help people as I intended to do so all my life. I walked out of my room and peeked in the twins' room, and smiled, watching them snore, sleeping on their backs with the covers pulled over their heads. At six years old, Josh and Johan were a force to be reckoned with. They were obnoxiously intelligent and handsome as ever, looking just like their dad with cream-colored skin, reddish-orange curly hair, and hazel eyes like mine.

I ended up falling asleep reading "Little Black Girl Lost 2" just to be awakened by the house phone ringing.

"Hello," I answered groggily.

"Helloooo," I repeated myself at least two more times before realizing nobody was going to say anything. I hung up the phone and looked over at Jason sleeping peacefully, and frowned, wondering why he hadn't woken me up when he came in. My thoughts were interrupted by the sound of a phone vibrating harshly on the nightstand.

"Hello?" I answered his vibrating phone, met with silence. I repeated myself a few more times before I ended the call and grabbed the house phone to see what number had called. Private. I looked in Jason's call log and noticed the only call was from whomever just called was also Private.

"Jason?" I said as I pushed his shoulder closest to me. He mumbled incoherently and remained asleep. I smacked my lips and stormed out of the room before I started yelling. I went and checked on my boys, kissing them both on the forehead before I went into our family room and turned on some pre-recorded shows I hadn't been able to catch up on. Before I knew it, I was out like a light.

"Mommy, Mommy," I awakened to Josh and Johan screaming in my face.

"Yes! Why are you yelling?"

"I couldn't find you!" Johan exclaimed with wide eyes. "Why not in bed?"

"Why not in bed?" I repeated back to him for him to correct his English.

"It's why weren't you in bed!" Josh corrected Johan.

"Whatever! Why weren't you in bed?" Johan asked, mocking Josh.

"I was watching the tv and fell asleep," I yawned, sitting up on the couch. "Where's your dad?"

"He went to work early! Mom, can we please eat pancakes and sausage with eggs and toast and watch cartoons all day since it's Saturday?" Josh asked, pulling on my shirt.

"I'll think about it! Go brush your teeth and take a shower, then come down for breakfast, guys!" I frowned while walking into my room. Why the hell wouldn't Jason wake me up to let me know he was going into the office on a damn Saturday. Weekends are family days. I grabbed my cell phone and walked into the bathroom with my bathrobe, and turned on the shower while dialing Jason.

"Hey Tamara," Jason answered, distracted as he talked to someone in the background.

"Jason, it's Saturday!"

"Yeah, I know I have this big case, and I have to focus on it and get it done, Tamara."

"Weekends are family days, Jason, your children, and I barely see you anymore. That's not fair to us."

"Do you want me to stay home and be a bum to appease my wife? We all don't have millions just sitting in the bank." He snapped.

"Excuse the hell out of me, Jason. I have a damn doctorate I could be putting to use, but instead, my husband decided I should stay home barefoot and fucking pregnant! So please don't talk to me about working! Is it wrong to want to see my husband at least once a week and not while he's sleeping or walking out the damn door!" I was fuming now, pacing the bedroom. "And as far as that "blood money," how dare you?"

Jason sighed and got silent. "I wasn't implying that, baby…I guess this case has me stressed. I'm sorry. I'll be home about two, ok?"

"Fine" I hung up the phone and hopped in the shower. Jason had a bad habit of throwing my money in my face every time I asked him about spending more time at home. At this point, I was sick of asking, and things were about to change.

Jason made it home a few minutes after two; we all watched movies together and made hamburgers and fries. Then, while the boys finished up their shower, Jason and I lay cuddled up in our bed watching reruns of Martin.

"Hello," Jason answered his vibrating phone. He paused and repeated himself once again.

"Hello?" He hung up the phone and looked at me. "That's strange."

"We've been getting private callers for the past few days," I sighed. "They even called your cell phone the other night and didn't say anything."

"Oh really?" He raised his brow and sighed. "The joys of being a lawyer." Before I could respond, Josh and Johan came running into the room full-throttle, jumping on the bed and jumping on Jason for a wrestling session.

CHAPTER 2 JASON

"Daddy, can we go to the park tomorrow?" Josh asked as I tucked him and Johan in bed that night.

"Sure, son."

"Daddy, you don't have to work?" Johan asked sleepily.

"Weekends are for my boys," I replied, kissing them both on the head. "Goodnight, big guys."

"Goodnight." they both replied in unison as I turned off their bedroom light.

I walked into my bedroom and picked up my ringing phone before Tam heard it. She was in the kitchen singing along to Beyonce's "4" album as she did her nightly cleaning.

"Why are you calling me right now, Lynn?"

"You said this was our weekend, Jason," Lynn whined into the phone.

"You told Jayla that you would tuck her in ton-"

"I know what I told her, but what do you expect me to do? Did you forget I have a wife and family?" I snapped.

"Apparently, you forgot you had a family "at home" when you decided to stick your dick in me four years ago and made a baby with me on your "wife," Jason!"

"Yeah, yeah, yeah Lynn, same damn song! I was honest with you from the jump! You knew I was married the day you stepped in my damn office! It was no secret my wife's face is plastered all over my damn office!" I mumbled lowlily, pissed, sick of this same damn argument with Lynn every week.

"Jason, that was a low blow," Lynn whispered with hurt.

"No! What's low is you calling my house all day and night private! So stop the bullshit, Lynn, now! And if you slash my wife's tires again, I'll put you on your ass and out of my damn house, you got that?"

"Jason I-"

"You heard what I said. Cut the shit!" I hung up and threw the phone on the nightstand just as Tamera walked into the room.

"What's wrong, baby? Who was that?" she asked as she stepped out of her jeans.

"Just a client who is hard of hearing," I sighed, eyeing my wife's body as she undressed. She was still as sexy as the day I met her, if not sexier. Her smooth cocoa skin, bedroom slanted eyes, and full lips were enough to drive any man wild. She was all of five foot four with the attitude of a woman twice her size.

"Oh? That sucks. Let them know your wife misses you at home and that you need to spend time with your family so that you won't need a divorce attorney." She teased, walking over to the closet in her bra and thong. I smirked as my dick hardened and got off the bed, starting towards her.

"Who you gonna divorce?" I asked, sneaking up behind her kissing her neck.

"Jason, that's my spot, baby," She moaned.

"Yeah, I know," I continued kissing her neck as I used my hands to pull her thong down. "Now you gonna divorce who?" I asked, sticking my tongue in her ear as I lifted her slightly off her feet, putting two fingers in her juicy pussy.

"Baby, nobody." She moaned as her breathing grew shallow as she looked over her shoulder at me.

"You love me, Tam?" I asked as I used my free hand to pull down my basketball shorts that sprang my dick to life.

"Mmmm hmm," She moaned as I bent her over, pulling my fingers out of her pussy and replacing them with my tongue. I continued sucking and fingering her till I felt her knees getting weak and stuck my dick deep in her as she cried out.

"Shit, I love you." I groaned.

"Baby…Jason…oh"

"Cum with me, Tam." I slowed down and ground into her just as she liked and pressed my palm on her clit. I did that for a few seconds as she moaned, and I felt her pussy swell up and came hard as she squirted all over my dick and thighs, falling against me. We laid in the closet on the floor, both catching our breaths, hugging, enjoying each other's company until the house phone rang—a private call.

The following day..

"Dad, can we get me new baseball cleats?" Johan asked, looking up at me as I strolled into the mall.

"Didn't we just get you new shoes, young man?" Tam asked, picking imaginary lint off his Ralph Lauren vest that he and Josh wore in different colors.

"Those were Jordan's mom. I need baseball shoes," he whined.

"They all go on your feet! What's the difference?" Tam rolled her eyes.

"There's a difference, honey," I interjected. "It's a man thing kinda like you and your shoes…."

"Guess you got a point," She laughed, looking up at me. "Let's go get little Jackie Robinson his "cleats."

We walked around the mall buying necessities for the home and the little guys. I stopped in a tuxedo shop and looked at a few suits I was interested in purchasing while Tam busied herself in another store, probably trying clothes on herself.

"Dad, I have to peeee!" Josh whined, pulling on my pants leg as I paid for the suits I chose.

"Come on, Johan!" I texted Tam, letting her know I was taking the boys to the restroom and I'd meet her in the food court.

"Yeah," I answered my vibrating phone as I waited outside the stalls as the boys handled their business.

"Hey, babe! What are you doing?"

"At the mall with Tamera and the boys."

"Really? I'm at the mall too, where are you?"

"I'm with my wife and sons!" I whispered on the phone.

"Yes! I heard you the first time, love!" She laughed.

"Where's Jayla?"

“Why do you want to see her!” she laughed again.

“Lynn, I swear to Go-“

“Relax…relax, baby. She’s with my mom at church!”

“Goodbye, Lynn!” I hung up the phone just as the boys both ran out of the stalls racing each other to see who could wash their hands fastest.

“Alright, guys, let’s go,” I said as I passed them both some tissue to dry their hands.

“I want pizza!” Josh yelled.

“I want chicken nuggets!” Johan yelled in rebuttal.

“Ok big guys, you both can get-“ my sentence cut short as my words got stuck in my throat as Tam waved me over from the food court to her, where she stood talking to Lynn.

CHAPTER 3
LYNN

I tried my hardest not to smirk at Jason. He had a mixture between amusement and anger on his face as he came towards me and his precious "Tam the Bitch." Those dark eyes of his that Jayla inherited sparkled with anger and I got hypnotized every time I looked at them.

"Baby, look who I ran into inside of The Gap." Tam the Bitch practically shouted across the food court. I don't even know what Jason saw in her. She was short with a big butt, small tits, and stupid big curly hair that needed a damn straightening comb. No wonder Jason stepped out on her ass, I was a tall glass of water with the right amount of ass tits, and I kept my hair short and done every damn week.

"It's good to see you" Jason gave me a phony smile and hug. I wanted to squeeze his ass so bad, just to shake his ass up. But I kept it "cordial."

"Right, I was just up here getting Jayla a few items. Her dad bought me a check, so I'm spending it on her, you know how men are about their "child support." I laughed. Tam the Bitch laughed and high-fived me as if she could relate. Bitch, please! If only you knew your husband was the one paying my child support. Laugh at that.

“How is that beautiful little girl?” Tam the Bitch asked as the twins called out what foods they wanted.

“She is wonderful, and she’s getting so big and beautiful that hair-“

“Baby, Ima take the guys and go order their food. See you, Monday Lynn.” Jason interrupted. I smirked and waved him off.

“Ok, baby,” Tam the Bitch answered him with such a loving fucking smile that it made my damn stomach turn. Then, she turned her attention back towards me. “She is so beautiful I told Jason she looks like she could be his daughter with those eyes and hair.”

“I know right! He jokes about that all the time” I laughed knowing the truth.

“Oh yeah, did Jason tell you we are having a Memorial day picnic? You and Jayla should definitely come!”

“He certainly did not! We would love to come.” Tam the bitch and I talked for a few more minutes and I gathered the information for the picnic and said my goodbyes. By the time I made it back to my car, I had several text messages from Jason and an incoming call.

“Keep fucking with me!”

I smiled as I threw the bag in the back seat and replied. “Now you know I love a challenge!”

I hung up and threw my phone into my bag and pulled out of the mall parking lot with the biggest grin on my face. Jason's time was winding down and my ultimatum was still on the table. His ass either leaves Tam the Bitch or everything will crumble right before his beautiful eyes.

Chapter 4 Jason

"Baby, can you run to Walmart and pick up a new belt for the vacuum? The boys spilled popcorn all over the family room, and I've picked up the majority, but it's those little specks that I can't get," Tam asked as she came into the room.

"Of course, beautiful."

"Thank you, and I love you, baby." She kissed me on the lips.

I stuffed the new vacuum cleaner in the trunk of our SUV and laughed as I pictured Tam fussing at the sight of it. Not my fault Walmart associates are never anywhere to be found. I couldn't find a belt, so I just bought a new vacuum. Problem solved. I got into the car and threw my wallet onto the passenger seat, pausing as the picture of Jayla fell out on the car floor.

"I need to talk with you," Lynn said five years ago as she walked into my office, closing the door behind her. I smirked because that was her code word for sit on my dick. "Is that right?" I pulled her onto my lap.

"No, it's serious this time, Jason." she sighed, moving my head off of her neck.

I sat back and looked at her. "What's up?"

"Jason, I-" She looked away from me, wiping her eyes. I rolled my eyes and sighed in frustration. Not this shit again the "I can't be with you while you're married" speech. "Lynn, not this again, I'm not leav-"

"Jason, I'm pregnant...by you."

I stuffed Jayla's Picture back into my wallet and started the car. Living a double life was taking a toll on me. Making excuses just to find a way out of the house to tuck my daughter in was devastating. Cowardly even. Part of me hated myself for having to sneak around, and the other half of me hated myself for doing this to Tam, knowing she completely put her dreams on hold for me to raise our children and help me follow my dreams. As much as she deserves to know, I'm too selfish to man up and be honest. I'm in too deep, and there was no way to make light of this situation. I set my car alarm and looked around as I got out of my car, walking up to Lynn's front door. I pitied my situation and shook my head as I looked at the hundred thousand dollar house I bought Lynn just so that my daughter could have a safe place to sleep at night.

"I knew you'd come," Lynn said as she yanked the door open before I could even put my key into the lock.

"Don't flatter your-"

"Daddddddyyyyyyyyyyyyyy!" Jayla ran into my arms with her wild curly hair bouncing everywhere. It was amazing how she looked so much like my boys, and at the same time, I hated myself for creating a child so beautiful that I knew Tam wanted herself.

"How has my baby girl been today?" I asked, kissing her forehead as I carried her into her bedroom.

"Good Daddy! I had fun at school today!"

"Did you? What did my princess do at school today?" I asked, tickling her as I placed her into bed.

"I played, and I had lunch!"

"Is THAT ALL?" I asked, making a funny face.

"Yeaaaahhhh" She mirrored my face.

"And you didn't do anything else?" I tickled her.

"NO!" she screamed in laughter.

"Alright, now you two," Lynn said, standing in the bedroom door. "Time for bed, Jayla"

"Indeed it is." I kissed her forehead, and we sang our song "You Are My Sunshine" before tucking her in. "Goodnight. I love you."

"I love you too, Daddy," she said as I closed her bedroom door.

"You could do that every night if you just moved in," Lynn said as she followed me into her foyer.

"Don't you start that shit with me tonight! I'm not leaving my sons."

"Oh! But it's ok for you to leave your daughter?"

"Lynn, I don't know why you sit here and try to guilt me when I was married with children when you met me. I'm tired of this argument with you!"

"Well, I don't care!" she yelled. " Jayla deserves a dad too!"

"And I've been her dad! Who bought this house? Who gives you money regularly for her? Me!"

"Jason, I'm not talking about material shit! I'm talking about a full-time dad, not a part-timer who has to sneak around his bitch of a wi-"

"Don't you disrespect my wife! You'll never be half the woman she is!" I snapped.

"If she's so great, then why are you still fucking me?"

"Men say anything for a piece of ass Lynn; you're thirty-five, and you don't know that yet?"

"Why, why are you trying to hurt me?" She stuttered with tears falling down her face.

"Puh-lease with this bullshit sob story Lynn. You want to place blame and say I did something, yeah ok, I fucked you, I got you pregnant, I had a child out of wedlock, my mistake! But I ain't the only one to blame in this shit. You laid down with me and sucked my dick in my office while staring at my wife's picture, so when it comes to placing blame, you better make sure the shit is fifty fucking fifty."

CHAPTER 5
TAMERA

"Divvaaaaaaaaaaaa!" I yelled out as I hopped out of my blood-red 2021 track hawk as my best friend Aerca (Erica) stepped out her chrome pink G550 dressed in Gucci from head to toe.

"Bitch, I know you are lying rolling in this bitch dripping in Chanel hopping out the brand new hawk!!!" She yelled as we hugged. "I miss you so much, baby!"

"I missed you! You are always on the run." I said as we walked into Capital Grille.

"Now you know I got to get to the bag, sis," Aerca said as she waved her hands over her body. Aerca was the first-generation Haitian from her family living in America. When we first met in the fourth grade, she was fresh from Haiti, barely speaking English. The things she witnessed and went through I would never wish on a child. So when I tell you sis has come a long way and got the bag, BE-LEE-ME!

"I know, love, I get it completely." The hostess showed us to our seats, and we sat down smiling, still passing compliments.

"So what's been up? How're my nephews?"

"Girl! Everything has been up!" I said and paused as our

waitress came over. We both ordered a glass of wine and lemon water. After the waitress left, I continued our conversation. "So I decided to go back into the work field, anddddd I need your help!"

"Aw shit, -I mean, I'm happy to hear that because you've been saying it for so long, but what made you decide this? And how can I help?" Aerca asked all in one breath as she tapped away on her phone and set it back down on the table.

"I need your help finding a building. I'm not sure exactly what I want to do with it yet, but I want to put my degree and money to use finally." I sighed, looking at the menu.

"And chile you sitting on some cash!" Aerca smirked as I gave her the finger. "Nah, but I got you love. So what kind of building are you looking for? How many levels? You want something key turn? Meaning, ready to get right to work, or you want something to redesign to your liking?"

"Ok, so I think I want a group home for troubled girls. Those girls who are suffering and nobody knows or going through things that they can't talk about. So runaways and shit like that, I have to narrow it down, but once I see the building, I'll know."

"Awww, Tam, you have the biggest heart. You have always had this soft spot for everybody, and I'm so grateful you're my best friend." Aerca said, looking at me over her menu she held up.

"Nah, I'm grateful for you. I wouldn't be here today if it weren't for you." I said while getting choked up. When I was nineteen, my parents were killed in a head-on collision by a drunk driver while away at college. That was a tough time for me. I went into a deep depression and began binge drinking and popping percs. It had gotten so bad that one night I overdid it and was unconscious, laying on the bathroom floor. I'll never get Aercas screams out of my head; had she not found me when she did, I would be dead. After that, I got my shit together in enough time to sue the drunk driver, and his family, who I found out later, was loaded. My lawyer was ruthless and no-nonsense and fought for me to get ten million dollars per every tenth that the guy was over the alcohol limit. I walked away with over forty million dollars in a closed settlement after paying my lawyer, and that money has been sitting in savings and stocks collecting interest. So I figured its time to go ahead and finally put my funds to use.

"Ok, enough of the mushy shit. "Aerca chuckled, dabbing her eyes with her napkin. "Don't go fucking up my top-tier beat now." We both cackled. "Now for this building, is there a budget? I know you loaded and shit."

"Girl, hush. No budget. I just really want to find something that speaks to my soul, you know? I feel like once I see it, I can know exactly what I want to do."

"I get it. This is going to be fun best friend!" We spent the rest of the lunch talking about everything under the sun, and you would think we didn't speak damn near every day the way we cackled and howled through the lunch.

By the time Jason made it home that evening, I was still on a high, Aerca had sent me over a few links of buildings, and I couldn't wait to go through them. So after getting the boys tucked in, I got into the bed with my laptop and waited for Jason to finish up in the shower. Out of the five links Aerca sent, two caught my eye, and I wanted Jason's opinion on them. So I continued going back and forth between the two and writing what I liked and did not like and what I would change if I could.

"What you doing shopping?" I looked up and shook my head no as Jason asked with a smirk. "Say whattt?"

"I do not shop that much; stop it!" I rolled my eyes. He

mumbled in disagreement under his breath and got in bed next to me. "I'm looking at these commercial buildings that I had Aerca send to me."

"Oh yeah, for what?" He asked, peeking over briefly before sending his attention to his phone.

"Well, you know I have wanted to work for a while. So lately, I've been researching a few things, and I want to open a center for troubled young women, and if that does well, I'd like to move on to shelters and things like that." After a few seconds, I looked over at him when I didn't get a response and nudged him. "Jason, are you listening to me?"

"Yeah, baby." He shrugged with a sigh sitting his phone on the side table. "That's nice and all, but I guess it's hard for me to understand why you want to work so bad when you don't have to for the rest of your life."

"What the fuck does that have to do with anything?" I asked, looking at him in disgust. This is one thing that annoyed me the most about him. Whenever I brought up working, he loved to throw the settlement money in my face. I would give every dime of this money back to have my mom and dad here with me. "Make that your last time saying that, Jason."

"Alright, alright." He said, throwing his hands up in defense before turning his back to me and lying down.

I stared at him in disbelief for a few moments before I turned my attention back to the computer; all of the excitement I previously had was gone that fast. I sat my Macbook Pro on the side table and turned out the light, now lying with my back to him, my thoughts running a mile a minute, and my mind was exhausted, but I knew sleep would not come quickly.

Chapter 6
Jason

"Yo!" I said, tapping my guy Kylans open door as I stepped in. He lifted his head from the documents he was reviewing and nodded his head to say what's up as he sat back and crossed his hands in front of him.

"You got court this morning?" I asked, checking out my Richard Millie, seeing that he was here early as hell. It was eight-thirty in the morning, and by the look of his desk and breakfast in the trash, I suspect he had been there for a while.

"Nah, but I just like to go over shit and make sure everything is together," he said as he took a peek at his computer as it made a noise for a notification.

"You making me look, bad man!" I laughed. "You be up before the birds.

He smirked and shrugged. "You know what they say about the early bird! So what's up tho?"

"Mannnn, look." I ran my hand down my face. "I barely got any sleep last night. Tamera was mad at me, so she did all that huffing and puffing all night while tossing and turning. She even elbowed the back of my head a few times." I chuckled a bit.

"What happened?" Ky asked with a brow raised. I closed his door a bit and sat down in the chair nearest the door, and sighed.

"She got mad with me cause I asked her why she wanted to work. She wants to open some type of center or some shit, but remember I told you my wife got millions from that settlement."

"The one where she lost her parents, right?"

"Yeah...But still, she doesn't have to work a day in her life but yet pressing it. Shit just makes no sense to me." I shook my head.

"It ain't about the money for her. I'm sure she would give anything to have her parents back."

"And I get that, but why not just-I don't know, man. I'm just saying Tamera doesn't have to work."

"What's the real issue?" Ky asked as he got up and stretched. Ky was about six foot seven or eight, dark brown, and had tattoos all over his body that he would cover up with jackets and shirts. Today he wore a khaki suit, with a burgundy shirt that he had rolled to his elbows.

"It's just weird being with a woman who has more money than me, wayyyy more my guy." Ky frowned and shook his head.

"Yo, you bugging. Does she treat you like a bum ass nigga?"

"Nah, never shes not like tha-"

"Enough said then, stop letting your ego fuck up what yall got! You got a good ass woman at home. That woman doesn't ask you for anything. She takes care of yall kids and still makes sure yall good. So why do you want to ruin that? Do you know how many men wish they had what you-" His sentence halted due to a knock on the door.

Ky sat back down in his seat as Lynn peeked her head in the door. "Goodmorning, fellas."

"Goodmorning," I said, looking her over. Lynn was looking beautiful as always, wearing a fitted eggplant-colored skirt that had her ass sitting up lovely, with a pink blouse and matching shoes.

"Yall have court this morning?" She asked, looking from me to Ky.

"Yep," I said as I stood grabbing my briefcase. "Ky, I'll holla at you later."

Ky waved us off and went back to looking at his work.

"That man refuses to talk to me." Lynn chuckled with an eye roll as we walked away from Kylans office.

"He's like that with everyone." I shrugged. Kylan was not a man of many words. He would rather sit back and observe more than anything. Years in the streets taught him how to intimidate others without even having to open his mouth. Also, Kylan couldn't care less for Lynn than he already does; he knew all about our affair and made sure he let me know how much he didn't approve whenever the conversation was brought up.

"Hmph," Lynn mumbled as she smacked her teeth. We held more small talk as I made my way into my office to grab my briefings for court. My paralegal Denison would be walking into my office any moment so we could get down to the courthouse in time. Denison was a lifesaver and would make a phenomenal lawyer once he completed school and passed the bar.

At Court

"Bail denied." Judge Eileen Braxton said as she hit her gravel. "The court believes that the defendant has the means to leave the country. However, the court has also been notified that the witnesses for this case have been threatened by the defendant or the defendant's family and friends, which we will not tolerate. Therefore, the defendant will sit in jail until trial. Court dismissed."

My leg shook in anger as I looked over at my client Corbin Peters. Corbin was being held for the murder of two men, and the only thing the courts had on him were witnesses. I specifically told him to sit back and let me do my job d to not reach out to the witnesses in any way. But yet, here we are. Now he has to sit in jail until his trial, which is set a year from now.

Corbin frowned at me and shook his head as the sheriff stood him up so that he could be transported back to jail. I followed behind him so that we could briefly talk and see where to go from here.

"Why?" I asked Corbin, dragging my hand down my face after the Sheriff left us to talk.

"You are taking too long to do your job, so I gotta step in." Corbin huffed, looking at me through slit eyes.

"And where did that get us? You are making this shit worse. I specifically told you to stay put. I had this shit in a bag."

"You ain't got shit in the bag nigga! I'm still in this bitch! But I tell you what! If you don't figure it out, you, your wife, and them three kids will be in a body bag nigga." Corbin said before the Sheriff came back into the room to take him away. I stared him down as the hair on the back of my neck stood up. Corbin was a Rick Ross look-alike who was rumored to be a drug lord. These two murders he was being accused of were nothing compared to how many people he was rumored to have killed in his thirty-seven years of life. Corbins reach was very long and if he wanted you touched, believe me. You got touched. I didn't take his threats lightly and knew I had to figure something out and quickly.

CHAPTER 7
LYNN

I watched Jason stalk past my office hastily. He had his jacket strewn across his arm and was undoing his tie. I knew him well enough to know this meant that he must've had a fucked up day in court. He was going to lock himself into his office and be here all night trying to figure out how to fix what went wrong. Jason was a driven being. He hated to lose. That's why we clicked so well; I was one and the same. Losing was not what we did, and we would never take a loss lying on our backs.

I continued looking through my case file for another hour before I got up and made my way to Jason's office. I tapped lightly on his office door before I heard a low "come in." I shook my head, seeing him look so heavily in distress sitting at his desk. I closed the door behind me and went over to his file cabinet that had a bottle of *Jack Daniels* behind one of his law books, along with a few shot glasses. I poured him a shot and walked back over to his desk and handed it to him; he looked me over before he threw the shot back.

"What happened?" I asked, sitting on the desk next to him and crossing my legs over.

"Some bullshit." He said, being vague while maneuvering, so his chair was in between my legs. "You know how we always gotta fix the mess our clients make… take this off." he tugged at the hem of my skirt. I nodded and rubbed my hands through his curls as I stepped out of my skirt. I wasn't wearing any underwear, so I hurried back on his desk with my legs spread eagle and bald pussy in his face. Jason wasted no time putting his whole face into my pussy. He took his thumb and rubbed my clit back and forth while he assaulted my hole with his tongue.

"Oooohh shit." I softly moaned as I threw my head back. Maybe it was the thrill of fucking on the job or behind his wife's back, but this shit here felt terrific. After I creamed all down Jason's chin, he stood up and dropped his pants and when I tell you this man has one of the most beautiful thick veiny penis I have ever seen, trust me when I say my mouth just instantly moves towards it. I squatted in front of Jason and opened my mouth as wide as I could, and took his dick into my mouth until my face was damn near touching him. I swirled my tongue and gagged over him, using as much spit as I could. His low groans always made me go crazy, and I knew he was close to having an orgasm because he squeezed his butt cheeks tightly. Finally, I popped his penis out of my mouth and pushed him back down into his swivel chair, and sat right on that horse dick. I whined my body and bounced until we both came, hard.

"Whew.." Jason huffed, leaning back in the chair, catching his breath with his flaccid dick covered in my juices sat on his thigh. "I needed that."

"I know," I smirked as I grabbed some feminine wipes out of my purse, passing one to him and wiping myself. We both got dressed in silence and made sure we both looked presentable.

"What time do you think you'll be coming by tonight?" I asked as I picked up my phone; it was time to make my way home to our daughter.

"I'm not," he mumbled as he ran his hands over his face. "I'm already up to my neck in bullshit, and I can't."

"So our daughter is bullshit now?" I asked with my hands on my hip.

"Did I say that?" he asked as he tapped away on his phone. "I'm barely at home now. I don't even have time for myself."

"Yeah, but I bet you make time for your sons and wife."

"I live with them, so it goes without saying that I'll see them, Lynn."

"It's not fair to Jayla. It breaks my heart that she seriously gets the bad end of the stick." I choked up, sitting in the chair in front of his desk.

"It's crazy to me how you love to sit here and pretend that this is about Jayla." Jason chuckled, shaking his head. "You don't care if I see Jayla. This is about YOU! You want me to come by so that I can see you and so that you can fuck me and boast about fucking Tamera'shusband because in some part of your sick mind, you think you have one up on her or that you're the winner here. But you're not. I'm not leaving my wife. Ever."

'Fuck you, Jason! You're not the prize that you think you are. "I said, stalking out of his office slamming his door behind me. I couldn't get back into my office fast enough before I burst into sobs. Every word he spoke broke my heart little by little. He was right. In some parts of my mind, I was winning and had a one-up on his wife. But my baby was the one who ultimately lost in this situation because she didn't have a dad. After a few more minutes of feeling sorry for myself, I paged my secretary and asked him to come into my office.

"You rang?" My secretary Terry asked as he knocked and

opened the door.

“Yes. Sit. I have something I need you to file.”

“Well, okayyyyy, this sounds...interesting.” Terry snapped his fingers as he sat and crossed his legs, and got his notepad situated.

“It’s gonna shake the table for sure,” I said with a grin.

Chapter 8
Tamera

One week later

I pulled up in front of Jason's building and was happy that I found an empty spot with an already full meter. It wouldn't take me an hour to convince Jason to come to lunch with me, so this was perfect. I got out of my car and rubbed my hand down my rose Zimmerman silk wrap mini dress from Saks Fifth and matching Epsom Birkin, and made my way to the entrance.

"Tamera?" I heard from behind. I turned around and came face to face with Kylan. Baby listen! If I wasn't married, Kylan could rub it down, flip it, and reverse it. The Lord above knew what he was doing when he created Kylan. Kylan had a dark brown complexion that looked just like hot chocolate with a hint of red. His almond eyes were so dark that they looked black. He had the thickest of eyebrows and waves so deep in his head that if you stared too long, you got seasick. I lied when I said I came face to face with Kylan because the man was six foot seven, eight, or nine. I don't know which one but babyyyyy, he was up there and was solid with it; I'm talking about muscles, quads, pecks, all of that just there!

"Tamera?" I snapped out of my delusion and came back to earth, and blushed from embarrassment.

"I'm sorry. How are you, Kylan?" I asked, looking up at him.

"Ky." He corrected me with a smile. A smile that almost got Jason divorced. "I'm good. Just came from court."

"Oh yeah? I'm sure you killed it there. You're a great attorney!"

"I do what I can." He shrugged modestly. "Coming to see ya boy?"

"Yeah, I figure I'd come and take him to lunch. He's been working his ass off from morning till night, and I barely see him."

"Well, lucky him, come on, let me walk you in here." Kylan opened the door and stepped to the side so that I could enter. We made small talk until we got on the fifth floor where their offices were located and ran into Terry, one of the paralegals there.

"Miss thangggg…" He dragged, snapping his fingers down the length of my body. "Every time you come through here, you snatch my damn edges with all your damn perfection. My gawddd!"

"You play all day." I snickered, blushing, looking at Kylan out of the corner of my eye, who was smirking while he checked his mailbox at the desk.

"And do! But I'm serious! I'm taking pictures of you to my surgeon as a wish list, honey! Anyways, are you here for your husband?"

"I am. Is he in his office?"

"And is. Come on, let me take you back there." Terry grabbed my hand and power walked me so damn fast I felt like I was galloping. He knocked twice on Jason's door and opened it, and zoomed off, leaving me standing there looking crazy.

"Tamera, hey baby," Jason said as he sat up in his chair. He and his co-worker Lynn appeared to be in a heated conversation as she sat nearest his desk.

"Hello," I said, pronouncing both syllables looking from him to Lynn. "What's this?"

"Just work shit," Lynn said, finally getting up and turning towards me. "You know how shit gets heated in the courtroom. Good seeing you, Tamera. You look beautiful as usual."

"What brings you by?" Jason asked after Lynn left the office.

"What was that?' I asked, pointing at his door where she exited.

"Work shit like she said." He tapped away at his phone without looking up at me.

"Like?" I asked, sitting my bag in one of the chairs and sitting in the other.

"Like client-attorney privilege that I can't share with you." he set the phone down and looked over at me. "You look like a snack. Where are you headed?"

"To take my husband to lunch if he's not busy," I said as I looked around, something in this office smelled funny. "What's that smell?"

"What smell?"

"I don't know, it just smells in her-"

"Probably was the lunch I had. We had an early lunch while we went over case files." I rolled my eyes so damn hard I'm surprised they didn't get stuck in my damn head.

"Ok, well, that's a bust."

"I'm sorry, I would've told you had I known you were coming up here," he said, putting his hand on mine that rested on his desk.

"Your phone not working? Because I'm positive, I've called you at least three times."

"Yeah? It must have been on silent. I'm sorry, Tamera. I should be home for dinner."

"Ok," I said as I stood up and grabbed my bag. Jason sat there staring at his computer, never getting up to greet me or walk me out. I walked out of his office feeling indifferent. I felt like Jason was cold these days; there was a time when my husband could barely keep his hands off of me. Now he hardly touched me or came home early enough to even hold a conversation before falling asleep. I don't even remember making it to my car, but once I got in and shut the door, I couldn't stop my tears from falling. I wasn't happy, and something had to change. I wiped my face and went to start my car and was startled by a knock on the passenger window.

"Yo, you good?" Kylan asked once I rolled the window down. I gave him a faint smile and nodded yes when my own damn emotions betrayed me and tears fell from my eyes again. "Open the door."

I unlocked my doors, and Kylan got in and looked at me. "You want to talk about it?"

I nodded my head no, not wanting to talk about my husband to another man, especially one that was his friend. "I'm ok. Just PMSing." I smirked. "You know how us women are."

He stared at me in silence before saying. "Yeah. I grew up with all women. I know."

"Did you? I would have never guessed!" I said in shock. I wasn't trying to be rude, but Kylan didn't seem like he had a soft side like most men who grew up around women.

"Yep, six sisters, plus mama. Of course, I was the only man." he nodded with a smile.

"Were you the oldest?"

"The baby." He laughed at my shocked expression. "But we were all step ladders. When I was born, my oldest sister Lay was only 9, then you had Sid who was 7, Micha was 6, Fran was 5, Nelly was 3, JoJo was 2, and then me."

"Wow! I'm jealous. I was an only child."

"I used to say I wanted to be an only child when they used to run my little girlfriends away. " We laughed. "But I wouldn't trade them for the world. They are some true Queens."

"I can't believe I'm watching you blush right now. Tough old Kylan." I reached over, sticking my finger in his deep dimple.

"Gone, now." he chuckled, grabbing my hand. "You good now, though?"

"Yeah. Thanks for this. Sometimes I just need a breather, you know?"

"We all do. Be easy, though, Tamera. Don't let nothing dim your light." he said as he opened my door and stepped out. "See you around." He tapped the top of my car and walked off before I could respond. I looked at him walk away in my rearview mirror before starting my car and merging into traffic. As I drove away from the area, I couldn't help but get lost in my thoughts. As I was cruising, a call from Aerca came through.

"Hey, Diva!"

"Uh Uh, what's wrong?" Aerca asked damn near screeching. I

laughed out loud because lord knows I couldn't get anything past this woman. She was so intuitive and spiritual that she could catch on to every single vibe around her.

"Nothing worth even talking about." I sighed.

"Well, let me be the judge of that, spill it. Then we can get into the real reason I called."

"Ok, so, I just left Jason's office. I was trying to take him to lunch-"

"Aw damn, had I known you were in downtown LA I would've told you to come by my condo. I spent the night here." Aerca said, cutting me off. Aerca owned plenty of property, and she's been trying to get me on the same wave, and I have yet to make that move because I didn't want the responsibility. But it's definitely been heavy on my mind lately to start putting my funds to use.

"Something told me to call you too! So what are you up to?" I asked, trying to change the subject.

"I'm about to be up your ass if you don't get back to the story. So don't try to change the subject, heifer!"

"Mmmhmm." I playfully rolled my eyes. "So anyway, long story short. I get there, and he's in his office with Lynn-"

"That shifty-eyed hoe," Aerca added in.

"AERCA! Stop," I laughed.

"Nah bitch eyes are shifty. I keep telling you to not trust that trick. But go ahead."

"So she's sitting on his desk near him. They're like in a hush-hush argument. You can tell it was heated before I came in there."

"Mmmhmm."

"So I ask them, well what's this? She finally gets up and turns towards me, talking about "Oh nothing, just work shit." I said, changing my voice to mimic Lynn.

"Work shit, my ass," Aerca mumbled.

"Right, so she leaves, and I ask Jason the same thing, and all of a sudden, he acts like he can't tell me what their conversation is about. Now this negro comes home any other time, and I can't get him to stop blabbering about his damn case files, but now yall top-flight security? Puh-lease." I ranted, thinking back to the conversation.

"Yeah, baby, I don't know about that one. But you know what I say! Keep your third eye open at all times. See shit for what it is and not what we want it to be, and everything in the dark WILL come to light, you hear me?"

"I know it. But it was just his whole demeanor, you know? You know how touchy-feely Jason is with me-"

"Yes, eww, boy like a newborn on the titty around you," Aerca said, and we both had a hearty laugh. "It's sickening."

"Don't hate." I laughed. "But even with knowing that, do you know he never got out of his chair to hug me, kiss me, or even walk me to the damn elevator? So even if you're busy at work, you're telling me you can't make time to do something that takes less than one minute?"

"Did you ask him about the lack of affection?"

"I didn't, I practically ran to my car and cried-"

"Bitch I KNOW YOU FUCKING LYING. I know you ain't run your ass out of there crying like no white woman in a romance film!" Aerca yelled.

"Bitch, all I needed was the rain, you hear me. "I screamed, laughing after thinking of how crazy I probably looked. We both laughed for a good four minutes before catching our breath. "I'm so done with your ass."

"No, I'm done with you!" She said back, still snickering. "She's a runner, she's a track star, she gon run away when it gets hard." She sang, causing us to laugh again.

"Bye trick," I said, threatening to hang up.

"No, no, no, Miss Celie. I's be good. Don't hang up on me now."

"You a damn fool! You gon make me crash this damn car! What did your ass call me for?"

"I think I found the perfect building for you! Like it's perfect!" Aerca said excitedly. "If you don't end up liking it, hell, I'm a get it and figure out what to put in it after because it's a beauty, is."

"Really? You getting me excited! When can we see it?"

"I'm on my way to a showing now, and I have two more after that. But how's tomorrow morning?"

"Tomorrow morning is fine. You could've said midnight, and I would've been there in my bonnet!"

"Uh Uh, now don't let our good sis Mo'Nique hear you say that," Aerca said, and we laughed. This was the news that I needed to hear to turn my day around. I had finally figured out what I wanted to do with the building, and I couldn't wait to get started. I feel like I was finally finding my purpose in life outside of being a mom and wife.

CHAPTER 9
JASON

Aww, don't they look like the perfect couple. A text and photo came through from Lynn of my wife and Ky in her car laughing. Although I knew it was most likely harmless, to a blind eye, they definitely looked like a couple having the conversation of their lives.

We all know what it is. Worry about yourself. I text back.

You sure? They were there for about 30 minutes, laughing and talking. Correct me if I'm wrong, but I remember that's how we started.

The difference is Tamera isn't you. Bye. I threw my phone on my desk and clenched my fist. I knew my wife, so I knew this was definitely not what it looked like. But just the fact that Lynn came to me with this was annoying as hell. Having to deal with her for the rest of my life is really just not something I'm looking forward to. I swiped my hand down my face and sighed, I was overwhelmed, and it just felt like more shit was coming my way, and I had no way to stop it. It was only a matter of time before it all fell down.

CHAPTER 10
TAMERA

"You have arrived." my GPS alerted me as I pulled into the parking lot. "Oh, my goodnessssssss," I said excitedly with wide eyes. I already loved what I saw. This property looked like a small community; it had many small joined businesses that looked like houses. The landscaping was just as I imagined, and I couldn't wait to see the inside.

"Where are we?" Josh asked as I parked my car.

"Hopefully, mommy's new business." I squealed.

"TITI AERCA!" Johan yelled, knocking on the window as Aerca came out of one of the doors. I laughed and hurriedly got the boys and me out of the car.

"What do you think so far?" Aerca asked with a huge smile.

"Girl, I already love it, and I haven't even seen the inside!" I clasped my hands together.

"Just wait! Follow me, guys." Aerca grabbed Josh and Johan's hands, and they walked ahead of me inside of the property. Inside, my vision came to life. I saw myself knocking a few walls down and adding on some parts. I was in my mind going crazy with images of everything I wanted to be that I could barely contain myself.

"It's approximately-"

"I don't care. I want it." I cut her off. "I want it, I want it, I want it. Now."

"Well damn shit. That's the easiest sale I ever had." Aerca laughed in a loud whisper, so the boys didn't hear her across the room. "You sure?"

"Aerca, I ain't never been more sure of anything else in my life. I see my vision." I said with tears in my eyes. "A group home for girls who were like me, lost, trying to end it all, but they don't have someone like you. I wanna be you for THEM."

"Why are you always messing up my beat?" Aerca said, wiping her tear ducts. "Remind me to start being barefaced around your butt. I spent two hours perfecting this face, and you come and mess it up in twenty minutes. That's beautiful best friend, you always had the biggest heart. It's key turn ready, but I'm sure you probably want to change a few things?"

"Yes. I definitely want to knock down a few walls and add some things to it. How soon can we get started?"

"Alright, so let me go ahead and put the offer in and see what I can negotiate, and then we can go from there."

"Perfect," I said, looking around.

"Girl! You don't want to know the asking price?" Aerca asked, laughing. "I'm sitting here waiting for you to ask."

"Aerca, I don't give a rat's ass. Just get me it."

"Oooooo, mommy said a bad word." Johan teased.

"You're right. I'm sorry. Do you guys like this place?"

"Yeah!" They both yelled. "But I'm hungry," Josh said, rubbing his belly.

"Well, how about we all go to lunch?" Aerca said as she tapped away on her iPhone.

"Sounds like a plan to me!" I could barely hold my smile in as I continued to look around at this building that I knew would soon be mine.

"So... I've been thinking…." I said, tapping the table with my pointer finger as I looked over at Aerca.

"What?" She rushed, waving her hand at me.

"I wanna get some more property like you've been telling me."

"Say swear!" Aerca said dramatically, sitting up straight. "Don't make me act like a fool in these white folks' establishments!"

"Swear!" I laughed as Aerca let out a muffled scream. "Girl, you tryna give me a few "m's," huh?"

"Why not you?" I asked, still laughing. "But yes, I've been thinking heavily about it. I know my money is collecting interest in a few places, but some passive income and property to pass down to my boys would be nice."

"More than nice! What brought this about? Not that I'm complaining, but just a few months ago, you were "I don't knowww Aerca."" She mocked me. I peeked over at the boys who weren't paying us attention and quickly gave her the bird.

"I just woke up one day and decided I wanted more. I want to feel like I have something to leave behind like I'm making a difference." Aerca nodded her head.

"I get it. So what kind of property are you thinking about? I'll start looking when I get home tonight."

"Ideally one or two multi-plex, I want to house some parents at low income so they can get on their feet."

"You're my sHERO, I swear!" Aerca said, putting her hand over mine. "You're always thinking about everybody else. But I want to be honest with you, it ain't always easy being a tenant; some of them don't pay, so you might not get any money for a month or two from some people. But it's still worth it."

"I know, sis. I also want to look into a few single houses and maybe a condo in the city."

"Ok, I see you, sis!" Aerca said as her phone dinged. She read over whatever was on her screen then looked up at me with wide eyes.

"What?" I asked, trying to lean over and see her phone.

"It's yours, sis! Your offer was accepted!"

CHAPTER 11
JASON

I sat at my desk waiting on this file to download as I held my phone against my ear.

"Did you get it yet?" Corbin asked me using a contraband phone. How he got an iPhone into the jail, I don't know. But, no matter how many times I asked him not to call me on it, he did it anyway.

"It's still loading. It's a pretty big file. What is it?" I asked as I sat back in my chair.

"It's what better get me up out this mothafucka." He said with menace. I shook my head and didn't respond and sat up as the file automatically began playing. It was a few security videos of what looked like Corbin at a resort of some sort. First, he walked through the resort; it changed to him walking into a suite and many other angles. You never directly see his face, but you can see the distinct tattoos on the back of his neck, arms, and legs, along with a defining scar on his right calf. The date on the video ranges from March 15, 2020, until March 26, 2020, which would mean he wasn't present when the murder took place.

"Well, I'll be damned." I laughed as receipts came through from his credit card company saying he was, in fact, in Jamaica.

"Yeah, you got it. "He chuckled. "I expect to be out of here by the end of the week, Jason. I'm only giving you until then because there's a nigga in here who owes me money."

"But how did-"

"The less you know, the better, ain't that what you always tell me? I was in Jamaica. I didn't kill anybody. Now send that to that fat back ass prosecutor, judge, whoever the fuck it needs to go to and get me out this mothafucka." Corbin said before he disconnected the call. I sat there and stared at the receipts and the video over and over again for about twenty minutes. I knew for a fact that Corbin committed the murders because he admitted it to me. How he was able to get this video footage and pull this off, I had no clue. But I'll just add this to the list of other unethical shit I've had to do in the name of winning a case.

I sent the file and other evidence over to the prosecutor on the case and smiled when my office phone lit up with a call from Denison.

"What's going on, Denison?"

"Prosecutor Hilton is on line one, and she sounds pissseeeddd." I laughed.

"When is she not? Put her on through. Thanks, buddy."

"Absolutely. When you're done, I have something vital I need to speak with you about." Denison said.

"Ok, I'll ring you when I get off the phone with the angry bird," I said as I took Hilton off hold. "Hilton, to what do I owe the honor?"

"You are a piece of shit, you know that?" She hissed.

"Call me what you want, but call me when you get the

paperwork together to let Mister Peters out of jail."

"You think you're so slick. You and I both know he did this. So why do you insist on keeping these monsters on the streets?"

"Guilty until proven innocent. If you can't prove shit, then he's innocent. Isn't that what the law says? Besides, all I KNOW is that there is physical and video proof that my client was not even in the country when your murder occurred. So you have no reason to keep him, Hilton. Don't make me file another lawsuit. Remember how many millions you cost the state last time. This time I might file a lawsuit for however many days he's been sitting in the county jail. What is eight months multiplied by thirty?"

"Oh, go fuck yourself, Walsh," Hilton yelled and hung up the phone. A few years back, Hilton kept trying to keep a client of mine on the hook for a murder she had no proof of; not only did I get him off, but we also successfully sued the state for over ten million dollars.

Hilton just got her job back a few months ago and knew this wasn't a route she wanted to go with me. If she could, she would lock my black ass up right along with the criminals she chased for a living.

Knock. Knock. Knock.

"Yeah? Come in." I yelled out as I closed out my screen on the computer.

"I know you said you would ring me when your call was over, but I just really need to talk with you," Denison said as he stepped into my office, closing the door behind him.

"No problem, is everything okay?" I asked with my eyebrows raised. I never had any issues with Denison, and he was a great paralegal. I hoped to God he wasn't about to quit on me.

"Yes and no. I'll kind of leave that for you to decide." He said as he sat in the chair in front of my desk and swung open his messenger bag.

"Okay," I said as I checked a few messages responding to Tamera asking what I wanted for dinner and a few others. I sat my phone down when Denison slid a case file in front of me and put his face in his palm.

"What's this?" I asked, picking it up and seeing my name in bold. Denison didn't answer me; he just sighed and sat back in his chair as he stared at me intently. I looked back at the file and began reading, and saw red. "This crazy fucking bitch." I seethed.

"I know it's your business, but I thought you should se-"

"How did you get this, Denison?" I asked, looking from the paper, him, and back to the form.

"Well...this is the part where I kind of messed up."

"How so?"

"Remember I told you my girlfriend is a clerk at the family courts office?" he said lowly. I nodded my head.

"Yes. What does that have to do with you getting this pa- OH!" I said, finally catching on. "Did she file this?"

"I asked her not to. Just so that I could show you and stall it. I know that was wrong, but I told her to just pretend it was lost if she was asked anything. So please don't fire me for overstepping. I just thought you should know."

"Denison. Calm down." I said, getting up and walking around, and placing one hand on his shoulder. "I'm not going to fire you, not at all. But I really truly appreciate this. That was very noble of you. Unethical, but noble. Does anyone else know about this besides you and your girlfriend?" He shook his head no.

"Terry handed it to her, and before she could file it, she noticed the name from me talking about you so much at home."

"Good, good. Let's keep it that way. I'll handle this."

"Ok." He said, standing up. "I'm going to go ahead and go to lunch before our court hearing at two pm. Let me know if you need anything from me."

"Thanks, buddy, I should be good. Enjoy your lunch." I said as he walked out of the door. I went back over to my desk and tried my best not to wipe everything off of it. I couldn't believe Lynn was going through these lengths for attention.

So this is what you're resorting to? I took a picture of the filing and sent it to Lynn. I watched the three bubbles appear and disappear for a few moments before she responded.

How did you get that?

You know I know high people in high places. The three bubbles popped up and disappeared before a call came through from Lynn.

"How did you get that?" She asked again, sounding agitated.

"I just told you, I know high people in high places. So you had to know I would find out about this. The question is, why? I give you more than enough child support, so why the petition for that? When we both know they'll most likely give you less?" I asked amusedly, shaking my head.

"No, they'll give me more. From what I've heard, Tamera is a multi-millionaire. So they'll take that into account too, you know?"

"I don't know where you got your information fro-"

"From you. I heard YOU say it. Remember that day you were

pouring your heart out to Kylan about not feeling manly enough?" She chuckled. "Checkmate."

"Checkmate? You're playing checkers, not chess. If you were playing chess, you would've been a bit more strategic like me. So what I'm going to do is file for custody of Jayla because you're not mentally stable enough. Remember those text and photos you sent me of all those pill bottles the other night where you threatened to kill yourself because I wouldn't leave my wife? So then, after I get custody of Jayla, I'm going to have her calling my wife mommy while you sit on the outside looking like the fool you are."

"Jason, you wouldn't, you know I would nev-" She whimpered.

"Checkmate bitch." I hung up the phone.

CHAPTER 12
LYNN

"What are you in here yelling about, child?" My mother said as she came into my room carrying a tray filled with soup and drinks. Today, I took a sick day after waking up for the fourth day in a row, not feeling good; only today, it accompanied a fever and a case of the chills. I went to the doctor, and now I'm back home resting up so that I can feel better sooner than later.

"Just work stuff." I rolled my eyes as she sat the tray on my lap. "This soup looks amazing, mama."

"Yeah, yeah, leave that work stuff be for the day. God is trying to tell you to rest for the day. Even he took a day off." She smiled as she rubbed my forehead with a cool, damp rag.

"I know, mama." I smiled at her. My mother, Gina Charleston-Williams, was a praying woman. All my life, my mother had me in church, from bible school to three services on Sunday. She loved God, and according to her, God loved her back. Even when my daddy died in her sleep, she gave glory to God, claiming he needed daddy more than we did. I call bullshit. Mama could believe whatever she wanted, but why did he take people if God was so great? The only man who loved me, he took him from me, but she wants me to believe he's some awesome God.

"I'm going to keep Jayla tonight so you can get some rest."

"Thank you, mama."

"Unless her daddy will be by to help with her tonight," Mama asked with a raised brow. This was mama's way of trying to figure out what was going on with Jason and me. She didn't know he was married, she just thought he was a man who got me pregnant, and we were working on the family thing. I'm sure by now you can see why I chose to not tell her the truth about who he really is.

"No, he has to work out of town this week. He has a huge case going on."

"Seems like he is always out of town. When is the ever here to help you?"

"Mama, he helps, ok?"

"You ain't got to lie to me, chile. Tell the truth and shame the devil." She rolled her eyes as she stood up, grabbing her purse. "Finish that soup up so that I can wash the dishes and head out to get my grandbaby."

TRUE TO HER WORD after I finished my food, my mom washed the dishes and left but not before praying over me. So soon as she backed out of my driveway, I tried to call Jason again just to get no answer. After cursing him a few times via text message, I laid down on my couch and watched some reality television before eventually dozing off.

"Happy birthday, my beautiful girl." Daddy said as he clamped a fourteen-karat gold necklace with a heart pendant around my neck. I opened the heart, and it was a picture of daddy and me from the day I was born. Daddy said that's the happiest he had ever been in his life.

"Thank you, daddy. This is the best day ever." I said as he kissed my cheek.

"Good. You make sure that the man you marry treats you like daddy does or better. You deserve the best, ok?" He asked, looking at me.

"I'll make sure he buys me nice things all the time, daddy!" I laughed.

"That's not what I meant." Daddy chuckled at my eleven-year-old humor. "What does daddy do every morning?"

"You wake me up?"

"How do I wake you?"

"You kiss my forehead and pray over me."

"That's right. The man who loves you will always pray over you because a family that prays together-"

"Stays together." We said together.

"That's right. " Daddy smiled. "What else does daddy do for you?"

"You pull my chair out, open the car door for me, you give me food. You always help me too."

"Yes, I do. That's because I respect you, love you, and want the best for you."

"My husband will too! He's going to look just like you, too, daddy!" My dad let out a hearty laugh and opened the front door so that we could leave.

"I don't know if he will look like me. Your old man is one of a kind baby girl. But you're a beautiful girl, so you will attract men

of all kinds. Just make sure his insides are as good looking as his outside, ok?" I nodded my head yes, not sure that I actually knew what he meant. But I trusted everything my daddy said because he was the most brilliant man I knew. My daddy was a big-time lawyer, and I wanted to be just like him when I grew up. Mama always said God blessed her when he sent Daddy and me to her, and she praised him every day for it. Daddy and I spent half of my birthday in his office where I was his little helper, then we went to the mall where daddy let me get a bunch of new clothes from all my favorite stores. After that, Mama called and said it was time for us to come home for dinner and that she had made all of my favorites.

"Go ahead and get cleaned up so you can see what I made for you, baby," Mama said, kissing me on the cheek once we arrived home. Daddy and I carried my bags to my room, got cleaned up, and returned to the kitchen, where I saw oven-baked mac and cheese, fried chicken, collard greens, and an upside-down pineapple cake for dessert.

"Oh, Mama! Thank you sooo much!" I hugged her around her waist and hurriedly grabbed a plate so I could begin feasting. At dinner, we laughed and ate until our bellies hurt. That night mama and daddy kissed me on my forehead and prayed over me. Finally, I went to bed grateful that God gave me such a wonderful family.

The next day I woke up and knew something wasn't right. I looked over at the clock on my dresser, and it read ten forty-eight am. Something definitely wasn't right; daddy would never let me sleep this long, or Mama. Even if it was a school night. I stood up and made my way into my bathroom attached to my room, used the bathroom, washed my face, and brushed my teeth before leaving my room. I walked across the wooden floor, and it was so cold on my feet that I wanted to go back and put on socks, but I decided not to. I got to Mama and daddy's door, and I could hear Mama crying. I've never heard Mama cry, so I was worried. I turned the knob and pushed the door open and saw Mama in bed with daddy pulled on her lap as she cried and cried. I felt stuck. My feet wouldn't move because I didn't know what was going on. Daddy just looked asleep to me.

"Mama, what's wrong?" I asked, moving towards the bed.

"Oh baby, I'm so sorry," Mama said, shaking her head with tears falling from her eyes. "I'm so sorry."

"What's wrong with daddy mama?" I asked as my eyes filled with tears from hearing her sobs.

"I'm so sorry, baby." She continued repeating over and over again as I climbed up on the bed and grabbed my dad's hand. It felt cold. It was stiff. It didn't even move.

"Daddy," I said frantically, with tears falling from my eyes as I touched his face. His face was stiff and cold, and once I paid attention, I noticed his skin looked dull. "Daddy" I screamed.

"Oh Father God, please God help us." I looked over, and Mama was praying as she held her phone to her ears. I laid down on Daddys cold body and wrapped my arms around him while Mama told someone over the phone she needed help and asked for God to help us.

I woke up in a cold sweat with tears falling down my face. I hadn't had that dream about daddy in years, and every time I woke up damn near sobbing. Even though I was young, I never got over losing my daddy. I rebelled after his death, I began acting out in school, got into so many fights over bullying, and I didn't want to hear anything about God for the longest. God let my daddy die, all the praying Mama and daddy did, and God still took him from us.

God didn't bless the faithful; he fucked over them. Mama used to tell me it was just a test of faith, but how much testing did one need? I shook my head and wiped my face as I looked for my phone that I heard beeping with notifications.

I had a few missed calls from Terry, one from my mom, two from Jason, and a few text messages. I cleared the missed calls, opened my mom's text messages, and noticed a few pictures from my mother and Jayla. They were with my stepfather Lance at Applebees, and Jayla was smiling wide with her front teeth missing. I couldn't help but smile at my beautiful baby. Although she looked like Jason, she reminded me of myself when I was younger, so innocent, full of life, and curious as can be. So instead of texting back, I decided to Facetime my mom instead, when the call connected Jayla in the bathtub with bubbles up to her chin laughing.

"Bathtime?" I questioned. "What time is it?"

"You must've slept great." My mom laughed. "It's a quarter till nine."

"Wow, yeah, I practically slept the day away. Hey pretty girl!"

"Hi, Mommy!"

"Are you feeling better?" My mom asked, turning the screen so that it was facing her.

"I am." I nodded with a small smile. "I can't believe I really slept all day like that."

"That's your body telling you to rest. I know you want to be just like your daddy was, but you have to rest, baby, you don't want to run yourself into the gro-" Mama cut her sentence off and bit her lip. She was speaking figuratively, but of course, it was literal for daddy. Mama swore he worked himself into the ground, so every chance she got, she was telling me I needed to take a day off and rest.

"I know, Mama. I know. I will, from now on, I'll probably only go into the office a few times a week unless I have appointments and court. Then, I can work remotely from home."

"When I say rest, child, I don't mean work from home. I mean rest. But I guess this is a start, right?" She smiled at me. "You may look like me, but you are your daddy through and through."

"But you love me, and that's all that matters."

"Always, baby. Jayla, tell mommy goodnight." She said, flipping the screen back to Jayla.

"Night, mommy!" Jayla waved as she blew bubbles out of her hand.

"Goodnight, baby. I love you."

"Love you too, mommy."

"Alright, Mama, thanks again. I love you. Goodnight."

"I love you more. Goodnight, baby." My mother said before disconnecting the Facetime. As the FaceTime ended, a call came through from Jason, I rolled my eyes, knowing I didn't feel like arguing, but Jason was relentless when he didn't get his way.

"Yes?"

"Did you get my text?"

"Jason, I just got up. I haven't even looked at my text messages yet. What does it say?" I said as I got off of the couch and made my way into the kitchen as my stomach rumbled.

"I asked, are you sure this is what you want to do? This child support thing." He mumbled. It sounded as if he was walking through the parking lot at work as I could hear the echo of the empty lot.

"I just want to make sure that I have guaranteed help with her. Yes, you do help me, but any day you can stop and decide you don't want to, and there's nothing I can do about that since you're not on her birth certificate and there's nothing on file."

"And this was the way you decided to go about it? Let's be real here. You and I are both lawyers. We could have done without the antics and gotten our own lawyer to do this internally."

"Internally? Putting everybody in the office in our business? You and I both know that's something you're against." I said, pulling out items to make a quick sandwich with.

"You don't know what I'm against. You never even brought it to me. This is some type of get back for you. You don't care about Jayla." he accused. This was the one thing I loved about Jason. He was no fool until he was. He was a wise man, funny, worked hard, and was sexy as all get out. From the moment I laid eyes on him, I was obsessed, and I think it was because he reminded me of my daddy, and every time he came around, I felt like a little girl in love.

"I did bring it to you. How many times a week do I ask you to spend time with Jayla? You're more concerned about your wife finding out than caring about being a dad. Yes, I know what we did is wrong, but how many more years do you plan on hiding from the truth? We will eventually have to deal with the consequences."

"And this was how you wanted to deal with the consequences?" He snickered.

"It shook you up, didn't it?"

"Not in the way you think. You won't win trying to battle me, Lynn."

"Yeah, ok, Jason," I said with strong antipathy.

"Yeah, ok. Where's Jayla?"

“With my mom for the night.”

“Why? I was about to come by and see her.”

“Well, too bad. I wasn’t feeling good today.”

“Are you sick?” He asked with an ounce of tenderness.

“Something like that. Just haven’t been feeling at my best.”

“Are you pregnant?”

CHAPTER 13
KYLAN

I pressed the button for the sixth floor hurriedly as I stepped onto the elevator. "Come on, come on." I seethed, waiting on the doors to shut. The elevator couldn't go any slower, and I was annoyed as I tapped my foot on the floor.

"Finally shit," I said, darting off the elevator when it was halfway open on the sixth floor. The nine one one text from my oldest sister Lake wasn't something that I took lightly. She and I barely talked, so I knew it was severe for her to send me a nine-one-one text. I got closer to room six twenty-eight and stopped taking a deep breath telling myself to slow and be harmonious. The quick meditation helped tremendously as I felt the stress leave my shoulders. I knocked on the door twice and waited for someone to tell me to come in before I stepped into the room. I immediately wanted to step back out seeing my sister Jedidiah or JoJo, as we call her, sitting up on the side of the hospital bed with a swollen black eye and a cast on her wrist.

"What the fuck happened, Jedidiah?" I asked irately as I clasped my hands together to stop me from flipping shit over in this room.

"Calm down, Ky. I'm fine." Jojo simpered, reaching her cast free arm out to me.

"You're not fine," Lake said, coming from the bathroom with a grimace. "She let one of your homeboys knock her ass around and leave her in the fucking street like a dog."

"One of my boys?" I asked with a raised brow glowering at Lake.

"Yeah, your niggas from the streets. The ones who used to run behind you, now they are beating on your sister like she's a drum."

"Yo, what the fuck are you even talking about right now, Lake?" I waved her off. Every time I was around her, she made sure she brought up the streets as if I was still in them. I've been out of the streets almost ten years, and you'd think I was still gangbanging by the way she talked.

"You know what I'm-"

"Nah, I don't, and I suggest you be real careful with the words you say before you piss me off."

"Kylan, don't nobody care about pissing you off nig-"

"Lake, please! Every time you come around, you start shit with everybody because of your guilty ass conscience. I don't even know why the hospital called you, but I'ma make sure I remove you as an emergency contact because I don't need your shit." Jojo yelled, trying to stand and almost falling over. I scurried over to her and helped her back onto the bed.

"Yo, chill out, JoJo. Don't even get yourself worked up like this." I squatted in front of her, so we were face to face. "Just chill."

"I'm not the one who put you-"

"Get out, Lake!" I said, pointing at the door.

"I ain't going no-"

"Get OUT Lake!" Jojo screamed with tears coming down her face. Lake stood there for a few more seconds like the rigid mule she was before she yanked her purse off the chair and stalked out of the room.

"Yo chill…" I said to JoJo, passing her some tissue off the side table as she quietly sobbed. "Stop letting her work you up like that."

"Ky, she left us for dead, and she thinks she can just come around and judge us like she's better than us. Fuck her!"

"I know. I get it. But you working yourself up like this ain't going to fix shit, and she damn sure ain't the reason why you in here, so quit bullshitting and tell me what happened." Jojo let out a heavy sigh before looking up at me with her good eye.

"Ky, I don't want you in my shit."

"Well, it's too late, so get to spouting."

"Listen, Ky, it ain't what it seems, me and Crip go back and forth. Just last week, he was in the hospital from me stabbing him. So it ain't like I'm innocent." She chuckled nervously.

"And that's cool to you? What type of shit you on?"

"Ky, ain't no such thing as a perfect relationship. YOU know that." I started to respond and stopped when the nurse walked into the room with her discharge information. The nurse explained how she needed to care for her broken wrist and black eye and told her to get plenty of rest. Jojo looked from the nurse to me the whole time, knowing I was getting more unbalanced as the nurse talked about each wound. Once the nurse left the room, we sat in stiff silence, me in fury while I'm sure JoJo was more in angst.

"Where am I dropping you off to?" I asked as JoJo got up, sliding her foot into her Gucci slides.

"You can just drop me off at my house."

"Ok, will your boy be there?" Jojo smacked her lips and shook her head.

"Ky, stay in your lane."

"Jedidiah, when it comes to my family, I have multiple lanes, and I ain't afraid to cross them bitches at a hundred miles per hour, feel me?"

"I know how you are, Kylan, and if you don't step off, I'll cut you off."

"Me? You'll cut me off?" I yelled bitterly. "I ain't the one- you know what? Fine. Let's go. You got it."

I shook my head and heatedly walked out of the room with JoJo, trying to keep up with my long strides. The ride to her apartment was filled with deafening silence, no music or anything.

"Ky look, I'm-"

"You good, bye JoJo," I said as we pulled up to her apartment. I could feel JoJo staring at the side of my face, but she knew when I got like this, there was no getting through to me. She shook her head and stepped out of my car.

"I love you." She said, closing the door.

"Love you too," I mumbled and watched her walk into her apartment building before pulling off. Part of me wanted to sit and wait for her boyfriend to show up or come out of the building, but JoJo meant it when she said she would cut me off, she had done it before when I was fifteen, and some guys from the gang and I jumped one of her boyfriends for hurting her feelings. She didn't speak to me for eight months, and it broke me because, at that time, I was closest to JoJo. Jojo was the second person to teach me how to detach from someone I love, first was my mother. A year after I was born, my sperm donor up and left; mama held it down for a few years before she started neglecting us. She would go to work, come home, and stay in her room; she stopped cooking for us and making sure we were good. She made sure we kept the bare necessities in the house, but it was like she didn't exist. Lake was about fifteen at this time; she had to step in and take care of us because she was the oldest. It was as if she became the mom. She missed out on everything that a high school girl like her should have been able to enjoy. There was no prom, no afterschool activities, nothing for Lake. With everything going on, Lake never slipped on her grades; she was valedictorian and got a full scholarship to college for physical therapy. She left as quickly as she could and never looked back until years after she graduated. She called here and there, but it wasn't the same.

When Lake left for college, I was eleven years old, but I was already five foot ten and knew my way around the neighborhood. Realizing I had no guardian, I had to find a way to get what I wanted and the attention I needed. From there, I joined a gang, began robbing, selling dope, and everything else you could think of. It wasn't until I was arrested at nineteen and sent to a federal prison that I decided to get my shit together. While locked up, I completed my degree in business and made friends with some important people who helped get my record sealed and erased before I even made it out of jail. Once I was out, I promised I would never go back, and I haven't been this far.

"Late night?" My sister Neliah asked as I closed the door behind me and set the alarm.

"Yeah.." I groaned. "I didn't plan on it, but your sisters pulled me into their melodrama."

"Oh lord. Who?"

I shook my head and sat my suit jacket on the back of the couch as I unbuttoned my shirt to get comfortable. “Jedidiah and Lake.”

“Lakkkeee?” She rolled her eyes. I snickered because it seemed as if we all held animosity towards Lake somehow, and she felt the same. “What happened?”

“Well, apparently-”

“Hey, baby,” I heard a familiar voice say. I looked from Neliah to my ex-girlfriend Onyx with obvious disdain etched on my face.

“Onyx, why are you here?”

“I let her in. I’m sorry, Ky. I didn’t know you guys were on the outs.” Neilah shifted her eyes from me to Onyx anxiously.

"It's all good, Nelly. Let me talk to you, Onyx." I said, walking towards the back of my house to the stairs. Onyx followed behind me, her heels beating the floor with every step. It's funny how loud they are now, but I didn't hear one step when she crept up on Nelly and me in the foyer.

"Rip, baby. I missed you." Onyx said, throwing her arms around my waist as soon as we made it to my room. I pulled her arms from around me and moved back, so there was some distance in between us.

"That doesn't explain why you're popping up at my house." I folded my arms in front of me.

"Well, it's not like you answer my calls." Onyx rolled her eyes, waving her hands at me.

"No, because you are blocked. Normally that means the person doesn't want anything to do with you."

"Kylan, you're tripping. After all these years!"

"After all these years, what? Be honest, Onyx. The relationship between us was done the moment I told you I was going legit. Remember, I'm boring." I shrugged, recalling one of our many conversations. When I got out of federal prison, Onyx thought I would go back to the streets, get fast money, and move recklessly. Onyx was a suburban girl who had a thing for bad guys, so this turnaround was a turn-off for her. The only reason she was still around is that we did fuck now and then, but I was done even with that.

"I didn't mean you per se. I meant your lifestyle. I don't see what's so interesting about being a lawyer."

"It ain't for you to see. It is not even for you to worry about. But I'll tell you one thing. I ain't going back to jail, not for you or nobody else."

"And I'm not asking you to."

"Yes, that's exactly what you're doing. You don't know anything about street life. If you did, you would know it's only two ways out of it, jail or death. I've already experienced one; I'll be damned if I aim for the other."

"Ky, I get it. Forgive me." Onyx sniveled, looking up at me with her big doll eyes. Onyx looked like an innocent doll baby. She had some of the softest features that often made her appear younger than she was, she was short in stature, around five foot six, and her body was filled out in the right places to give her a curvy shape. She kept her hair in a black bob and had a button nose in which she wore a small nose ring.

"I'm cool, Onyx. Grab your stuff so I can walk you out, make this the last time you pop up unannounced." I nodded my head at her items sitting on my bed.

"Really, Ky, damn. I said I was sorry." She fussed, stomping her feet. I raised my eyebrow at her and moved towards the bed to grab her stuff; she was getting her ass out of my house and now. I was tired as hell, I had some cases to look over, and I didn't need this shit right now.

"Yeah, I heard it all before. Let's go." I opened my bedroom door and nodded my head towards it.

"Can I use the bathroom first? Damn Ky." I stared at her for a few seconds and rolled my neck side to side in irritation.

"Go ahead and don't play with me, Onyx. Tonight is not the night."

"Fuck it and fuck you. "She stormed past me and down the stairs at record speed. I stood at the top of the stairs watching her from one of my double-hung windows get into her car and zoom off. Good fucking riddance, one more thing from my past I can close the door on for good.

CHAPTER 14
TAMERA

"Oh, my goodness, is that my grandbabies?" Phylicia, Jason's mom, squealed as we walked into one of her many bakeries called Phynomenally Baked Goods.

"Yes!" Josh and Johan chuckled as they sprinted towards her wrapping their tiny arms around her waist. Phylicia was a godsend. Ever since I met her, she became like a second mom to me, and when I had the boys, she stepped up tremendously. She gets the boys constantly for days at a time, they even go on yearly vacations, and I won't even talk about how much she buys them. She's just as bad as I am.

"Hi, baby." She kissed my cheek once she reached me.

"Hey, mama." I returned the gesture, and we all filed into one of the empty booths.

"How are you guys?" She said as she ran her fingers through their curly mane. "You boys are so handsome."

"Good." They simultaneously answered.

"We just came from practice!" Josh said excitedly. The boys loved football and baseball, so I made it a goal to get them into everything they loved and more.

"Well, look at my little athletes." She beamed.

"Yeah, I'm good at baseball, and Josh is good at football! Our coaches said Y'all are going to be some damn hall of Famers." Johan mimicked his coach. We all guffawed loudly before I scolded him for cursing.

"He's right. My babies are some superstar-"

"Hey, guys!" The bakery manager Samantha said as she came over to the booth waving to everyone. "I'm about to make some top-secret cupcakes and could use some big help!"

"Oh! Mama, please, please!" They both said with their hands clasped together and pleading. I pretended to be pondering over it for a few seconds before nodding my head yes.

"Go ahead, and listen to Mrs. Samantha!" I winked at her and helped the boys out of the booth. They love going to the bakeries for that reason alone; they knew every time they stepped foot in one, they would leave with a satisfied sweet tooth.

"Whew, they are something else," Phylicia spoke with a sparkle in her eyes as she watched them go into the back.

"Indeed they are. They are all the exercise I need."

"Well, you look good, baby! But, hell, I need to get them more if that's the case."

"Oh puh-lease, you know you're fine! Daddy Jo told me about the young boys in your neighborhood calling you Miss Parker." I snickered as she rolled her eyes playfully and tapped my hands.

"They better gone! They don't know Josef back in his day used to rip these jokers a new one for even looking at me."

"Now I know Daddy Jo wasn't out in these streets like that." I proclaimed, clutching my fake pearls.

"And was!" She smized. "My baby calmed down a lot when we had Jason. I'm grateful for it because I just knew his behind was going to end up in jail the way he used to carry on about me."

"I'm in shock. I can't even see Daddy Jo being like that. That man is so chill." I chuckled, shaking my head.

"Yep, he was a mess, honey! Anyways, how are you, baby?"

"I'm ok. I guess I can't complain."

"But you can. What you can't do is bury yourself in your complaint and let you become your troubles, ya hear?" I nodded my head yes and smiled. Mama Phyl always knew what to say. "Now, what's wrong?"

"Something is just troubling my spirit, Ma." I exhaled heavily, shaking my head.

"In what way?"

"With my marriage, and I know he's your son an-"

"Aht, stop it right there. Son or not, I'm a woman first. So I'ma always have my blinders off." She hushed me as she flipped her arms above her brows as if she was lifting glasses from her face. I nodded and filled her in on everything from him not having time for his family to what happened in his office and more.

"Wow, yeah, something ain't right in the mix, that's for sure." Mama Phylicia spoke as she drummed her fingertips on the table. "Let me ask you, something baby." I nodded my head for her to proceed. " What is your spirit telling you?"

"Like there's more to the story. I honestly try not to even think too hard about it because I feel like I'ma lose my mind." I whimpered, dabbing the inner corners of my eyes to stop the tears from falling.

"Don't ignore what you feel. That feeling in your spirit and that sickness in your stomach is your intuition. It will never steer you wrong, understand me?"

"Yes, I just don't know what to do; it's like I'm just waiting for the ball to drop in the meantime."

"Don't, if you live your life worried all day long, you will stress yourself into sickness. So keep living your life, and trust me, anything you need to know will fall into your lap."

"You're right." I agreed with a small simper. "But in the good news. I found me a building!"

"Did you?" She screeched, throwing her hands up as if she was praying. I nodded my head yes and guffawed at her response.

"Sure did. It's so beautiful, ma. I can see me truly opening this group home for girls that are like I was."

"That's amazing, baby! You are a great woman, so they will be grateful for you."

"Aw, thank you, ma!" I reached over the table, meeting her halfway for a hug.

"So when do you think you will be able to open the group home? Will you have a grand opening? I know I'm bringing some goods!" She babbled excitedly.

"Calm down, Ma." I chuckled. "I go and sign the papers for the purchase next Thursday, and then I have to narrow down an architect so that I can get assistance with the blueprint, then I have to meet with the city to make sure I'm following proper protocol for the group home. So I've been doing a lot of research, and I'm hoping that I can have the renovations done in six to eight months and then open up in about a year from now."

"That's not bad, and it can definitely be done. As a matter of fact, I still have the architect's number and the company who did the renovation on all my bakeries. Do you want their information?"

"Of course, I don't know why I didn't think to call you, to begin with!" I smacked my hand against my forehead as I shook it.

"You have a lot going on, don't stress yourself. Come with me to my office so I can get his card."

That evening

"Mama, did we do a good job setting the table?" Josh asked, pointing at the table.

"You guys sure did," I said with a chuckle before kissing their cheeks. They had different color dishes and placemats all over the table, along with coffee cups and tumblers, but I was still very much grateful for their small help. As I brought the dish of Tuscan chicken pasta into the dining area, I heard the alarm sound for the front door; soon after, I listened to the boy's footsteps, and they yelled out, "Daddy."

He's home early. I said as I looked at my watch while I grabbed the dinner rolls and lemonade.

"Hey, baby," Jason said with a smile as he came into the kitchen. Before I could respond, he had taken the items out of my hand to take into the dining area. "How's your day?"

"My day has been good. Go wash your hand's guys." I shook my head in amusement as I heard the boys take off towards the downstairs washroom to cleanse their hands. Jason and I made our way into the kitchen to do the same. "How was your day?" I asked as I dried my hands.

"It was a good day. Finally, I was able to wrap up a hard case. I'm so relieved to be done with this damn case." He said with a heavy sigh, sounding like the world was on his shoulders.

"If it was causing you that much stress, I'm happy that you're done with it too," I said as he pulled out my chair for me to sit in.

"I'm happy that I can spend more time with you and my boys." He pecked me on the lips and sat on the other side of the table. Shortly after, the boys came zooming into the room, hopping into their seats. "Hey, hey easy, fellas. How was baseball practice, guys?"

"Good!" Johan said with a huge smile. "I had two home runs, Josh had one home run, and he hit the ball out the park. The coach said I'm one of the fastest baseball players he's ever had!"

"Did he?" Jason asked, showing all thirty-two teeth as I put food on the boy's plates.

"Yep, daddy, I run like this," Johan said as he pushed away from the table and quickly ran in place with a severe look on his face.

"Daddy, I'm fast too; my coach said I'm one of his fastest too, and he said I got a meannnn arm!" Josh said, standing up, running in place, pretending he was throwing a football.

"Alright, boys, that's enough." I chuckled, tapping their chairs. "Let's sit down."

"Look at mama. She's jealous she can't run like yall." Jason teased as the boys sat down.

"That's a lie, dad. Mama is fast!" Josh exclaimed, shaking his head. "She beat both of us on the track."

"Daddy knows better. He knows I ran track in college and was one of the fastest and would dust him any day." Jason laughed heartily, throwing his hands up in surrender.

"I don't want no problem from the too fast crew."

"That's right." I winked at him. We joked around a bit more through dinner; afterward, Josh and Johan retreated to their rooms for reading time before taking their nightly shower. While they were occupied, I used that time to clean up the kitchen and figure out what would be for dinner the following evening.

"Practice wore them out today, huh?" Jason asked as he came into the kitchen.

"Why do you say that?" I said, turning towards him and had to do a double-take. He was wearing plaid pajama pants, no shirt with his v cut on display.

"They are knocked out. Josh's book was sitting on his head, Johans was hanging out his hand. So I just moved the books and tucked them in."

"Wow. Yeah, they go hard every practice. They compete so much with one another and then go twice as hard at every other team player. It's amazing to see."

"They get that competitive streak from me. I don't ever like to lose." Jason walked up to me and pecked my lips.

"Don't I know it," I said before Jason took my mouth hostage right there at the kitchen island. Jason was kissing me like he was making up for lost time while he assaulted my mouth. His right hand was wrapped around my neck, lightly choking me while he used his left hand to pull my dress over my ass, pulling my thong to the side and strumming my clitoris.

"Oh, Jason." I moaned against his mouth. "Wait, are you sure the boys are asleep?"

"Positive baby, they were drooling." He said as he rubbed his fingers faster against my clitoris. That's all I needed to hear, my knees buckled from how good his fingers felt, and I threw my head back in pleasure.

"Mmhmm, you like that. She's dripping all on my fucking hand, shit Tamera."

I succumbed to my impending orgasm and panted for air as Jason began kissing my neck, only stopping to pull my dress over my head. My body was on fire, and right now, Jason was the only thing that could put it out. Once I calmed down from my first orgasm, I yanked Jason's pants down and was hit against my stomach by his hard veiny dick. He was so hard he had precum oozing from the head. I wrapped my small hand around his thick dick and began to jerk him at a slow pace. Jason moaned in my ear, letting me know how good it felt to him. Not the one to be outdone, I squatted in front of him and put his dick in my mouth and brought it back out, making a popping sound.

"Shit, Tamera." He groaned, gripping my hair. I opened my mouth and let slob drip onto his dick as I continued jerking him off. Once I felt like he was fully salivated, I put his dick back into my mouth. I put my hands on his thighs and pulled him further into my mouth until he hit the back of my throat, where I swallowed to keep myself from gagging. Then, I slowly moved back to the tip while I twirled my tongue around his length.

"I don't want to nut yet." He groaned out as he pulled me back by my hair.

In one swift motion, he sat me on the island and dove into my dripping tunnel. My mouth hung open as he strategically and slowly stroked me. Jason pulled out and then came back in using only half of his length as he tapped on my clitoris with his pointer finger. I couldn't even moan because my body felt like it was on another planet. I could feel the island beneath me getting slippery as my ass began to move at a faster pace.

Jason's strokes went more intricate and more profound, and before I knew it, we were both climaxing together.

"Hopefully, that was my daughter," Jason mumbled against my lips.

"Now you know I am on the pill," I said as I slid off the island, pulling my dress back over my head. I didn't want to roam the house naked if one of the boys woke up on my way to my room.

"I thought we decided you would get off the pill?" Jason asked as he followed behind me. I silenced him with my hand as I opened the boy's bedroom door quietly to see if they were still sleeping.

"No, we discussed that we would discuss in the future me getting off the pill," I answered once we got into our room and closed the door.

"Hmph. Well, let's discuss it now."

"Now isn't the right time. You know I'm trying to open my business. I'm going to be way too busy for a baby right now."

"Ok, so when?" He asked as I pulled my dress off as I walked into the attached bathroom in our room.

"I'm not sure, Jason. I didn't know that we were in a rush. Since when?"

"I mean, I just figured since the boys are getting older, we could have another baby in the house." He said, turning the shower on.

"WE?" I huffed in disbelief. "WE are not the ones who are here day in and day out with these children. That's all me. You barely beat the clock home."

"By then, I will."

"It's a no for me right now, Jason." I stood firm as I stepped into the shower. Jason stared at me in the shower with a frown on his face before he stalked out of the bathroom. I shrugged and continued to wash up; I said what I said. I was not about to have a baby right now. Right now, I was building my career, getting back to Tamera, and Jason would have to deal with that.

CHAPTER 15
JASON

"So yall just been walking around not talking to one another?" Kylan inquired, looking up from his phone as he sat at his desk.

"I mean, we talk, but it's short. Yes and no answers and nothing else."

"Wow, is it worth it? Are you good at walking around, not talking, touching, or checking in on your wife?"

"Nah, I ain't saying I'm good with it. But I want another baby, and we talked about it, now she is acting brand new talking about her career and shit." I shrugged. I knew I sounded selfish, but I didn't care. I knew that if I got Tamera pregnant and she found out about Lynn, there was less chance she would leave me having three kids.

"It's her career, though. She ain't out here fucking off."

"Yeah, I know, and this shit with old girl is driving me up the wall." I shook my head and told him about Lynn's attempt at filing papers on me.

"You up Schitt's Creek right now, huh?" He shook his head. "What you gon' do, my boy?"

"I don't know. I want Tamera to find out because I'm sick of hiding my kid, and I'm sick of having this shit on my shoulders. But at the same time, I'm not ready for the aftermath of her knowing. She might be little, but she ain't no joke. She doesn't take no shit." I said with a nervous chuckle. Kylan nodded his head as if he understood but didn't respond. So we sat there in comfortable silence, both in our thoughts, until we were interrupted by my phone going off loudly in my pocket.

"Hey, woman!" I said, answering for my mother after her name flashed across the screen.

"Where are you at?" She asked, sounding out of breath.

"I'm at work. What's wrong?"

"What do you mean what's wrong? Why aren't you at Tamera's signing?"

"What signing?" I asked, genuinely confused.

"Wow." She huffed into the phone. "She needs to leave your sorry ass. Come and get me from my bakery in Bunker Hill now!"

"What are-" I looked at my phone, and my mother had indeed hung up on me.

"Everything ok?" Kylan asked, looking from me and back to his computer, where he was typing away.

"Apparently, there's a signing I'm missing."

"Oh, Tamera is signing for her building? That's what's up."

My eyes widened as I realized that's exactly what it was. I had been so out of touch with my wife that I hadn't even asked about anything she had going on. I hurried up and grabbed my shit and threw out a see you later to Kylan before rushing to my car. I tried to call Tamera and got her voicemail, so I had no clue what time the signing was, but I hoped I hadn't missed it. I had my foot damn near through the floor of my G-Wagon as I floored it to my mother's bakery, which wasn't far at all. So soon as I pulled up, she was standing outside tapping her foot while holding her phone to her head and going off. Most likely about me. I got out of my truck and kissed her on the cheek, and she swatted me away, following me as I opened her door.

"Well, he's here now. I'll call you back...mmmhmm...love you too. Yes, that's fine. I'll be ready. Ok bye." She hung up her phone and put it into her purse that she had sitting on her lap.

"Daddy?" I asked as I merged into traffic.

"You know it. Do you even know where we are going?" She asked with her brow raised, looking over at me.

"Uhm...I think the building is-"

"Now, why would we be going to the damn building Jason?" She huffed, rolling her eyes at me. "We need to go to Aercas office where the signing is. Not to the building. Do you know where Aercas' office is?"

"Yes, it's about ten minutes from here. What time is the signing?"

"Wow. You are something else. You really haven't been supporting your wife? After all, she has done for you?"

"It's not that I don't support her. I've just been busy, that's all." I mumbled, lying. "Heyyyy! Are you trying to kill us?" I yelled as I ducked my mother's flying purse.

"Clearly, you forgot who I am and who I married. Don't try that busy shit with me." She hissed.

"What? I am very busy."

"I am very busy." She mocked me. "You are full of shit, is what you are. It's your practice, and you have a paralegal, hell you can go in when you feel like it and leave when you want! None of that excuses why you're neglecting your duties as a husband."

"Who said I was?" I asked, glancing over at her.

"Me! I said it! Your ass isn't present for one of the biggest events in your wife's life. That lets me know you are slacking. As her husband, you should've been by her side the whole time. But you're selfish, always have been. If it's not about you, then it is not important. I told you when you were thinking about marrying her to make sure you were ready, and you whined to me, Mama, I'm ready, I'm a man. Now, look at you."

"I'm here now. I just have to find balance." I shrugged.

"You better find it quick before you find yourself divorced." My mother said as we pulled in front of Aerca's real estate office. "Your ass don't have any flowers or anything."

I didn't respond as I got out and walked around to open my mother's door. I knew I was definitely on thin ice with Tamera and needed to get it together quickly before losing her. We walked into the office building and got on the elevator to the fourth floor, where Aerca's office was. Through the glass, I could see Tamera and my boys sitting in the reception area waiting.

"Daddy!Gram!" The boys yelled simultaneously as we walked through the glass double doors of Peters Realty.

"Ok, calm down." Tamera chuckled as she hugged my mom and kissed her on the cheek. "What are you doing here?" She asked, giving me a quick hug.

"Came to support my wife," I said, pulling her back in for a more prolonged hug pecking her lips. She gazed up at me questioningly and nodded her head.

"You guys can come on back. Miss Peters is out of her meeting." The receptionist said, standing up and guiding us to the back of the office into a large conference room.

"Congratulations, Tamera!" Aerca squealed as she ran to hug Tamera. Next, Aerca said hello to all of us before introducing us to everyone who needed to be present for the signing, from the real estate attorney to the title insurance agent. Once that was over, everybody went through the documents, and I was thoroughly impressed with the deal that Aerca could get for the building, especially with it being a cash sale.

I sat there looking goofy with a massive smile on my face because although I had not shown my wife as much support as I should have, I was proud of everything she was accomplishing. Tamera had a beam in her eyes that I hadn't seen in a long time, and I promised myself that I would be more involved from this day forward.

“Alright, now that we have everything signed, here are your keys!” Aerca slid keys and a gift bag over to Tamera. “Also, the sellers wanted to give you a gift.”

“Thank you, God.” Tamera grabbed the items and wiped her eyes as tears fell.

“Congratulations again, baby,” I said as I passed her some tissue and hugged her.

The following evening

Today I decided to take the day off work since I had a day free of court. Monday morning, the courts would be dismissing the charges against Corbin, and I needed to be there bright and early to make sure everything went accordingly. I was out picking up pizza, and we would spend the night watching movies together as a family. As I pulled into Pitfire Pizza parking lot, my phone began to ring, and the dashboard showed that it was Lynn calling. I quickly ignored the call and proceeded to get out of the car.

"Yeah?" I answered my phone in annoyance as Lynn called back for the third time after I ignored the call once more.

"I need you to get Jayla." She blew out in a weak voice.

"Why?" I stopped in my tracks.

"I don't feel well, so I'm going to the hospital, and I have nobody to get her."

"What about your mom?"

"She's out of town for her anniversary. I tried her first. Jason, I need you to step up right now." Lynn wept.

"And where am I supposed to take her?"

"Are you kidding me right now?" She screeched.

"You take her to your freaking home! She's your kid, not a stray dog!"

"Now you know I can't take her to my house," I said, wiping my hand down my face.

"Ok fine, since you can't TAKE her to your house like a man, I'll drop her off and let your wife know everything." She shouted out before disconnecting the call.

"FUCK!" I yelled as I got back into my car, slamming the door. I called Lynn back as I reversed out of the parking lot.

"What, Jason?"

"I'm on my way," I growled.

"Just meet me at Cedars-Sinai, please."

"Ok, I'm not far from there. Let me know when you pull up." I said before hanging up. My knuckles were turning white from me gripping the wheel as tight as I was. I didn't know what I was going to do, and right now, my back was against the wall.

It's packed at this Pitfire. I'm going to try the one on West Washington. I text Tamera.

I can cook, babe, no worries.

No, I'll get the pizza. I'm already out. Just relax.

"FUCK! FUCK! FUCK!" I yelled, punching the hood of my car. All of this was becoming too much for me.

Ok, babe. Love you. Be safe.

I will. Love you too.

I pulled into Cedars-Sinai and was able to find an empty parking space near the front. I sat there for a few minutes in silence and placed the pizza order online as I waited for Lynn to pull up.

Pulling up now, parking in the lot across the street.

Don't come swap places with me. I'm in front of the hospital.

Ok.

I started my car and waited until I saw Lynn and beeped my horn twice to get her attention before pulling out so that she could pull in. Then, putting on my blinkers, I jumped out of my car and went to hers.

"How long do you think you will be here?" I asked as she got out of the car. Lynn was a beautiful woman, but right now, she looked pale and very sick.

"I have no idea. I will let you know soon as they tell me what's going on."

"What's wrong?" I asked as she handed me Jayla's car seat.

"I don't know. I have a fever, can't keep anything down. I'm just not well. Do you need me to put that in for you?"

"No, I think I can manage." I buckled Jayla's car seat in as I heard Lynn tell Jayla she would be spending some time with me while she got better.

"I love you." She kissed Jayla's cheek while buckling her into the car seat.

"Love youuuu." Jayla squealed.

"I'll call you," Lynn said as she turned to walk towards the emergency room entrance.

"Ok." I waited until I saw Lynn enter the emergency room before I hurried and pulled off. Jayla and I made small talk before I reached my destination.

"Is this your house, Daddy?" Jayla asked. I sighed and looked at her through the rearview mirror and watched her look around curiously.

"Come on, baby," I said as I got out of the car. I opened the back door and unbuckled her, and picked her up. My thoughts were jumbled, and I knew this was the start of everything falling down. I knocked on the door and bounced Jayla on my arm with a small smile as she giggled.

"I knew that was your car- Jason, who is...this?" My mother

said as she opened the door with a smile, and it fell almost immediately as she laid eyes on Jayla.

“Jayla.” My daughter yelled out.

“Jayla.” My mother repeated, looking from me to Jayla.

“Mom, I need a huge favor. Please.” I said, passing Jayla to her. “I will explain over the phone.”

I rushed back to my car as my mother called my name out. I ignored her and got in my vehicle, waving to her and Jayla as they both stood on the porch looking at me. I just knew my mother would be blowing my phone up immediately and was shocked when ten minutes went past before she called my phone.

“Hello,” I mumbled, answering the phone.

“I am so angry with you right now I can’t even think.” my mother started as soon as I answered.

“I finally got that baby settled so that I can call you and for you to explain this to me.”

“I know, mama.” I sighed heavily.

“Do you, Jason? Correct me if I’m wrong, is this little girl my grandbaby? Tell me the truth.”

“Yes,” I said as I pulled back into the parking lot of Pitfire Pizza.

“How old is she?”

"Almost five." My mother gasped loudly.

"Jason! And Tamera doesn't know?"

"She knows of her. But not that she belongs to ME."

"No….no...how could you?" She sniveled.

"I know. I know. I just don't know how to tell her....pick up for Jason." I said to the cashier as I walked into Pitfire Pizza.

"Now I know, and now I have to pretend that I don't know. Who is this child's mother? Did she know you were married?"

"I work with her. She knew and knows."

"You WORK with her? Jesus! Can it get any worse? Tell me it's not that hussie that I warned you about years ago?" I thanked the cashier as she handed me the food and walked out of the restaurant without answering my mother. Lynn was indeed the hussie she had warned me about.

"Hmph. So I'm guessing that means she is the hussie. How did this happen?" I shook my head and told my mother everything up until that point.

"Wow. My son, what have you done?" She said lowly. "This beautiful baby doesn't deserve this. Tamera doesn't deserve this."

"I know, ma, I know. I don't know what to do."

"I can see that!" She hissed. "Send me the hussies number, NOW! I want you back here soon! You hear me, son! And I'm telling your daddy about this mess too."

"I hear you, ma. I have to go. I just got back to the house."

"Mmmhmm. Send me her information." She said before disconnecting the call. I quickly sent Lynn's contact card to my mother, grabbed the pizzas, and went into the house to pretend nothing ever happened.

CHAPTER 16
LYNN

"Miss Charleston, what you have is something called hyperemesis gravidarum. With your severe case of nausea with this pregnancy, it's causing your blood pressure to be low, not to be able to keep anything down, and causing the dehydration leading you back here to us." The emergency room doctor advised me as she stood at the end of the bed. "What I would like to do is keep that IV going so that we can get you some more fluids, get an ultrasound done to make sure the baby is fine. From there, we will either monitor you overnight or discharge you with something to help alleviate the hyperemesis. Sounds good?"

I nodded my head and set the bed up so that I was sitting up straight. Yes, you heard it. I was pregnant again, and yes, it was by Jason. I know, I know dumb, right? I couldn't believe it when I heard the doctor tell me that I was eighteen weeks along, my stomach was still flat, and my periods had always been irregular, so I had no clue early on. If it weren't for this morning sickness coming about, I probably would not have known until I was in labor. But anyway, I picked up my phone to call Jason and was interrupted by an unsaved number calling.

"Hello?"

"Hi, Lynn?" A syrupy woman's voice asked.

"Yes? This is she. Who's this?" I asked as I put my AirPods earpiece into my ear and hurriedly looked in my phone's calendar to see if I had an appointment I forgot to reschedule.

"This is Mrs. Walsh. I got your number from Jason. I hope that's ok?"

"He didn't say anything to me about a Mrs. Walsh. How can I help you? Right now really isn't a good time." I said, a bit vexed.

"Wow. So you have a baby with this man and don't even know his mother's name? All you know is that he's married and what his penis looks like, huh?" She asked back in the same tone. I gasped and quickly apologized.

"I'm so sorry, Mrs. Walsh. The name didn't click for me, I'm in the hospital right now, and my mind is fog-"

"I understand. Jason told me everything."

"He did?" I asked, astounded.

"Yes, this beautiful baby is here with me, and I had him give me your number so that I can call to check on you and also to let you know she's fine."

"Hmph. So you have Jayla right now?"

"Correct."

"Is there a reason why Jason doesn't? No offense, but she doesn't know you."

"Offense taken. Let's not be brash here. You KNOW why Jayla is here. Even though I disagree with how Jason is doing things, fingers need to be pointed in both directions, not just one."

"As his mother, don't you think it's time for him to step up?"

"As his mother, he should have stepped up years ago. However, he hid it from me until he dropped her on my porch an hour ago. From my understanding, you have been ok with him doing the bare minimum as long as he continued sexing you and throwing you a check, correct?'

"I don't know what he told you-"

"It's not about what he told me, Miss Lynn. It's about what I can see. You knew he was a married man, and now that you want more, you want him to wreck his wife to appease you.

"Listen-" I attempted to cut her off by raising my voice.

"If you want better for you and this baby, be better. Stop trying to cause havoc on someone else's marriage and get one of your own. I didn't even call to go back and forth with you. I called to say I wanted to keep my grandbaby the whole weekend. Save my number and let me know you're ok, and when you get home, call me so we can video chat so she can talk to you. Talk to you soon." She said and disconnected the call.

"The fuck!" I cursed, slamming my phone down next to me on the bed. When I told Jason to get his daughter or else, I just knew that meant it would be time to come clean, and yet he found another way to sweep his mess under the rug.

You are such a coward. I texted Jason as I trembled in anger. *Just can never be the man your daughter needs, can you?*

What are you talking about now?

Your mother just called me. Why does she have Jayla instead of you?

Why is that an issue?

It's an issue because she should be with her father!

Nah, that's not the real issue. I know what the problem is.

It's you. You are a coward.

No, you want me to tell my wife about you so bad. Even if I tell her and she leaves me. I still won't be with you.

It'll never be you, Lynn.

I never planned on it being you. I love my daughter, but I don't love you.

Well, I don't love you either. I texted back as my heart caved into my chest and tears poured down my face.

Yeah, ok, I take it you're feeling much better since you found time to harass me.

Fuck you, Jason. Every dog has its day.

Woof. Woof. You would know since you're a bitch.

"Mrs. Charleston?" The nurse said as she knocked on the door and walked in. "I'm here with transport, and they will take you down to get an ultrasound so that we can be sure everything is ok with you and baby. Once you're done down there, they will bring you back up. Is everything ok?" She asked, looking over at me.

I nodded my head and grabbed the tissue that she passed to me.

"I'm just drained." I lied. "And emotional."

"I understand, completely." She chuckled. "I just had a baby nine months ago, and every time I turned around, I was crying."

"Yeah, I'm so over it." I shook my head as the transporter began moving my bed. Then, I closed my eyes and sat in silence as we got on the elevator down to the basement for the ultrasound.

A few hours later

After confirming everything was great with the baby and me, the doctor discharged me with a prescription that I declined. One of the nurses suggested Pink Stork Morning Sickness bites from Target instead of taking promethazine, so I made my way there immediately after leaving. Along with being dehydrated, I had not had anything to eat all day because I couldn't keep it down.

After parking, I made my way inside Target and grabbed a cart, knowing that I could never just get what I came for. So I roamed around aimlessly, grabbing household items, clothes, toys, and shoes for Jayla while ensuring I grabbed what I needed along with the soup. The lines were long but moving pretty fast, so while I waited in line, I scrolled on social media laughing at the blogs.

"Excuse me." A voice said. I looked up and came face to face with a Lamman Rucker look alike. I raised my right brow in question.

"I have all of three items. Can I wait in line with you?"

I nodded my head and moved a bit to the left so that he could fit in next to me; after doing so, I returned to social media as we waited.

"I appreciate that. I came in here for these little items expecting the self-checkout to be open, and to my surprise, it is not."

"Yeah, I came for two items, and boom, full cart." We guffawed.

"See, that's why I didn't grab a cart because I would've been in here the same way."

"I tried that trick before and walked down an empty aisle, and there was a cart waiting for me to snatch it up."

"This store must have seen you a lot and knew what you needed...Davis." He said, sticking his hand out for a handshake.

"Lynn," I said, shaking his hand.

"Everything ok?" He asked. I gave him a look of confusion before he nodded his head at my wrist, which still held my hospital band.

"Dehydration. Workaholic." I said, giving him the short answer.

"Ah, we all have been there before. Or at least I have." he chuckled as we moved up to the cashier. He placed his items on the belt and then turned towards me. "Put your items up."

"No, it's fine. You go ahead. I have a lot of things here." I shook my head, waving him off.

"Come on, Lynn, it's the least I could do. It won't break the bank." He said, reaching for my items in the cart. I shrugged and let him continue and froze up when he looked at the morning sickness bites.

"Pregnancy," I said lowly with a nervous smile.

"Congrats." He continued to place my items on the belt. Davis paid for our items and walked me to my car, making small talk. After he put everything in my trunk, we stood there in comfortable silence.

"Soooo.."

"Soooooo," I repeated back to him. We both chuckled, and he shook his head.

"I feel like high school Davis right now. Lynn, can I have your number?"

"I don't know about that. I have A LOT going on right now."

"I understand completely; I'm not here to add on to what you have going on. I'm here to offer an ear, a prayer, whatever it may be that God wants."

"Hmph, that God wants, huh?" I asked, rummaging through my purse for my phone.

"Indeed, and I'm just a servant."

"That's what they say, huh? Here, put your number in here." I said as I passed him the phone.

"Wow, is that your baby girl?" He asked, looking at the wallpaper of Jayla and me.

"It is." I smiled.

"She's beautiful like her mom." He smiled at me as he handed the phone back. "I put it under my name Davis Marshall. Text or call me anytime."

"Thanks, Davis." I nodded, opening my driver's door and getting in. "Will do."

"I sure hope so, Miss Lynn. Drive safe." He said, tapping the top of my car before walking away. I started my car and made my way home.

I was able to make a quick call to Mrs. Walsh to talk to Jayla without incident. Once I got home, I took a quick shower, made my soup, and cuddled up on my couch with my laptop to check my work email. After reviewing my work email, I noticed it was a bit after nine pm, and I was exhausted from a day of being in the hospital and dealing with Jason's drama. So I picked up my phone and hovered over Davis' contact before quickly putting my phone back down. I had enough men problems and didn't need to add to them.

It's just a text, Lynn. You're not marrying the man. I told myself.

Hey. It's Lynn. Thanks again.

I didn't want to seem desperate for a response, so I made myself busy cleaning up my mess and straightening up the couch I was on. Once I made it back into my room, I looked at my phone and noticed Davis had responded.

No worries. I'm glad you text me. Part of me thought I would never hear from you.

Am I that bad? I asked, followed by a few sad face emojis.

It's not you per se, you're a beautiful woman, and well... I'm just me.

And who exactly are you?

Just a simple man called on by God to lead his people.

Wow. Are you very big on religion?

I am. I am a Deacon at City Hope Apostolic Church.

I dropped my phone like it was on fire. The last thing I needed right now was another church-going being in my ear about all the wrong I've been doing. As nice as Davis seemed, I would have to pass. I picked up my phone, put it on the charger, and lay in bed, consumed with my thoughts before dozing off to sleep.

CHAPTER 17
AERCA

Tamera is going to kill me. I fussed as I hopped out of my car, damn near throwing the valet my keys and snatching the ticket as I sprinted inside the tall building. Today was her meeting with the architect, and she demanded that I be there every step of the way. I had my day set up so that I would be on time. I had one meeting this morning at eight am that I didn't expect to go three hours long. The meeting with the architect was for eleven forty-five, and I was pushing it now at eleven thirty-eight, beating on the buttons on the elevator hoping that it would come sooner than later. Instead, it came rather quickly, and I pressed the button for the thirtieth floor and stepped back to take a deep breath to calm myself.

Everything is fine.

I am amazing.

I am enough.

I am fine.

Everything is going great.

I am grateful for my life.

I continued with my affirmations until I felt the weight come off my shoulders and the elevator door opened. I was taken aback to see that Suttles Architecture Inc had taken over the whole floor instead of many suites as soon as I got off the elevator. I nodded my head, impressed with the decor, and walked over to the receptionist desk, who watched me and smiled welcomingly.

“Welcome to Suttles Architecture Inc. I’m Marcia. How can I be of assistance?” She asked, standing and shaking my hand.

"Hi Marcia, I'm Aerca. My client Tamera had an appointment with a .." I hurried and looked through my and Tamera's text messages. "Mr. Benjamin Lee at eleven forty-five."

"Ah, ok, let me walk you on back. I just took Mrs. Walsh back a few minutes ago. Can I get you anything to drink? Water? Tea? Coffee?"

"Wow, thanks a lot, but I'm great," I said, following behind her. I admired the structures and design as we continued down a hall until we reached a door with the name Benjamin Suttles on it. Marcia knocked two times before opening the door.

"Alright, Mister Suttles and Mrs. Walsh, I have the other half of your company here," Marcia said, stepping aside so that I could walk in.

When I walked in, it felt like my breath got caught in my throat. This man before me was gorgeous as can be. He was a pretty pecan brown complexion with a head full of tapered curls, thick eyebrows, slanted eyes that gave off that he was of Asian descent, long curly lashes, a broad nose, and the most kissable lips. He was fucking gorgeous.

"Aerca?" Tamera said, snapping me out of my daze. I looked at her confused, and she waved her hand in my face. "She asked if you needed anything?"

"Oh, I'm sorry. My mind is all over the place. But, no, thank you, Marcia. Thanks so much." She chuckled, nodding her head, and left out of the office, closing it behind her.

"I'm Benjamin Lee Suttles. You can call me Ben Lee." Fine ass said as he stood up, putting his hand out for me to shake. But, damn, he just got even better. I was five foot nine without shoes on, and he had a few inches on me, appearing to be at least six foot four.

"Aerca Peters. You can call me Aerca." I shook his hand. I went and sat next to Tamera, who looked at me with her eyebrows up and nudged me under the table. "Sorry for being late. I had a meeting that ran over."

"It's fine. Mrs. Walsh was just letting me know what her building is for. We have yet to get into the good stuff yet."

"Ok, good, glad to know I didn't miss much."

"Mrs. Wals-"

"Call me Tamera, please. Mrs. Walsh is so informal." Tamera interrupted. Ben nodded his head and turned his head to me, showing all thirty-two teeth.

"Mrs. Wal-Tamera was telling me that you two are best friends, and you're also her realtor?"

"That is correct." I nodded my head.

"That's dope. Keep it all in rotation. What realtors office do you work for?"

"Peters Realty in downtown LA."

"Oh, I've heard good things about your group. Is it a family business? With your husband or something?"

"I'm not married. It's just mine."

"Really?" he asked, sitting back in his chair and crossing his legs while staring at me. "Hmph. That's interesting. Alright, so Tamera, were you able to find any wish photos for inspiration?"

"Yes, I have some right here in my folder. I was thinking that we could…." Tamera started as she went into her folder. I found it hard to concentrate on what she said as Ben Lee and I traded looks back and forth. I was a bit more sneaky with mine, but he stared boldly at me during the entire meeting.

One hour later

"Bitccchhh," Tamera squawked as the elevator doors closed.

"Whatttt?" I chuckled, shaking my head.

"He was ready to dick you down as soon as you came into the office, and you were looking like you were going to let him." She shrieked with a giggle.

"Absolutely not!" I shook my head no. "Don't get beside yourself, Tam. You know I don't do that."

"I know, but you have to admit he is FINE!"

"Umm, yo ass is married!"

"Bitch, I'm married, not blind!" She said as we got off the elevator on the main level. "It's cool, front all you want, but I felt the tension in that room, and it was all sexual."

"I don't have the time for men. I'm trying to get this bag." I returned as I went into my clutch to retrieve the valet ticket.

"I know, diva. But you do deserve love. You know that, right?" She asked, touching my arm.

"I know, boo. I'll meet my husband, don't worry, and he will be fine, paid, and have a big donkey dick." I joked, sticking my tongue out.

"I know that's right." She gave me a high five as the valet pulled her car around. "Well, let me get out of here and get my babies. Call me, and I love you."

"I love you too, Tam." I blew her a kiss as she climbed into her car.

I waited for the valet to bring my car back around before making my way back to my office, where I just had a few documents to review, sign and fax. I scouted out a few more homes and wrapped up my day. I was exhausted and ready to get home, smoke some weed, meditate and go to bed, but of course, my life could never be that simple. I would get home and find more work to do.

"Bonswa!" I announced myself as I walked into my parent's home. They lived in a modest five-bedroom, five-bathroom home with a vast yard housed a small pond and garden. This was the first house I ever purchased, and it felt good to be able to do something nice for my parents after everything they sacrificed for us.

"Bonswa!" I heard from the kitchen. I sat my purse on the living room couch and followed the voices.

"Manman! Papa!" I said in Haitian creole as I hugged and kissed my parent's cheeks. Manman was standing at the stove cooking as usual, and Papa was keeping her company as he read over the newspaper.

"How are you?" She asked in her native tongue. My parents spoke broken English around other people, but they always spoke Haitian Creole growing up and around family. Being bilingual has helped my business tremendously as I also picked up Spanish, Mandarin, Russian, and French in which a lot of Haitians speak.

"I'm well. Just a bit tired, long workday and an early day tomorrow!" I said back in our native tongue as I sat at the table.

"You don't work. You don't eat." Papa teased, sitting his newspaper down. "I kid. You need to settle down and have some babies."

"I would love to see some pretty grandbabies from you, Cheri mwen." Manman smiled at me. I rolled my eyes playfully and waved them off.

"I don't have time for that right now. Right now, I need to make money so that we are all taken care of."

"I keep telling you that we are fine, bél. You have done enough for us." Papa sighed.

"Yes, we saw the five thousand you sent us this morning, and Nadia told us you sent her money for school too. We told you she has scholarships." Manman fussed at me.

“I know, I know. I just don’t ever want you guys to struggle as we did before.” I said, choking up, thinking back to us living in Haiti.

“Let that go,” Papa said as he rubbed my hand. “Everything is ok now.”

I nodded my head and wiped my face as a few tears fell from my eyes. I’ll never forget what we went through living in Haiti. Even though I was a young girl, it still feels like yesterday.

“What an animal,” Manman yelled in her native tongue as we all sat in the living room watching the news. I was only eight years old and didn’t understand politically what was happening, but I saw many Haitians being killed. Every night it got worse and worse.

"He doesn't care about the people." Papa fussed, looking at our President "Papa Doc" on tv.

"What did he do, Papa?"

"He's killing us." He sighed, shaking his head as he went into the back room. Manman pulled me into her arms and hugged me tightly. As I dozed off, I felt her tears drip onto my mane.

"I love you." She said, kissing the top of my head. I said it back and fell asleep.

Hours later, I was jolted awake by the sound of a loud sob. My eyes widened as I looked around and noticed I was no longer on the couch with Manman but in the closet in our back room. Over and over, I heard thumps and screams, and I covered my ears and closed my eyes, trying to quiet the noise.

"Get off of him." I heard Manman yell out, then a loud thump. I started shaking as I heard more thumps and my daddy scream out before I ran out of the closet.

"No," Papa yelled, looking at me as he laid on the ground, face barely recognizable as the Haitian militia beat him down.

"Get off of my Papa," I yelled, pushing on one of the guy's legs. He pushed me off of him, and I landed on Manman, who was unconscious, and began screaming and praying for them to please leave us alone.

I heard my dad sobbing "No" over and over again before the men turned to look at me and walked out of our home.

"Why did you come out of the closet, bél? They could have killed you." Papa cried, grabbing me close to him. "They could have killed you."

Shortly after Manman came to we were on our way to the

United States of America. I'll never forget that night for as long as I live, and I'll always make sure it never happens again.

That following morning

I knocked on the second apartment of the multiplex I owned and stepped back so they could see me out of the peephole. Every month I had to come and collect rent personally, or some of my tenants would try and play dumb as if they didn't know rent was due the first of every month.

"Who is it?" Johnessa yelled.

"Aerca," I said back.

"Hold on." I heard scrambling around before she opened the door with an attitude. So here it was the fifteenth of the month, and she got an attitude as if I was doing something to her.

"Rent," I said with my hand out.

"Oh, I thought I paid already." She mumbled, turning away from the door and walking away. I stood at the door tapping my left foot, annoyed; every month, it's the same shit with her ass. She gon make me knock her the fuck out one of these days.

"Here." She said with a stack of bills in her hand. I frowned my face up at all the ones having to remember she shook her ass for a living.

“I’m about to count it right now. Hold on.” I snatched it out of her hand. Johnessa and I had a bit of tension between the two of us due to the little sneaky-ass comments she would make, and think I didn’t catch on. I stood in the doorway and counted the money carefully to make sure all sixteen hundred were present.

“Here.” I passed a five-dollar bill back. “You gave me too much.”

“Aren’t you nice?” She said sarcastically as she took the money back.

“Yeah, I’d be even nicer if you had my shit on the first. Bye.” I said, putting the money in my clutch and walking back to my car. I made sure I was mindful of my surroundings as I pulled off and made my way to the bank. There was no way in hell I would get caught with money on me and be robbed or beaten. After putting the money in the machine, I made my way to a showing I had. Before every show, I do a background check to ensure I wasn’t walking into any ambushes. Way too many realtors have died at the hands of some shiesty people.

I pulled up to the property thirty minutes before the showing to make sure everything was neat and add a few signature pieces. As I got out of my car, my phone rang with a phone number that wasn’t stored.

“This is Aerca Peters,” I answered from my Airpods earpiece.

“Um...Miss Peters?” HIS voice came through my phone. I paused in step and looked confused.

“Ben Lee?”

“Y-yeah..” He said, equally confused. “Mrs. Walsh gave this number as a means to contact her.”

“Did she?” I snickered as I continued to the house. “She is something else.”

“Pardon?” He asked.

“Nothing Mister Lee. What’s going on?”

"Ah, well, I finished the blueprint sooner than expected. Mrs. Walsh's vision is so big and pure that once I got started, I couldn't stop." He nervously chuckled.

"That's amazing, and I'm sure Tamera would be pleased to hear that. She's ready to get this started and open as soon as possible."

"Absolutely. Once she approves the blueprint and if changes are needed, we can go ahead and get construction set up."

"Awesome, and Ben Lee, from your experience, how long does construction for something this size generally take?"

"Well, it can take anywhere from six to eight months in general, but the great thing about Suttles Architecture Inc is that we are not to be generalized, and we get things done faster than most companies, so with us, she would be looking at five months tops."

"Yasssssss…" I said, and we guffawed.

"I take it you like what you just heard?" He questioned.

"Absolutely. So what's next? Do we need to come up there again, or -"

"I can send the file via email. It's a permit drawing and four d architectural drawings."

"Ok, perfect," I said before giving him my email address.

"Alright, I'll get that sent over in a moment."

"Alright, and you cc'd Tamera on there as well, correct?" I asked as I walked through the house, making sure everything was nice and neat.

"Yes, ma'am, I did."

"Ok, just checking."

"I got this, Miss Peters." He chuckled.

“That’s what they all say, MISTER Ben Lee.”

"I'm sure you will let me know if I'm not meeting your standards."

"And will."

"I like that about you."

"Do you now?" I snickered with a grin on my face.

"I do…" We both got quiet. I'm sure he was in his thoughts as I was in mine. Ben Lee was a fine, hardworking man, and I wondered if his lips tasted as good as they looked.

"Miss Peters?" I jumped as he snapped me out of my thoughts.

"Yes? I'm sorry I'm at a showing and got distracted." I lied.

"No worries, I was asking if you wanted to grab lunch soon."

"Um, I-I don't think that's a good idea." I stammered.

"Why?"

"Well...every time I try to date, the men get upset because I work so much. So I just don't anymore."

"Boys."

"Huh?"

"Boys. You said, men. Only a boy would be upset about his woman working hard." I closed my eyes and had to force myself not to squeal. It ain't nothing like a real man.

"And which one may you be?"

"All man, baby. Now about this date?"

CHAPTER 18
KYLAN

I completed my thirty-second sprint on the treadmill before I winded down and got off. Every workout session ended with the song Everybody Mad by O.T. I related to this song, especially once I decided to change my life.

I wiped the sweat from my face and made my way to my room to take a shower so that I could get dressed and leave for work. Today I opted for an all-black classic fit Burberry suit, with matching logo detailed topstitched derby shoes and a charcoal Burberry short sleeve check stretch cotton poplin shirt.

"Ok, G.Q.," Nelly said as I walked into the kitchen. I chuckled and went into the cabinet to grab my cup for my morning shakes. "It's in the fridge. I already made it for you while you were in the shower."

"See, and that's the reason why I love you." I kissed her cheek and went into the fridge to grab my shake that sat on the top shelf. "How are you feeling this morning?"

"I'm ok. We have a field trip today, so that should be interesting." Nelly smirked as she grabbed her purse off of the counter along with her binder where she stored work and tests she graded. Nelly teaches sixth grade at Nordonia Middle School and has been doing so for the past five years. She loves those kids like they're her own.

"Interesting indeed, didn't the one boy run off the last time, and y'all had to spend half the field trip looking for him, just for him to be on the bus sleep?" I laughed.

"Honey, yes, he's not coming this time. Thank goodness. I refuse to spend my day playing hide and seek."

"You used to love that game, Nelly."

"Yeah, when I was six. That shit ain't no fun now." She rolled her eyes playfully, grabbing her bags. "Anyways, I love you, and I'll see you later."

"I love you too, and I'm right behind you." I grabbed my messenger bag and followed her outside, locking the door behind me. "Let me know if you need anything. You know I got you like -"

"Four flats on a Cadillac." She finished cutting me off, chuckling. "I know, baby brother, I know."

"Long as you know," I said as she pulled out of the driveway in her 2021 Jeep Renegade that I surprised her with for her birthday last year.

Nelly and I were the closest of all my siblings; when my mother fell into a deep depression, Nelly took it the hardest because she was my mother's shadow. She wanted to be just like our mom, from how she talked to how she cooked. When my mother fell ill, she pushed Nelly away, and she soon after became depressed too. While in school, they noticed the change in Nelly's behavior and got her counseling. She was diagnosed with major depressive disorder and bipolar disorder, and she's been on medicine every since. Some days she's fine, and other days she won't even get out the bed. After not being able to contact her for almost two weeks, I called the police, who did a welfare check, and although she hadn't physically harmed herself, mentally, she checked out. That was two years ago, I convinced her to move in with me, and she's been here since.

After deciding to drive my black 2021 Mercedes Benz GLS Class, I got in and let my device sync before I started my morning ritual. I turned my business phone back on because I refused to bring my work home with me if it wasn't necessary. Having balance was far too important for me. Plus, I always make sure my clients know I am not available until after eight-thirty am even though I am always in my office before that time. Once my personal iPhone synced to the car, I went ahead and listened to yesterday's voicemails so that I could make sure I returned calls today.

Ky, it's me again. I know you got my message. Call me back. I pressed seven to delete another message from Lake. I would call her back when I felt ready to do so. I had enough to deal with, and playing the blame game wasn't on the agenda.

Hi King Ky, it's me, Fran. Your nephew wanted to know if there was practice this weekend. You can shoot me a text or call me when you get a chance. I love you, and I'm always praying for you. Talk to you soon. I smiled and saved the message, that was my older sister Fran, she was married with children and was a loving, prayerful woman. She's the one who taught me the art of meditation and using affirmations to stay at peace mentally. When I was locked up, it was her letters that kept me grounded the whole time.

Rip, it's me On- I pressed seven to delete immediately. I didn't need to hear the rest of Onyx's message to know she was on some bullshit. Calling me by an old street name, knowing I was trying to disassociate myself with that past life, was her way of being passive-aggressive, and she could do that shit with somebody else.

After checking my voicemails and returning calls or texts to whom I wanted to, I made my way into the parking lot for the office and parked into my assigned space. The best thing about arriving at work before everyone else was that I could do my work uninterrupted. It seemed like as soon as everyone arrived, my office door would begin revolving nonstop.

I had court this morning at nine-thirty, and I wanted to make sure all my paperwork was together along with the plea deal my client opted to take against my advice. She was arrested for having less than a gram of weed, and I knew I could get it dismissed since she didn't have any prior criminal history, but she allowed them to bully her and waived her rights during the interrogation, now all that's left is just for us to finalize everything in court today. I answered emails and completed a few motions for discovery by the time people began arriving at the office.

"Goodmorning." Zelon, my paralegal, said as she knocked on my door. Zelon was an immigrant student from India here on a student visa. She had a year left of school and would be taking her bar exam and getting married. Zelon was an excellent paralegal, and I planned to take her with me to my firm that I planned on opening and making her a partner once she passed.

"Goodmorning Zelon, how are you?" I motioned for her to come into my office and close the door.

"I am well, Sir-"

"Kylan." I corrected her as I did every day. In her culture, they had specific ways to address men, but I let her know that although I respected it, the culture between her and me was one of equality.

"I am well, Kylan." She said as her face flushed.

"That's good. How's Aaron?" I asked about her fiance. He was an accountant a few floors under our office and was always bringing her flowers and lunch.

"He's great. You just missed him."

"Aw man, I gotta see my guy the next time he's up here. Did you guys get a chance to get a babysitter so that you could go to the golf tournament the other night?"

"Yes, Aarons parents love keeping little Aaron. Aaron also told me to tell you thank you once again, and he enjoyed the tournament. He can't stop talking about it."

"No worries, you both are like family."

"We truly appreciate you." She smiled.

"As I do you. Are you ready for court in about forty minutes?"

"Yep, I got the documents you left on my desk. I wish you would let me do my job." She rolled her eyes playfully.

"Hey, it's our job. I was here early and figured I could knock it out so that we can both get out of here on time today."

"You're a great man. Do you know that? When are you going to get married and have some babies? You would be an amazing dad and husband."

"When that time comes, you'll be the first to know." I chuckled.

"I better be." She smiled. "I'm going to get ready for court. I'll see you shortly."

I nodded, picked up my ringing phone, and sighed, noticing Lake was calling for the sixth time in the past three days. Let me get this shit over with.

"Yes, Lake?" I asked with a heavy sigh rubbing my temple.

"Hello to you too, Kylan." She said sarcastically.

"Goodmorning, Lake. How can I help you?"

"I've been calling you."

"And I've been working. What's up?"

"Hmph. Well, you know JoJo is still with that boy, right?"

"No, I didn't know, but I'm not surprised."

"So she's going to just keep letting him knock her head around?"

"That's her man, and she gon stick beside him," I said, mocking the popular video going around.

"Wow. Ky, I don't like this. We need to do something."

"Lake, she's grown. She's going to do what she wants to do at this point. She needed help when she was a kid, not now."

"And let me guess that was my fault?"

"I never said that, Lake."

"You don't have to; none of you do. But yall feel that way. I can tell by how you treat me. It's like yall hate me." She said with her voice cracking.

"Lake-"

"No, Kylan, yall have to understand I was a kid too. Yes, I was the oldest, but I was a fucking kid. I had to learn how to survive on my own and with yall when mama checked out. I had to learn how to put a pad on by a teacher at school when I bled all over the fucking seat. I was a kid too." She sobbed. I pinched my eyes closed and shook my head. I hated thinking back on those times. We were all so alone, and we did look at Lake like she was our mom, so once she left and went to college, we all felt abandoned and began resenting her.

"Lake, calm down," I said with my voice heavy with emotion.

"I never wanted this for us Ky, I wish we could have had a perfect life, but we didn't. I had to go and make something of myself so that I could come back for all of you. If I stayed, I would've been just like mama. I swear, Ky, I didn't turn my back. By the time I came back, you had already had your mind made up and hated me."

"I know, I know. I'm sorry."

"I'm so proud of the man you are, but you hold so much animosity towards me that I feel like I can't even tell you how proud I am." She sniffled into the phone.

"Thank you, Lake, and I'm proud of you too. I refer people to your clinics all the time."

"I know, they always tell me about the fine chocolate man that sent them to me. I make sure I bend their arm back far too for it." She giggled.

"Aw hell, I'm a be having to defend you next. Yo ass is crazy." We guffawed.

"I ain't never played about you, Ky. Hell, I ain't never played about none of yall."

"Yeah, I know, you beat up all my girlfriends."

"And still will." She said.

"Ain't nobody to beat up. I'm single. But I always let them know I got a bunch of sisters about that life." I said with a smile.

"Yeah, we all would flip a table about you, even Fran peaceful ass, she can go from kumbaya to kick yo ass with a blink." We both laughed hard because it was true. Fran was the peacemaker but would turn into Laila Ali on anybody if they tried her.

"I love you, Ky, and I'm sorry if you felt like I abandoned you, ok?" She said once we stopped laughing.

"I love you too, Lake, and I'm sorry for putting that burden on your shoulder for you to carry. That was mama's burden, not yours, and I was just a kid who needed somebody. I didn't realize we both needed somebody."

"Absolutely, but I'm here now, and if you ever need me. You can call me. I don't care about the time of day, ok?"

"Same for you."

"I gotta go, my break is ending, but I want all of you to come over for dinner Sunday. Are you free?"

"I am. I'll be there."

"You remember where I stay?"

"I do."

"Ok, thanks for talking to me, Ky."

"Anytime. See you Sunday."

"See you Sunday, Ky." She said and disconnected the call. I sat my phone down and took a few deep breaths to calm the anxiety that was brewing. Anytime I had to think back on the past, it made me emotional for the whole day, and I needed a clear head before court. I checked the time and noticed I had forty minutes till court. The courthouse was within walking distance and took less than ten minutes for us to get there. I got up, stretched, and decided to go to the break room for a drink out of the vending machine.

"Rip!?" I heard somebody call as I made my way to the breakroom. I ignored it because I knew nobody could be talking to me, figured it had to be just a part of a conversation being had until they called it out again with more force. I stopped in my tracks and turned around, and came face to face with Doc, who was standing in Jason's doorway.

"Motherfucking RIP!" He said, showing all thirty-two teeth and clasping his hands together. I shook my head and walked into Jason's office, closing the door behind me.

"Nigga I'm Kylan here." I joked, playfully throwing a two-piece at him in which he ducked and came back with a weak right. "I see that right hook is still weak af."

"Shut up nigga." We both laughed and hugged one another. "Motherfucking Rip! Man, I ain't seen you in forever. Fuck you doing here?"

"I work here! Got my shit right in jail and then switched up." I said, speaking in code. He nodded his head and smiled at me again.

"So you a lawyer and shit now?"

"Yep."

"Wow. I never would've thought. But you have always been a smart mothafucka. Had I known, I would've hired you instead of this nigga." He said, throwing his head Jason's way.

"I'm offended," Jason said with his lip turned up.

"Nigga me too!" Doc said, shaking his head. "Had me out here getting myself out of jail. I should file a dispute with my bank and get my fucking money back."

"Well, at least you're out. So you two know each other?" Jason asked, looking back and forth between Doc and me.

"We do," I said, keeping it short.

"Where yo office at Rip, lemme holla at chu for a minute… I'll be back." He said, throwing over his shoulder at Jason as we walked out of the office and down the hall to mine.

"I can't believe this shit," I said once he closed the door to my office.

"Where the fuck you been nigga?"

"Shid, after you got locked up, I got hit with a bid that next week. I just got out eighteen months ago, and they just tried to set a nigga down for life." Doc said as he looked around my office. "Motherfucking Rip a lawyer now. Niggas would never believe me if I told them."

"I had to do something. So I took my money when I got out, flipped it into some legal shit, and got my life together."

"So you done, done?" He asked, looking at me with a skeptical look on his face. I nodded my hand and did a birdman hand rub.

"Completely."

"That's crazy even to hear. You wasn't shit to fuck with out here. I just knew when I got out you would've been the plug. Niggas acted like you dropped off the face of the earth." he shook his head in disbelief.

"Shid, I damn near did. But I had to so that I wouldn't go back. That street shit in our DNA, and if I ain't distance myself, I would be right back out there, you already know."

"I know nigga. That's what got me in this shit now." He shook his head. "But this is all I know. I ain't never been book smart like you. This street shit I'm a genius at."

"I get it nigga trust me. But check it, I got some people who can help you. They can help clean up your dirty money into some legal shit. That way, you will always have some shit in your name if they question where you are getting money."

"Now you know I don't trust mothafuckas with my money or my business." he frowned.

"And you think I do? Listen, he was doing a bid with me. He knows his shit. He only got locked up because his partner did some foul shit, and since they were in business together, he got caught up too."

"And you used him?"

"All the time. Right hand to God. I trust him."

"Shid, alright. Slide me that information. You know I trust you with my life." he said as he absentmindedly rubbed the scar on his cheek.

I pulled my hood over my head as I ran out of the alley like I was a track star. I just got through robbing this punk ass nigga Chauncey from the neighborhood and wanted to get away before anybody heard all that squealing his ass was doing. So I jacked niggas to get what I wanted. I know you probably think that shit ain't fair, but it's life. Plus, these niggas I usually robbed was some braggadocious ass clowns who wanted everybody to know they got money. Well, I knew, and I got it now. I didn't have time to stop and count what I jacked Chauncey's bitch ass for, but I knew it was a few stacks. That should be enough to get me, Nelly, and Jojo, some school clothes for sure. I slowed my stride once I hit my block and opted to walk instead, so I didn't look suspicious.

"Bitch ass nigga, where the fucking work at." I heard ahead of me. The street lights didn't work on half the street, so I couldn't see shit from afar. I stopped walking and bent down and started creeping so I could check out what was going on, so I ain't end up chalked.

"I ain't giving you shit, kill me nigga."

"You're saying that shit like I won't."

"Then stop talking about it and do that shit, pussy ass nigga." I was able to see across the street onto the side of a house where a dude was standing in front of somebody with his gun pointed at them. I couldn't see the other person's face, but I knew it was Doc by the shoes on his feet. Doc was a nigga from my hood who sold dope and was always fresh as fuck. Just earlier, I saw those Jordans on his feet and said to myself I wanted them bitches. So I crouched down and quietly tipped across the street just as I heard Doc yell out.

"Don't make me shoot your dumb ass, give up the fucking work nigga." the other dude said as he pistol-whipped Doc again. Usually, I'd mind my business, but for some reason, it ain't feel right letting no nigga from my block get jacked.

"Fuck you nigga." Doc spat on the guy. The guy cocked his pistol back and aimed it at Doc.

PEW! PEW!

The nigga fell to his feet as both bullets split his head open. He fell forward, almost landing on Doc, who hurried and scrambled out the way.

"Shit!" Doc yelled. "Got this shit all over me nigga."

"I mean, your shit was about to be all over the fucking ground. You're welcome nigga." I grimaced, putting my pistol back in my pants.

"Aye, what's your name, man?" Doc asked, wiping his face looking around.

"Kylan."

"I'm Doc. You saved my life, my boy. Where you from?"

"I'm from around here." He nodded his head as he pressed buttons on his phone.

"Man, you let that bitch rip, a nigga just knew he was a fucking pack. You ain't even have to do that shit, but you did, and I owe you my life. Whatever you need, I got you."

That's how I got my nickname Rip. I was known for letting my pistol talk for me if I needed to. From that day on, Doc and I became thick as thieves, he put me on to selling dope, and I began to see more money than I had ever.

"Bet, get with him as soon as you can. Trust me. He will get you right and quick." I said as we exchanged contact information.

"So you really work here with all these stuffy ass mothafuckas?" Doc joked. "Every time I come in this bitch, I feel like my throat about to close the fuck up."

"Nigga you a fucking fool." We laughed. "But yeah, I've been here for about a year now, I'ma open my own shit soon."

"Oh shit, I'm a have all the Lil homies put you on retainer and shit. I ain't fucking with that other clown ass nigga no more. Nigga was about to have me sitting down for life." He shook his head.

"That bad?" I asked, looking at my watch. It was almost time for me to get ready to leave out.

"That mothafucking bad. Like he ain't give a fuck or something."

"Damn," I said, shaking my head.

"Right, I gotta go over here and holla at his ass now about some shit and then get the fuck on this plane. Hit me up nigga, and I'm a call that dude later on today."

"Aight bet. Be safe out here, my guy." I said as we did a brotherly hug.

"You already know." He said as he opened the door and made his way back to Jason's office.

CHAPTER 19
JASON

"So, is there any way that they can arrest me again for this shit?" Corbin asked, sitting across from me with his arms folded in front of him.

"They shouldn't."

"But they can?"

"If they somehow find evidence that directly links you besides witnesses, then yes."

"But what about the footage?"

"They would have to prove it's altered footage."

"Hmph." He said, staring at me intensely.

"You should be in the clear now, Mr. Peters."

"That's what you say. So what do I have to do to ensure this shit don't come back around?"

"I don't follow," I asked with a frown.

"Nah, you follow very clearly. So who the fuck...do...I...have... to....eliminate?" Corbin asked lowly as he stood up over my desk.

"I-I," I stammered as I pushed my chair back so that we could have some space in between us.

"Do you have time-" Lynn walked into my office without knocking. "Oh, I'm sorry, is everything alright?"

"Yes. What's going on?" I asked with my eyebrows raised.

"I just wanted to speak with you about creating a schedule, but it can wait until you're done."

"Ok." I nodded as Corbin looked between Lynn and me. She hesitated before she walked back out of the door, leaving it open a bit.

"Wow. You cheated on your wife for that?" Corbin shook his head, still looking behind at the door.

"Huh?"

"Yeah, you did. I can tell. Anybody who comes around yall can tell that yall are fucking."

"You're incorrect." I shook my head.

"Nah, I'm not. I'm from the streets. One of the things I do best is read the fuck out of people. She's pregnant too. That's your kid?"

"What? No!" I shrieked.

"Shid. You ain't see the ginger ale and crackers in her hand? She's fa'sho pregnant."

"Doesn't matter, even if she is, it ain't mine." I shrugged.

"Yeah, ok, I thought lawyers were supposed to know how to lie?" He frowned.

"That's a prevalent misconception. We don't lie. We force the state to prove their case, and we disprove it with facts or reasonable doubt."

"Either way, your ass sucks at it. I'm out. Hopefully, I don't have to see yo ass again." He tapped my desk before making his way to the door and out of it without looking back again. I sighed, relieved that I wouldn't have to deal with him anymore for the time being. If he were smart, it would never be again.

Knock. Knock.

"I saw your client leave, so I thought it would be safe to come back now," Lynn said with a slight chuckle. I smirked and took a hard look at her as she came and sat at the chair in front of my desk. Her nose did look a bit swollen, right along with her lips, she had been missing a lot of work lately due to not feeling well, and I did notice the crackers and ginger ale she carried around often. "So I talked with your mom, and she was saying that she wants to-"

"Are you pregnant?" I blurted out, cutting her off.

"What? No." She rolled her eyes. "Do I look fat or something?"

"No. Just asking. So what did they say at the hospital?"

"Dehydrated, that's all. But like I was saying before, I was rudely interrupted. Your mother called me last night and asked if she could get Jayla this upcoming weekend, and I said yes. So I wanted to make sure that was ok with you."

"Whatever she wants is fine. She cursed my ass out like I wasn't her son, then tagged my dad in. So I'm in the doghouse right now."

"As you should be." She nodded.

"Don't start," I said with my brow up.

"Oh, I'm not trust me. It's just nice to see Jayla finally be around her family. It'll be even better when she can be around her brothers so she can quit asking me for one."

"Well, that part will take some time. I doubt once Tamera finds out that she will be ecstatic to bring Jayla over."

"So you think she will stay once she finds out?" Lynn asked, amused.

"We are married. Not dating."

"The woman that I met is not staying. Trust me."

"Well, the good thing is that I know her more than you do. Family is everything to her."

"That educated, strong woman will not let you make a fool of her. You better hope she doesn't pack her shit and move out in the middle of the night."

"And again, even if she does, I still won't be knocking on your door asking you to replace her. Did you need anything else?" Lynn shook her head and stood up.

"Remember Jason; every dog has their day. Toodles." She snickered, waving at me as she opened the door.

"Thanks, Lassie." I mocked, giving her the finger.

I picked up my phone to call my mother, hoping she would pick up the phone this time since I was on her shit list.

"Hello, son... Give me one second." Her background was extremely loud, letting me know she must've been in one of her bakeries. My mother was one of the most hardworking women I know. She didn't need to work but chose to do so anyway. With her working so much and my dad always being gone at work, I spent a lot of time with the nanny or grandmother.

"Alright, I'm back. Had to get back to my office."

"How are you?"

"I'm ok. One of the stoves went out today, so we have been trying to get everything cooked as good as we can with three."

"Wow. I know that's stressful. When can they come out and fix it?"

"The man is here now. He's saying it might cost more to fix it than to just replace it. So I'm a call and see if I can get one expedited."

"Oh, ok, well, let me know if you need anything." I offered.

"Mmmhmm. So what's going on with you? I know you ain't call to hear my mess."

"I've been calling you." I chuckled nervously. "You been ducking me."

"Yeah, I had to calm down first. But, you, my child, I love you, and I'm a always stand beside you, but I'm a always let you know when you wrong."

"I know, mama."

"I love Tamera, and God knows I don't want to hold this from her. I love that girl like she came from me, and I'm a lose her." Her voice broke.

"Why would you lose her?"

"This is betrayal in the worst way. Once she finds out, and she knows I knew and didn't say anything...." She got quiet.

"I don't know, mama."

"I know."

"She just left out of here saying you want to get Jayla this weekend?" I asked, changing the subject.

"Yeah, I called her yesterday and asked if that was ok. I want to get to know my grandbaby more. She seems like such a sweet baby, and your daddy is just head over heels for her pretty self."

"Yeah, she is a sweet girl."

"Jason?"

"Yeah, ma?"

"You are not your father."

"Huh?" I asked, taken aback.

"That man has always been your role model." She giggled. "You wanted to be like him in all ways. The good and bad."

"What kid doesn't want to be like their parents?" I questioned.

"You got a point there. But it's the parent's responsibility to be a great example for their children to want to be. Unfortunately, your daddy wasn't always the best example for you, and now you're following in his footsteps."

"He did the best-"

"No, he didn't. No parent should ever take their child with them while they cheat on their spouses. Your daddy was wrong for bringing you with him to do that. That changed you, I saw the change in you, but I didn't know what it was from. If I had caught on sooner than I did, I would have stopped it. I'm sorry for that."

"You knew?"

"I found out when you were sixteen." She sighed heavily. "Tore me up. I'll never forget that woman walking into my bakery and telling me how my husband and son were at her house the day before. She had photos of you playing one of your little games in her living room eating pizza and your dad in her bed."

August 2001

"I'll just be about thirty-five to forty minutes in here. I need to talk to this client about her case. Once I'm done, we can go to the mall and grab those shoes you asked about." My dad said as we pulled up to a small two-family house.

I nodded my head and didn't say anything. Whenever my dad offered to buy me something, he previously told me no to I knew he was up to no good. This wasn't the first time he took me with him while he cheated on my mother. He just liked to pretend I was too dumb to know that's what he was doing. This had been going on for five years, and it made me mad that my mother was too busy with her bakeries to even notice what was going on.

I dragged my feet behind him as we walked up to the house, and he knocked on the door. A woman came to the door in a short robe, she was nice looking, but I still think my mom was the most beautiful woman in the world.

"Oh, I didn't know you were bringing company."

"Yeah, just my son. He's going to wait in the living room while I talk to you about your...case," My dad said as we stepped into her house. At least it was clean.

"Oh, ok." She stammered. "Well, I just ordered some pizza. It should be here in a moment, and I have a game system there he can busy himself with."

"I'm sure that's ok with him, right, son?" My dad asked with his brow up. I nodded my head and trotted over, and sat down on the worn couch. She had a PlayStation that sat in front of the tv, so I grabbed the remote and controller to play.

I was halfway through a race on Mario Kart when the doorbell rang.

"Son, can you grab that for me?" My dad yelled out to me. I shook my head and got up so that I could answer the door. I looked through the peephole and saw a Pizza Hut delivery guy. Assuming she handled the tip, I took the pizza and sat it on her dining room table before grabbing a few pieces. Thirty more minutes passed before my dad made it from wherever he was in the house.

"You ready to go, son?" He asked, walking towards me. I nodded my head, noticing how he looked damp in the face but very put together everywhere else. I followed him outside and back into the car, where we made our way to the mall for whatever I wanted in exchange for my silence.

"I'm sorry, mom-"

"You were a kid, and you have nothing to be sorry about. Having to choose between parents is a very tough thing to do."

"Yeah, I didn't want him mad at me, and I didn't want you to leave."

"I left. You just didn't know. I didn't want to disrupt your life, so I made sure every morning I was there, and before you went to bed, I was there. But immediately after, I left to my sister's house, and that went on for almost a year."

"Really? How come I didn't know that."

"It wasn't for you to know. Our issues were ours, and you didn't need to be brought into that more than you had already."

"Yeah, you're right." I groaned.

"I also regret not getting you therapy, but I thought since it stopped that you would be ok, but I can see how that's the furthest from the truth. That was a trauma you internalized, and it shaped you into what you are now, and for that, I apologize."

"It's ok, mama."

"No, baby, it's not. Get yourself some help before it all falls down."

CHAPTER 20
TAMERA

"Boy, please, I'm a be flyer than you. You dress like Carlton Banks." Josh said with his lip turned up, roasting Johan.

"Carlton Banks? Boy, you over there dressed like a Halloween costume, you think you, Batman?" Johan asked, lifting Josh's batman shirt he laid out for school tomorrow.

"Yep, and Batman will beat you."

"Batman can't even fly without gadgets boy get yo I only have powers when I got my toys HEAD out of here."

"You just mad cuz Carlton Banks don't have powers." Josh teased, snatching his shirt back from Johan.

"Alright, that's enough." I laughed. "Yall are a mess. Thing one and thing two, that's for sure."

"That's that dude." Josh pointed at Johan, who swatted his hand away.

"Whatever."

"Anyways, let's say our prayers and get in this bed. Y'all wore me out today!"

"Don't forget me," Jason said as he came into the room, he had been doing a lot better coming home at a great hour, even making it to practice with the boys.

"Ooo, Ooo, can I say the prayer tonight, please?" Johan asked.

"Absolutely, baby." I kissed his forehead before we all formed a prayer circle.

"Dear God, we humbly come to you to thank you for life. We thank you for letting us live another day. God, we ask that you continue to bless us as we seek your guidance. God bless mama, daddy, my brother, and my family. In Jesus name-"

"Amen," We all said together.

"That was awesome, man!" Jason said, giving Johan a tight hug. "We gon have to let you take over prayer more. Where did you get that one from?"

"Gram does that prayer when we spend the night with her," Josh said as he hugged Jason and me.

"I felt that one in my spirit," Jason said, doing a holy dance, and we all chuckled heartily.

"Alright, I love you guys," I said as they got into their beds.

"Love you too." They both said back. Jason and I kissed their foreheads and turned on their nightlights before leaving out of their room.

"That boy prayed with some conviction back there, voice got deeper and everything." Jason joked as we walked into our room. I guffawed and hit his arm.

"Don't talk about my baby. He's passionate."

"Nothing wrong with it. Hell, he might end up a pastor one day. He already dresses like one." He snickered.

"I'm telling him you said that too." I teased, sticking out my tongue.

"Snitches get stitches." He said, running his finger across his neck.

"Yeah, yeah, yeah." I rolled my eyes playfully as I grabbed my laptop and sat on the bed.

"How's the architecture phase going? I know you told me earlier he had sent the drawings. Were they to your liking?" Jason asked, getting in bed scooting next to me.

"Baby, yes!!!" I squealed. "I'm so excited I don't know what to do. His drawings are amazing!"

"Yeah, he's pretty good. He remodeled all mamas bakeries, so I know he can hook your building up."

"True. I'm just ready to see it happen and be completed." I said, pulling up the file with the drawings to show him.

"I get that, so what's the next step now?"

"So now he has to send the design and drawing to the Department of Building, then they have to take a look at it and make sure everything is good so that they can approve it. The thing I like the best about Ben's drawing is that he has separate drawings for everybody. For example, he has one drawing for the electrician, which is strictly for him so that he's not confused with what everybody else is doing. He said that the biggest complaints are normally that they all get the same drawing instead of what's needed for their exact job. He also said this makes his job easy." I showed him the different drawings for him to see, he nodded his head in approval.

"That's dope as hell. He is really on his shit. So how soon can they start?" He said as he tapped away on his phone.

"Well, he's adamant that in good business, there are bids on contracts. So he wants me to see the bids from other construction companies to see if there may be something better for me instead of just going with his company. But I already know I'm going to go with him."

"Right. You already see the kind of work he can do, so I get that." He sat his phone down on the side table.

"Yeah, I'm just so excited."

"I'm proud of you, baby," Jason said as he leaned over and kissed my neck.

"Thank you, baby. OH! Before I forget, I have something to run by you." I said, going into my email and opening an email from Aerca. "I'm also looking into owning property. Aerca found this duplex, and it already has tenants, so I would just buy the house and start getting income from it."

"Wow. Are you sure that's something you want to do?" He asked, still kissing my neck.

"Yes," I said, nudging him off my neck. "Look, it's a nice property. They only want two hundred and fifty thousand for it. Aerca thinks that if I offer a cash deal, we can knock off at least sixty of that."

"IF" is the keyword. You sure this won't be too much on you?"

"No." I rolled my eyes. "I can manage, and even if I can't, I could always hire a property management company."

"Well, baby, sounds like you have it all planned out."

"No, but it's nice to have your support and help if I need it."

"And you do. Whatever you need, I'll do. I know things have

been rocky lately, and I acknowledge it's my fault, but I'm doing better and will continue to do better for you and my kids, ok?" Jason said, turning my head and kissing my lips.

"Ok." I closed my laptop and put it on my side table before getting back in bed.

"So I was thinking that this weekend, let's get away, do a staycation or something."

"This weekend? Jason, tomorrow is Friday!" I shrieked, thinking about all the shit I would need to do in order to get ready for a vacation.

"Yeah, I know, and?" He asked, confused.

"Do you know all the shit I would need to do? My hair needs to be done, my nails, my feet. I need some clothes for it. Why are you just now saying something?" I asked, jumping out of bed and going over to our walk-in closet. Jason laughed and came behind me, dragging me back to the bed.

"Calm down, crazy lady. I just thought about it as we laid here. Get up early tomorrow and go do all that shit you claim you need to do because you're perfect to me."

"Blah blah," I rolled my eyes playfully. "What about the boys? They have school in the morning, and where would they go?"

"Now you know my mom would kill for a weekend with them. Look, I'll take tomorrow off from work, you can run whatever errands you need to do, and I'll take the boys to school. You just be back before four pm." he said, tapping away in his phone again.

"You ain't said nothing but a word," I said, doing a happy dance in the bed. "Let me call Aerca real quick and see if she can come with me."

"Oh lord. You do that, and I'm a go call, my mom, to set things in motion." He said as he got up, grabbing his phone before walking out the room. I grabbed my phone and went to Aercas contact, calling her before walking back over to my closet to see if there was anything I may have wanted to take with me.

The Next Morning

"Good Morning, Ladiessss." Our stylist Staci said as she opened the door for us. Staci had a beautiful full-service salon, and you can come here and get your hair, nails, feet. Brows, lashes, and facials done. Everything was appointment only unless you were one of her VIPs, and even then, if it's last-minute, you have to pay an extra fee.

"Hey, beautiful," I said, hugging her. Staci was indeed beautiful, thick as hell, most would call her plus-sized, and she had the most blemish-free cream color skin with pouty lips, a cute button nose, and almond-shaped eyes that gave her a sexy cat look.

"Goodmorning," Aerca said behind me, hugging Staci.

"Sorry we called on you last minute, but I need you, girl," I whined. "My husband came to me last night talking about a trip today knowing damn well all the shit us women have to do to get ready."

"Oh hell, he plays too much. But I know exactly what you mean. So what hairstyles are y'all getting today?"

"I'm a get a blowout and silk press. Then nails, feet, and a facial."

"I'm going to get a wash and go. Curls for the girls and all the rest, she said." Aerca joked, snapping her fingers in a circle.

"Yall are so crazy. Do yall want something to drink? I got some water in here, I'm about to run across the street to Starbucks, and I can grab something from there if you want."

"I'll take Starbucks for 500, Alex," Aerca said. We all guffawed.

"Same." I nodded my head.

"Alright, cool. So Aerca, you want to roll with me over there and then come back, and we can get started on your nails, and Tamera, I'm a have Samantha get you washed and conditioned right now. Cool?"

"Cool! Perfect!" Aerca and I said at the same time. I gave Aerca my order before being led to the shampoo area by Samantha. We made small talk while she grabbed the products I told her Staci normally uses on my hair. I almost moaned out when Samantha started washing my hair, and lord knows her hands felt like heaven as she massaged my scalp.

"Girl, you know you got them magic hands!" I said after we finished the shampoo rinse.

"Everybody says that." Samantha laughed as she put a deep conditioner in my hair. "I love your hair. Have you ever thought about any color?"

"Yes, I've been thinking about it lately. I will soon. I have to figure out what color I'm a go with."

"Some golden blonde would make your eyes pop even more."

"I'll keep that in mind." She nodded and asked me to lean back so that we could rinse the conditioner out.

Three hours later

"Alright, call me yall. Y'all be forgetting about me." Staci pouted playfully.

"Girl, bye. Your ass was down at the jailhouse every other day. Every time we called you to come out for lunch, you were talking about "I gotta go see my mannn." Aerca hissed, rolling her eyes playfully.

"Oop. Please don't do me. He home now." Staci laughed.

"Well, hell, that means you got even less time now. You probably been on your back all day every day when you not working." We all laughed loudly.

"And is!" Aerca joined in.

"Yall some damn fools. Call me! I'm not playing with yall uppity asses."

"Ok, ok." I threw my hands up, laughing.

"Bye, hoe." Aerca hugged Staci before we walked out of the salon.

"Now, let's get in this mall and spend a check," I said as we hopped into my truck.

"That's what I do best!"

"So…" I teased. "Are you nervous about your date tomorrow?"

"Bitch... I'm about to get bubble guts thinking about it now." Aercas dramatic ass said, rubbing her stomach.

"Why?" I asked as I pulled into traffic.

"Did you see that fine ass man?" Aerca fanned herself.

"He is handsome! Y'all would make some pretty ass babies!" I gushed.

"See! That's what I'm afraid of! You know damn well I'm a virgin, and I've never even been kissed." Aerca mumbled that last part as she dug in her clutch.

"Oh, I know you lying!" I screeched. "Are you serious?"

"Yes, you know I don't play that. Especially with the parents I have. My whole life, it's been *keep your legs close and wait for marriage*." She mimicked an accent.

"And there is nothing wrong with that boo. Jason is the only man I've been with." I said, shrugging my shoulders. "He's taught me whatever I didn't learn from porn."

“Porrnnnnnnnn.” She said mocking soulja boy.

"Yes, ma'am. I ain't heard a complaint yet." I stuck my tongue out, rolling my hips.

"Ugh, stop all that before you crash." She rolled her eyes. "I just don't feel like getting my feelings involved, and then he leaves because I'm holding out."

"I get that, but as long as you let him know that's what it is upfront, it's on him to be a man and say he can deal with it or he can't; and if he can't, then shit, he ain't the man for you no way."

"Preach!"

"I got faith in him, though. He seems like a sincere and upfront man."

"Yeah, but you never know."

"Yes, you never know. But you have to be optimistic as well. You can't go into a situation with a wall up thinking he's out to get you, or you will ruin it before it even starts. So stop overthinking and have fun."

"You right." She sighed heavily.

"I know I am. Plus, once he sees how good you're going to look, he ain't going to want to let that go." I smiled as we pulled into the mall parking lot.

CHAPTER 21
JASON

Picking up the boys and dropping them at my mom's house. I'll meet you at home. Love you. I pressed send on the text to Tamera. I knew my wife, and I knew how she prided herself on being a superwoman and getting everything done. That was my fault, I left the burden of taking care of our family on her shoulders most days, but I swear I'm going to help out more.

Before I went to the boy's school, I had run into a local flower shop and grabbed Tamera a bouquet just because I knew shit like this meant a lot to her. It's like I had an epiphany of all the shit I needed to do to keep my wife by my side.

Ok, love you too. I'm almost done at the mall.

Remember four pm. I texted back as I got out of the car and walked towards the boy's school.

I'll be there, baby.

And not on CP time. I sent back with a side-eye emoji. She responded with a bunch of laughing emojis.

After grabbing the boys, I called my mom to see where she was before I dropped the boys off, and she let me know she was at home. She was adamant about me not bringing them anything, saying that she had more than enough for them at her house in their rooms. Yes, she had rooms for them at her home as well.

"Well, boys, you guys are going to be spending the weekend with gram and pop pop!" I said, looking in the rearview mirror. They both yelled out, yay and started talking about everything they would be eating and doing. "Don't let gram or pop pop tell mom or me that you guys have been fighting or acting up, or you guys are going to be on restriction."

"We won't." They both said.

"Good." We sang along to a few songs on the radio before I pulled up to my mother's house, where she was in front of her house checking out her beds of flowers.

"Ain't they looking good?" She said as I got out of the car.

"They are! You always had the prettiest flowers. I just got Tamera some. I should've come and stole yours." I laughed as I opened the door for the boys, who ran over to her immediately.

"You touch my flowers, and I'll break your fingers." She said, pointing her finger at me.

"I know you would. Remember I stepped on one before, and you tried to fight me?" I laughed while hugging her.

"I sure did. Talking about you ain't see my dang on flowers. Come on, wash your hands. I made some cookies."

I followed her into the house, and the boys ran into the bathroom so they could wash their hands as I did in the kitchen.

"How are you, son?" My mother asked as she laid three cookies out on two napkins for the boys, along with cups of lemonade.

"I'm good." I nodded my head as I grabbed a few cookies off the platter.

"That's good. So what do you have planned for Tamera this weekend?"

"Well, I'm gonna-"

"Done!" The boys yelled, running into the kitchen; after scolding them for running in the house, my mother handed them their drinks and snacks and told them to go into the back yard, where she had a patio and play area.

"Ok, now you said y'all are going where?." She waved her hand at me.

"I bought tickets to Vegas, and she's never been there, so I know she will be happy. Then going to take her to the Usher concert they have down there and then wing it from there." I shrugged.

"That's good." She said with a small smile. "But you know doing all this nice stuff won't lessen the blow, right?"

"I know."

"As bad as this all is, you just gotta rip the bandaid off and let things fall where they may."

"Yeah." I sighed. "So what time is Jayla coming over?"

"That girl should be pulling up any minute now." My mother rolled her eyes. "I will never understand why a woman that looks like her with such a good job and seems like she has so much going for herself put herself in this situation."

"How long will Jayla be staying?" I asked, changing the subject.

"Just until Sunday evening." I nodded and peeked out the window to see what the boys were doing in the backyard. They were still talking and eating their cookies.

"The boys will probably ask who she is…." My mother said lowly as she looked at me.

"I thought about that."

"And what do you suppose I say?"

"Nothing. Just say she's Jayla." I shrugged my shoulders.

"Wow." My mother shook her head. "I don't even like being-" she was cut off by her ringer blaring on her cellphone. "This is Tamera now."

"Answer it."

"I am. I just don't like this." She said before pressing the green answer button. "Hey, pretty."

"Hey, mama! How are you?"

"I'm good, baby. How are you?" My mother asked as she squeezed her eyes tight.

"Same. I know Jason has this weekend trip planned for us, but let me know if you have a lot going on. I'm sure we can find a way to bring the boys with us."

"No, we can't!" I interrupted.

"Uh! Jason!" Tamera laughed. "I didn't know you were at mommy's house."

"Yeah, I've been here since I dropped the boys off."

"Mmmhmm. Well, don't be over there driving her crazy with the boys." Tamera fussed.

"Now you know I ain't going to let them worry me. I got plenty of switches in the back." My mom joked.

"Yeah, for decoration, you know doggone well you don't be

whooping nobody," Tamera said, and we all laughed.

"I can pretend I am. They are scared enough when I give them the look."

"You ain't never lied. All black mamas got that look that straightens kids up quick."

"Sure do! You all packed up?" Mama asked.

"Just about. I just grabbed a few things from the mall and just have to put them in my suitcase."

"You act like we are leaving for a week. All you need is three outfits!" I shrieked, shaking my head.

"Three?" My mom and Tamera said at the same time.

"Oh, he's tripping."

"He sure is, mama! But you know men, they'll wear one outfit all day from breakfast to a nice event without changing or showering."

"Yes, little funky selves." My mother teased me by sticking her tongue out.

"Yes! They sure are. It's quiet over there. Are the boys napping?"

"No, they're snacking on the back patio. Gave them some cookies and lemonade."

"Oh, that's why they're quiet, the only two times. Food and sleep."

"You know it! Wanna talk to them?"

"Yeah, thanks, Mama." I walked over to the patio door and told the boys to speak to their mama. They sat on the phone with her for a few minutes while she inquired about their day, told them to behave and how much she loved them before letting us know she was about to drop Aerca home and would see me shortly.

"Alright, well, let me get out of here so I can beat her home," I told my mother as I checked my email notification.

"Ok." She sniffled, causing me to look up.

"What's wrong?" I asked, encasing her in a hug.

"My heart is just broken right now, Jason. I love that girl like she came from me, and I'm a lose her." She sobbed. "That hurts me to my heart. I don't know why it's not hurting you."

"I'm just not trying to think negatively about it. You stayed with daddy."

"That was me! Don't base your marriage off of mine. Me and Tamera are two different people."

"I know, mama." I groaned.

"I hope so, son." I kissed my mother on her forehead and walked out to my car. As I was pulling out, Lynn was pulling in. I was not in the mood to go back and forth with her. So I just nodded and continued home. By the time I made it home, Tamera was pulling in as well.

"Hey, baby." She said as I opened her door, kissing me.

"Did you get everything you needed? You look beautiful." I noticed she was wearing her hair straight which she rarely did.

"Yes. I grabbed you and the boys some things too." She popped the trunk, and I shook my head when I saw that it was packed.

"Don't judge me." She laughed as she opened the front door. I went back and forth carrying the bags in the house. She had brought her suitcase down by the time I was done; mine was already positioned in the foyer.

"I'm just going to add some of the things I have, and then I'm all set."

"Ok, baby." I nodded my head before going back to my car to get her flowers.

"I'm ready whenever you are." She said as she looked down, zipping up her luggage.

"I'm ready," I said, holding her flowers out in front of me. When she looked up, her eyes ballooned.

"Oh, baby!" Her eyes watered. "Thank you so much. You know I love flowers. Let me put these in water really quick." She said as she took off towards the kitchen.

"I have another surprise," I said, reaching in my back pocket.

"Really?" She beamed with her eyebrow raised.

"Check me out," I said, passing her the Usher concert tickets. She took a second to read over the tickets before she let out a scream and jumped on me.

"We going to Vegas? AND going to see Usher?" She kissed all over my face.

"Yes, we got two hours to get to the airport and make our flight. We need to go like now." I laughed, looking at the wall clock in the kitchen.

"You ain't said nothing but a word!" She jumped down and scrambled out of the kitchen.

CHAPTER 22
AERCA

Honayyyyy, that yellow dress is the one! It looks like skin, and you are serving some serious bawdy! Tamera texted back after I sent her two photos of me in an hourglass midi dress by x Momma Malika NW, one in the color yellow the other in black.

You sure? I don't want to send the wrong message. I text back as I twirled in the mirror. This yellow midi did look bomb on me, and it accentuated all the curves I possessed and honey! I was a stallion. I had a flat stomach, legs, ass, and titties for days. No matter how much I tried to downplay my curves, it never worked.

DING

My text notifications went off. One text from Tamera, the other from Ben Lee. I went to Ben Lee's notification first, scared that he was canceling at the last minute.

Hey beautiful. I blushed and texted back, feeling like I was a high school girl with her first crush.

Hey, handsome (smiley face).

As I waited for him to text back, I went back to Tamera's text to confirm that this was the dress I should go with.

I'm sure! Clothes don't give the wrong message! Women are not fucking objects.

You're right, sis. I'm just nervous.

You're not backing out on me, are you? A text from Ben Lee popped up.

Nope. You think I'm passing up a free meal? (tongue out emoji with crossed eyes).

Don't be nervous, babe. You're an incredible woman. Just relax. Tamera texted back.

I will, but don't be surprised if I call you for guidance to have you in my ear.

Freeeee? (Soulja Boy gif) I thought you were paying (shocked face emoji). I laughed heartily before texting back.

Let me put this bomb-ass dress back in the closet and get my clown suit out since you thought that.

Aht Aht, don't call me. I'ma be VIP with Usher heaux! Tamera texted back.

I'm still mad at you for going without me, so I'm calling for sure. (tongue out emoji).

Clown suit? Oh, you like role-playing?

I only bring out the clown suit when I'm being taken to the circus.

Let me go ahead and block you now (purple devil emoji).

You block me, and I'll be waiting for you in your hotel room with vaseline on my face so I can whoop your ass. I text Tamera back.

I don't plan on being the ringmaster today, so you can keep that one in the closet. What time should I pick you up?

Bitch please! I'll kick you right in them strong ass kneecaps.

Yeah, because that's all you can reach, leprechaun. But anyway, should I let him pick me up or meet me there? I felt like it would be safer for me to drive myself there. That way, if I wanted to leave, I could just hop in my car and go. However, I don't get bad vibes from him, but you never know.

Either or. We know where he works, so if he is on some fuck shit, we can blow his shit up. (laughing emoji).

You right. (laughing emoji)

You can certainly pick me up. Are you going to ring my doorbell too? (questionable face emoji)

Yes ma'am. My daddy raised me right.

Good. Don't be late. I said before sending my address. We agreed on a seven pm date, and it was now four pm, so I had time to sit and get my mind right. I had already meditated that morning, so now I was just about to get high and check on my investments. I had just pulled up my stock portfolio on my laptop when a FaceTime from Nadia came through.

"Hey, my love," I said once it connected. We both burst out in laughter, seeing how we looked identical in our underwear, both smoking a joint.

"See, that's why you, my favorite sister!" Nadia smiled as she took a hit on her joint.

"Girl, bye. I'm your only sister."

"You sure?" Nadia asked with her brow raised. "You know what they say about them Haitians."

"I'm sure. You know Manman would crack papa right over the

head with her skillet if she thought otherwise." We both chuckled, thinking about how many times we have been threatened with manmans cast iron skillet.

"She stayed tryna hit somebody."

"And did. She swears she, Serena Williams." I joked, causing us to laugh harder.

"What you up to? I'm surprised you not out working right now."

"I would've been, but I got a dateeee." I stuck my tongue out doing a happy dance.

"Oh, God. With who?" I ran down the story of how we met up until today.

"Oh yes, this sounds like a good time. Hopefully, he can get you to give up that snatch." I started choking on smoke, shaking my head.

"Bye, hoe."

"Nah, don't try and hang up." She laughed. "You let mama and daddy keep you from enjoying your life. You don't even date. Probably ain't never been kissed."

"Nah...big sis, say it ain't so!" She said, getting close to the camera after noticing I was quiet. "You ain't never been kissed?"

"I don't want everybody's mouth on me!" I shrieked, shrugging my shoulders.

"BITCH, PLEASE!" She screeched. "What are you going to do if he tries to kiss you tonight?"

"I'm a curve his ass like the letter c!"

"And he gon' leave yo ass at the curb that starts with the letter c." She shook her head. "I guess I can tell you what to do. It depends on the kiss-"

"I am NOT about to let my little sister teach me to kiss." I waved her off as I finished off my joint, sitting it in the ashtray nearby.

6:58 pm

DING! DONG!

"Well, aren't you early?" I said after looking out my peephole and answering the door.

"Well-I-...shit," Ben Lee said as he looked me over. I nodded my head with a smile and twirled around.

"Ain't I fly?" I joked, pulling the door closed behind me.

"Fly ain't the word. Yo ass is trouble." He hissed as he put his hand on the small of my back to walk me towards a 2021 Cadillac escalade that was blacked out. Before he could touch the door, a big black man came from around the other side of the vehicle scaring the shit out of me.

"Relax, baby, that's just my driver Adam," he said, nodding towards the man. The man opened the door and closed it after we both got in.

"Oh, you got a driver? You got monaaayyyyyyyy." I said, mocking the viral video causing him to laugh loudly.

"You are something else." He shook his head. "That's my guy. He's been with our family for years."

"Oh, y'all got monaayyyyy then and not just you."

"We do ok." He smiled.

"Better than ok, Mister eighteen million net worth."

"I see somebody did their research."

"As you did me." I nodded at him with a smirk. "A man like you would never come over here without doing his research. I'm sure you already had my address before I even gave it to you... Am I right?" He smiled and shook his head.

"Smart woman."

"Mmmhmm. Is there anything that you don't know about me?"

"So Haiti, huh?"

"Yes. Ever been?"

"No. I would love to someday. When is the last time you went?"

"Not since we left when I was a little girl."

"Do you want to go back?"

"I don't know. Haiti didn't leave me with good memories." I sighed heavily. He nodded his head and rubbed my hand.

"My mother is from China. Whenever we visit, people stare at my sister and me like we are aliens and take pictures of us."

"Wow, really?" I asked with my brow raised.

"Yeah. They act like it's a culture shock to see black people. More so my sister than me. She's around your complexion with Asian features, so they try and touch her or take photos of her the whole time. She hates it."

"I can imagine. Are you all close?"

"Yes and no."

"Meaning?"

"We love each other obviously, but I feel like my sister, and I resent our mom just a bit. Asian culture is no joke at times."

"Oooohh, I know about parents and their cultures. But, unfortunately, my parents have wrecked my mind with what I should and shouldn't do all the time."

"Oh, we have a lot more in common than I thought, Miss Peters." He joked as the car came to a stop. We both got quiet as Adam got out and opened the door for us. That's when I noticed that we were at the new restaurant Chef Amor.

"I didn't know this place was open yet," I said, pointing towards the restaurant.

"They're not." Ben Lee said. "I constructed this place, and I'm cool with the owner. So I called him and told him I had this beautiful ass woman I needed to impress, and he opened it for me."

"You're kidding!" I squealed. He shook his head no, put his hand on the small of my back AGAIN, and led me towards the restaurant door where a woman stood in hostess uniform.

"Welcome to Chef Amor, Mr. and Mrs. Suttle. Chef Thomas has everything set up already. Let me get you to your tables so that we can begin." She said, smiling. I looked at Ben Lee with my brow raised at her, referring to me as his wife, and he smirked and shrugged his shoulders.

"Manifestation is real." I blushed and followed behind the hostess, who walked us over to a dimly lit area. A circular table was covered in an ivory satin table cloth that housed two chairs covered in black fabric with a white bow tied around the back. On the table sat a beautiful bouquet and candles that illuminated the area.

"This is beautiful." I beamed, looking at Ben Lee, who waited for me to sit down so he could push my chair in.

"Not as beautiful as you, though." He smiled as he sat in his seat.

"Benjamin Lee, my man!" A man yelled as he walked upon us in a chef uniform. He was an older tall white man with a peppered beard and dark eyes. "She is beautiful! You didn't lie. Some guys say beautiful girl, and I see the girl, and she looks like my mom's dog. But you were telling the truth." He joked as he winked at me.

"Come on, man." Ben Lee laughed as he got up and hugged the man.

"Jasper, this is Aerca, Aerca Jasper." Ben Lee introduced us.

"Nice to meet you, beautiful." He said, kissing my hand that I put out for a shake.

"Aye, hey!" Ben Lee laughed. "Don't be trying to steal her away. I haven't even gotten the chance to woo her yet."

"You're lucky this time, buddy. If I weren't happily married, I'd make her fall in love with me by giving her some of the chocolate cake in the back."

"I love chocolate." I joked, winking at Ben Lee.

"Aw damn." Ben Lee laughed, shaking his head.

"That chocolate will do it every time." Jasper laughed. "Benjamin's a good guy. You're in good hands with him. We aren't even open yet, and he offered me a car full of money to make this night special for you, so let me tell you what I have for you guys this evening." Jasper ran down the whole menu, and my eyes ballooned. I couldn't believe Ben Lee had him do that for our date. He was surely winning brownie points.

"So tell me something, Miss Peters-" Ben Lee started before I cut him off.

"Oh, I'm not Mrs. Suttles anymore, damn." I teased fake mad as I bit into the stuffed mushroom appetizer.

"Don't play, woman. I'll drag you to the courthouse soon as they open." He teased back.

"Anyways." I rolled my eyes playfully.

"As I was saying, Mrs. Soon to be Suttles. Why are you single?"

I wiped my mouth and took a sip of my wine before answering. "Cultural differences."

"Like?"

"Like I'm a virgin who has never been kissed," I said coyly while staring at him, expecting a big reaction in which I got none.

"I'm still not understanding why you're single."

"You know how you men are."

"You mean boys. Boys are pressed for pussy and a few kisses. Real men know there's way more to a relationship than that."

"Ok then, grown man. So that's not a problem for you, is what you're saying?"

"That's what I'm telling you." He nodded his head. "So when you say cultural differences in regards to your virginity, in Haitian culture, they want you to wait for marriage?"

"I'm not sure about all Haitian households, but my parents prefer for me to wait until I'm married. They wanted me to stay with them until I married, but I wasn't having that." I snickered.

"It's that bad?" He laughed.

"I just like my peace. Manman and papa are very friendly people, so they think I want to talk all day and be up under them when I'm at their house. I like my space. Plus, I smoke weed and play loud music, and manman would try and iron skillet me if she knew."

"Iron skillet?"

"Yes, manman would swing that skillet at you if you got on her bad side," I said, mocking her with my hand, and he laughed loudly.

"That reminds me of my mother, she's a small Chinese woman, but she would whack you with anything that she saw."

"See, you get me." I nodded my head. We both stopped talking once Jasper approached our table with dinner. He wasn't playing when he said he made the whole menu. He got to go back into the kitchen a few times just so that he could bring it all out. The rest of dinner was terrific. Ben Lee and I got to know one another, and I hoped that we could do this more often.

"What are you over there thinking about?" Ben Lee asked as we were driven back to my place.

"I'm thinking about how you didn't ask me for another date yet," I smirked. Ben Lee mirrored my smirk and nodded his head.

"See, that was going to be the grand finale at the door, but you done ruined that." I chuckled, slapping his shoulder.

"Stop playing Ben Lee!"

"Alright, alright. You ain't got no skillet in that purse of yours, do you? The way you swinging that arm."

"Not in this expensive ass Gucci clutch!" I fake clutched my purse in shock.

"You never know." He shrugged. "So you want to see more of me?"

"I think I can grace you with my presence more." I teased, shrugging.

"I'd like that Mrs. Soon to be Suttles. When are you free again?"

"Just let me know the time, and I'll make sure that I am free for you."

Chapter 23
Kylan

"Alright, we are going to do these cone drills. I set up each of the cones three and a half yards from one another. There are three groups, and I want all three groups to line up in a straight line behind these cones, so group A here, group b here, and group c here." I pointed at each cone.

"When I blow my whistle, the person at the front of the line will run around the cones, whichever team finishes accurately and first wins doesn't have to run five miles today, only three."

"Oh yeah!"

"We gon win!"

"Yall better not make us lose, man!" All the boys yelled out something in regards to not losing this drill.

"Alright, yall, just better bring your best foot forward," I said as I moved back so that I could watch them all.

"What up, my boy?" I heard from behind. I turned around, and Doc was walking up on me, shining like always.

"Aye, what's up, man! Your late ass! I said nine am." I joked, hugging him.

"Listen, I'm barely up at noon, so this was a miracle." He laughed.

"Either way, I'm glad you could make it. You know how much sports meant to us being in the streets; that's the only time we were able to be regular-ass kids, ya dig?"

"You know I know." He nodded his head.

"Hell yeah, let me introduce you to the guys," I said, walking back towards the boys who stood there watching our interaction. "Boys, this is my guy Doc. If you from around here, then you've heard plenty about Doc from high school games and games around the neighborhood. Doc was one of the best quarterbacks around! He could knock the fastest and biggest man down quicker than you could think. So he's here today to give you guys some pointers and help us out. Is that cool?"

"Wow."

"I've heard of him."

"My dad was talking about him." All the boys chattered.

"They're about to do cones now. I told them the group to win only has to do three laps on the track. The rest gotta do the full five."

"Oooo, I hated that shit." Doc shook his head with a smile.

"On your mark… get set… GO!" I blew my whistle. Every week this is what I did. I helped boys in the neighborhood get into sports to keep them off the streets. I charged them nothing and paid for everything. After practice, we sit and eat lunch while we talk about what they have going on. I even reward them for good grades.

After Practice

"So what do you think, man?" I asked Doc nodding towards the empty field where the boys just left.

"That kid Lance is nothing to fuck with on the field!" Doc said, nodding his head with a beam in his eye.

"I told you! My boy is lightning fast." I smiled, thinking about my nephew. He was athletic and competitive as hell and had it in him to go pro if he stayed in football as he got older.

"He is! They not fucking with him."

"Yeah. When the school league starts, I told him to let me know the fees and shit, and I'll pay it. I told him I'll even pay for a tutor."

"That's some solid shit, Rip. Niggas ain't built like that these days. You walk it and talking it."

"I got to. I lived this street shit. How many of our niggas didn't make it? We did."

"You right. Speaking of, I called that stuffy ass nigga you told me to call."

"Who?" I asked with my brow raised.

"McDowell, McDougie, Mc some shit," Doc said, waving his hand. "The clean money nigga."

"McNaulty?" I asked, snickering.

"Yes, him. His ass was talking about making an appointment. I kept telling him I wasn't on that type of time, so I just went up there to his office. Should've seen his face nigga. Boy was red as a fucking tomato talking about "this is not how I do business." Doc mocked McNaulty as he frowned his face up, and we both guffawed.

"Mannnnn…" I said, trying to catch my breath. "So, what did you do when he said that?"

"Now you already know. I threw a duffle bag full of money on his desk and told him how he do it today. He changed his tune real fucking quick."

"I already know! Money talks no matter what color you are."

"You feel me? So he put my shit into some stocks, I told his ass if I lost a dime, I was gon' bust his ass too."

"Nigga!" I laughed. "Stocks are tricky like that. What else he do?"

"He told me that I should open up a few more salons for Staci and be a silent partner, and that will help clean my shit up too. She's been talking about opening more, so that's right up my alley. I gotta find a turnkey and shit."

"Bet. I got somebody who can help you with that. She's cold at finding the best buildings and shit her name Aerca. She's been helping me look for a spot for my practice. I've been picky as hell. That's the only reason I haven't found shit yet, but trust me, she's solid." I said as I went through my contacts and texted him the contact card.

"Ok, bet. I'm a hit her up as soon as I leave from around here."

"It's Sunday!" I said with my brow up.

"And nigga?" Doc asked, mirroring my look. I threw my hands up in surrender, knowing he didn't give not one fuck. "Anyways, I saw your one shorty the other day."

"Who?"

"Ozen, or whatever her name is, the little mouthy big-faced one I couldn't stand."

"Onyx."

"Yeah, she was on the block the other day, tried to ask me about you and shit."

"Asking what? I told her ass the last time I saw her to keep it moving."

"Shid, I asked her did it look like you were in my mothafucking back pocket. Don't ask me about the next nigga."

"She's crazy. Started beefing with me because I got out of the streets. She doesn't like this legit shit and thought that talking crazy to me would make me want to get back in, but all that did was get her ass tossed."

"Shorty wild'n like that?" Doc shook his head. "These bitches just want the title of being with a street nigga, don't give a fuck if you in the dirt or doing eight to ten."

"Exactly. I ain't on that shit."

"Staci ass been on me, shorty gave me an ultimatum, told me I had a year to wrap this shit up, or she was out. Said she done holding a nigga down just for me to get locked up or die, said she wants a family and shit." He shook his head. "I ain't mad at it. That's why I jumped at that opportunity to clean my shit up. But like I said before, this all I fucking know ya dig?"

"Real shit. Staci got my boy ready to be a family man?"

"Shut up, man." He gave me the finger. "She deserves that shit. She stood ten toes down while I was in and out. Every bid I did shorty did it with me. I know she's fed up. I can't keep making my shorty cry."

I nodded my head, understanding. "I get it. Ain't too many out there like that."

"At all. As a matter of fact, let me get up out of here. She told me to bring her some lunch an hour ago, so I know she gon' light my ass up. So I'm blaming you."

"Tell sis I'm sorry!" I said before dapping him. We made small talk as we both walked to our cars. I looked at my watch and noticed I had an hour to get home, shower, and make my way to Lake's house. We have been talking more lately, and I even have dinner on Sundays when I'm available. I turned on some music and made my way home while in my thoughts; as I neared my house, I noticed a for lease sign on a fairly new building right off the highway. I pulled over and took a picture of the for lease sign, and peeked in the windows. Maybe I can get my shit sooner than later. I got in my car and sent the address and picture to Aerca, asking if she could find out information on this property when she got a chance, and made my way home with a smile on my face. Today was a good day.

Chapter 24
Jason

"Thank you so much, baby. I enjoyed myself. That was truly the trip I didn't know I needed." Tamera said, kissing my cheek as I put my seatbelt on. We had just made it back from Vegas and were back into the car on the way to get the boys. I had already confirmed with my mother that Jayla had left already, so that was one less thing on my mind.

"You heard me, baby?" Tamera asked, snapping me out of my thoughts.

"Shit, my bad baby, I'm jet-lagged." I shook my head.

"You should've rested on the plane as I did. Do you need me to drive?"

"Nah, I'm ok. I'll get some rest when we get home. Wanna stop and get some takeout on the way home?"

"Good idea because I would need to defrost something and then cook. I'll be in the kitchen all night. What do you have a taste for?" She asked as I merged into traffic.

"What about some Chinese? I haven't had any of that in a while."

"Ok. I'll call and place an order once we get to your mom's house. What you want some orange chicken?"

"You already know. We gon' sleep good tonight. Those beds weren't bad at the hotel but ain't nothing like your own bed."

"You ain't never lied about that, plus I miss my babies." She pouted as she texted on her phone.

"Well, they will be causing chaos in less than twenty minutes."

"Right, I'll regret my words in a few hours." She laughed. "Hey babe, did you put all this together on your own, or you used a travel specialist?"

"I used a specialist. It was so last minute, but she got it done. I found her right on google too. Her name is Dena or something. I'll have to look in my email. Why?"

"Aerca jealous little ass wants to go on a girls trip since she claims we snuck out on her."

"Oh, ok, when is she thinking about going?"

"It's got to be in a few weeks or something because I want to be there for the start of construction to make sure nothing is going wrong."

"Oh, ok, when I get home, I'll go through my email and send you her information. She should already have my card on file, so use that."

"You sure, babe? Aerca was bringing her sister Nadia too."

"It's fine, baby. Your husband got it." I joked. "I know you balling, but I ain't doing too shabby."

"Oh, hush!" She swatted at me. "Don't say anything when you get that bill in the mail."

"I won't. I'll make sure to get it back another way." I stuck my tongue out nastily.

"Say that then." She winked at me.

A few minutes later

"Hey, my babies!" Tamera shrieked, jumping out of the car running towards the boys. My mother and I laughed at the image because Tamera wasn't that much taller than the boys. She could pull off telling people she was just their big sister, and they would never question it.

"I missed you, Mama!" Johan squealed as she kissed all over his face.

"I don't miss this part tho." Josh frowned as Tamera made her way to his face.

"Boy, hush! You gon wish somebody kissed and loved on you like that when you get older." My mother teased Josh.

"Sure will!" Tamera said, sticking her tongue out. "Hey, mama. They didn't raise your blood pressure too much, did they?"

"Honey, no! We had a good time!" My mother smiled with her mouth falling short of reaching her eyes.

“Good! I appreciate you! I’ll be by this week to take you to lunch! Go hug your gram and tell her you’ll see her later.” the boys did as she said and made their way over to my mom before running to the car.

“Alright, mama. I love you.” I said as I got into the car.

“Everybody buckled up?” Tamera asked before I pulled off getting a series of yes.

“So, what did you guys do with gram?” Tam asked, looking back at the boys before they could answer. I cut them off, telling her not to forget to place the order for takeout.

"Thanks for reminding me. I forgot that quick." She said as she picked up her phone and scrolled through it.

"We did a lot," Josh said from the back. "We went to the park, the mall, target, and everywhere!"

"That's not everywhere," Johan mumbled.

"So! It's a lot!" Josh shot back.

"Hey, hey, no arguing!" I said, looking at them through the rearview mirror.

"Sorry." They both said.

"Yes, I'll hold," Tamera said and looked back at the boys. "Did you guys go with gram and pop-pop?"

"Yes anddddd Jayla!" Josh said, and I almost crashed into the car in front of us.

"Jason!" Tamera screeched, looking at me in confusion.

"They brake checked me." I groaned and shrugged.

"Idiots." She hissed. "And Jayla?"

"Yeah, she-" Johan started, and I cut him off.

"Yeah, my mom said they saw her at the park or something like that."

"Oh. I wonder what park they...yes, I would like to place an order for pick up…." Thank goodness for that save. My boys would tell you everything if you asked, so I needed to dead this conversation before it even started. So while she talked on the phone, ordering our food, I handed the boys my phone and told them they could watch youtube until we got home. By the time Tamera got off the phone placing the order, Aerca was calling. As long as she was distracted, my secret could stay in the closet for another day.

CHAPTER 25
LYNN

I'ma assume you're sleeping, beauty, and that's why my text have been going unanswered, and you need me to come and save you. I rolled my eyes and smirked at the lame joke Davis had just sent to my phone. It wasn't like I was ignoring hi- ok yes, I am. But I just don't feel like we have much in common, plus everything I have going on. It's just not a good time. I continued my stride to my office, getting settled in before I debated over texting him back and telling him why I wasn't responding.

I certainly don't need to be saved.

I just don't feel like we have much in common, and I didn't want to waste either of our time. I'm guessing my response wasn't good enough because he immediately called.

"Yes?" I answered.

"You're breaking my heart." He said jokingly.

"And why is that?" I asked as I looked through my calendar to see what was on the agenda today.

"I don't feel like we had enough conversation to determine if we have much in common."

"No? I think so." I said with conviction.

"Ok, so if you don't mind me asking, what part of our text conversation helped you to determine that?"

"You being a deacon."

"Ahhhh," he said as if he had an epiphany. "So that's what this is about?"

"I'm just not that kind of woman. I don't go to church for bible school, Sunday's best, first service, or none of that."

"What does that have to do with me?"

"Everything. Your calling is to lead as many people to God as possible. That's not for me. I don't believe in God."

"And that's your choice."

"Wow…" I was shocked at his response. "So you not gon' get all preachy on me?"

"No. Being a deacon is a part of who I am, not ALL that I am. So when it's time to be "preachy," as you call it, I do. But I don't see why I would need to right now."

"Wish my mother was more like you," I mumbled, smacking my teeth.

"See, you thought you had me figured out over there."

"I won't lie. I thought I did."

"It's ok, no apology needed. You can just meet me for lunch today."

"Slick one, aren't you?" I snickered. "I'm at work, I have court at eleven, which will run until probably about twelve-thirty, so it would be a late lunch around two-ish when I'm free."

"It's your world, Miss Lynn. Two is fine with me. Shoot me a message and let me know what restaurant you're craving, and I can either pick you up, or you can meet me there."

"My hands work fine, Davis. I'll meet you there." He chuckled at my comment.

"Can't blame a man for trying to get in as much time as he can. You might go missing on me again." He joked.

"You never know. I'll see you at two." I said before disconnecting the call.

KNOCK KNOCK

"Hey, you got a minute?" Jason asked, standing in my doorway. I nodded my head, and he came in, closing the door behind him. "I heard Jayla had a great time this weekend."

"She certainly did." I smiled. "She said Dosh and Dohan taught her how to count to ten in Spanish, and she made sure I knew she knew how from yesterday until I left for work this morning." We both chuckled.

"She is something else." He shook his head.

"Ain't she?" I said with pride, looking at her smiling photo that sat on my desk.

"Well, I had just got off the phone with my mom, and she wanted me to thank you again for allowing her to spend the weekend with her. She's hoping it can happen regularly now."

"That's fine with me." I nodded my head.

"Okay, cool, I'll let her know. Talk to you later." Jason said before he left my office. I was happy Jayla was getting to spend time with her dad's side of the family. However, it was still a shame that he was hiding it from his wife in plain sight. I no longer envied her; now, I just pitied her. I couldn't imagine being the butt of a joke that everyone knows about except you.

Panera Bread seems to be the lucky winner today. So I text Davis along with the address to the one nearest my office.

Really? I thought I was going to have to dig in my savings for this date.

I snickered before texting back.

If you get a next time, I'll be sure to meet your expectations. See you soon.

CHAPTER 26
TAMERA

Two months later

"Everything is looking so good!" I squealed as I walked towards Ben Lee. He nodded his head and handed me a hard hat and goggles.

"It is! My guys have been working around the clock. At this rate, things will be done in three months, four at the max."

"I'm so happy to hear that! I'm ready to get this going!"

"It's a great thing you're doing here. Did you get a chance to link with the grant writer I sent you?"

"Yes! She's amazing. Thank you so much for that. We already got a lot sent out, so we are waiting on responses now."

"You'll get some responses. They'll be foolish not to. E-mail me what you all put together, and I'll send it around to some people I know too."

"Really? Thank you so much, Ben Lee. You have been accommodating during this process. I don't know what I would do without you."

"Don't even worry about it. I'm just amazed seeing black women take over entrepreneurship."

"Okay! That good old black girl magic!" We both chuckled. "Alright, I'm a gon head and get out of yall hair. You know I'm good for coming here every day. It's just so amazing to see the progress as it happens."

"I understand. It's not an issue. I'm just here to oversee and make sure they are doing as they are supposed to."

"Don't be too hard on my guys now. I don't wanna fall through the floor because you pissed somebody off." I joked.

"You know I'm half Chinese, right?" He joked back, doing a light karate move. "I'll chop their ass in the throat and go eat lunch right after."

"See!" I cackled loudly. "This is why you and Aerca mesh so well. Yall both crazy on the low."

"Balance." He smirked. "I'm going to be leaving here in a little while to take her to lunch."

"Aww, that's so sweet. You're good for her. She's always glowed, but now she's glowing differently. In a good way!"

"That woman is good for me." He cheesed, showing all thirty-two. We chatted a bit more before I left. I needed to head to the store so that I could grab some items for dinner. I was passing up one of Mama's bakeries and saw her car outside and figured I would stop in and say hi and grab the boys some snacks while I was at it.

When I walked in, it was busy as usual. I waved to some of the staff who recognized me and made my way to the kitchen to see if Mama was there since she wasn't out front. It's only two other places she would be, in her office or kitchen if she weren't out front helping out.

"How yall doing?" I asked, peeking into the kitchen. "Where's Mama?"

"Oh, she back there in her office with her grandbaby." One of the bakers yelled out. I frowned because she didn't tell me she was picking the boys up from school early, so that was new to me. I pulled out my phone as I walked towards her office, checking for a message I may have missed while at the construction zone. Hmm, that's weird. There were no messages from her.

"Grammy, I want another cookie!" I heard a little voice squeal. Oh, that's not one of my kids. Maybe she just calls one of her staff kids her grandbabies. I started to get a funny feeling in my stomach like something just wasn't right. When I made it to the doorway, it seemed like everything went in slow motion. My mind starting moving at one hundred miles per hour. Things that previously didn't make sense now added up. Questions I once had, were now answered. In Phylicia's office sat Jayla, Lynn's daughter. The daughter I said looked like she could be my son's sister because of the uncanny resemblance. *How fucking dumb am I?* I thought to myself in disbelief.

"Grammy?" I questioned, my voice cracking.

"Tamera, I-" Phylicia sighed heavily. "Give me a second, come on, baby. Let grammy take you to get some more cookies."

Grammy. She only had one child, Jason. There's no way everybody sat in my face and let me look foolish. Ain't no fucking way.

"I just found out about this Tamera. I told Jason to tell you!" Phylicia groaned as she came back into her office, closing the door behind her.

"When?" I asked lowly as I closed my eyes, trying to keep my tears at bay.

"When what?" She asked, reaching for me. I side-stepped her and shook my head no.

"When did you find out?"

"He's been telling me over and over again that he would tell you. I'm so sorry."

"I don't care about your sorry! How long?" I asked again. She shook her head and sighed as tears fell down her eyes.

"Almost three months ago. He dropped her off on my doorstep, begging me to keep her for him."

"THREEEEEEE?" I screamed. "Oh my God! She's four! Four! Oh my God."

I felt sick. I rushed over to her garbage can and threw up my breakfast. I was throwing up so much I started dry heaving.

"Oh, baby.." Phylicia whimpered. "I know, I know. Take a deep breath."

She patted my back and led me to a chair in front of her desk, and passing me bottled water from her fridge. My husband has a four-year-old daughter. I started sobbing into my hands, not believing this was happening.

"I never wanted you not to know, and I certainly didn't want you to find out this way. She asked me to get her because she was at home not feeling well, and Jason-"

"I'm done with this." I snarled as I stood up.

"Tamera-"

"No. I don't want to hear it. You had three months to let me know what was going on. But you didn't! You sat in my face smiling every week, pretending you didn't know a THING! I understand Jason is your son, but you're a WOMAN first! The woman in you should've come to me immediately regardless of the outcome. But I see where your loyalty lies." I stormed out of the bakery and climbed into my truck, where I broke down. I was sobbing so hard my head was throbbing. I was hurt, sad, angry, and I wanted to destruct some shit.

I wiped my eyes and took a deep breath before grabbing my phone and calling Jason. After getting no answer, I contemplated driving to his office, but a text on my phone caught my eye, sending me in a different direction.

CHAPTER 27
LYNN

I decided to stay home today. I felt horrible for the past few days, and it did nothing but get worse. My back was killing me, and I had a fever out of this world. Right now, Mrs. Walsh was a godsend. Her checking on Jayla and finding out I wasn't feeling well and getting her was helpful. All day, I had been lying around in my bra and underwear, drinking water and eating soup, trying to get this fever to break.

"If you don't feel better by the time I'm out of this meeting, I'm going to come and take you to the emergency room. I knew I should have just taken you yesterday." Davis groaned.

"I'll be fine.." I mumbled, taking a sip of water. Davis and I had gotten close since our first lunch date. We weren't officially dating, but we talked all day and spent most of our free time together when he wasn't at church or creating websites for someone.

"That's what you said yesterday and the day before. So I'll be there after my meeting, and you can fight me all you want, but I guarantee you'll win."

"Look at you bossing up on me-" I was cut off by someone banging on my front door like the police.

"What is that?" Davis asked, concerned.

"Hold on." I sat my cell phone on the coffee table and pulled the door open without thinking, not bothering to even look through the peephole. Had I looked through the peephole, I might have seen the slap coming that caused my whole body to fly into the door.

"You dirty ass bitch! You had the audacity to sit in my fucking face knowing damn well you were fucking my husband and had a baby with him?" I heard the screaming, but my head was hurting so bad I had to take a minute even to get my thoughts together.

"Is that his baby too?"

"Look.." I said as I held on to the door tightly, feeling dizzy. "You need to talk to your husband. I told him to tell you what was going on, and he decided to keep it from you."

"You don't have to worry. I'll talk to MY husband about what he did, but I'm talking to you right now. YOU sat in my face having conversations with me, pretending we were buddy-buddy. YOU let me say to YOU that your daughter looked like she could be my kid's sibling. YOU did not come to me as a WOMAN. You're a fake ass bitch!" Tamera spat, pointing her finger at me.

"I had no obli-" I couldn't even finish my sentence before I felt myself fall forward, and everything went black.

CHAPTER 28
TAMERA

"What the fuck." I yelled out as Lynn fell forward, I started to let her ass hit the floor, but she looked so fucking pale I didn't want to go to jail for literally slapping the life out of her ass. I was small as hell compared to her ass, and she wasn't light. So I did my best to carefully lay her inside of her house, right in the doorway. I knew I shouldn't have brought my ass over here, but I just couldn't resist after coming across the text she sent me with the mailing address that she had sent to me in the past.

"Shit, shit, shit!" I screeched as I leaned close to her mouth to see if I could feel her breathing. I could feel light puffs and knew I needed to hurry up and call an ambulance so I could get my ass out of there. I ran over to her couch and grabbed a pillow to put under her head when I heard somebody yelling,

"Hello."

"Hello?" I picked her phone up off the coffee table as I rushed back to put the pillow under her head.

"What's going on over there?" A male voice asked.

"She passed out. I didn't do anything, I swear. I have her laid down and put a pillow under her head now."

"Ok… I'll call an ambulance." He said, sounding as if he was rushing around. "Stay on the line with me."

As he called nine one one, I noticed Lynn's eyelids fluttering, looking as if she was trying to come back to but was struggling.

“They should be there any minute now.” the man said, coming back onto the phone.

“Ok.” I whimpered, shaking my head. “I can’t believe this shit.”

“Do you mind if I pray right now?” he asked. I nodded my head no as if he could see me, and he started to pray. I don’t know what it was, but his voice caused me to start sobbing, sad about my own situation.

“Can I pray for you, sister?”

“Pl..ea..se.” I continued sobbing.

“Everything will be ok. This one is Isaiah 40:31, but those who hope in the Lord will renew their strength. They will soar on wings like eagles; they will run and not grow weary. They will walk and not be faint.” Shortly after he finished, EMT came running into the house, asking me what had happened. I told them she passed out, and they moved her from the floor to the gurney while taking her vitals.

“What hospital are they going to?” the voice on the phone asked. So I asked the EMT and relayed the information to him.

“Ok, are you riding with her?” the voice asked. I frowned my face up at his question but looking at her pregnant and helpless lying on the gurney; I knew I couldn’t leave her lying there like that. “I understand if you don’t, sister. God bless you for staying as long as you have.”

"I'm going to go. I can't leave her like this," I said into the phone as I climbed into the back of the EMT with her.

"Ok. I'll see you there shortly. Can you look through her phone and call her mom?"

"I will." I closed my eyes and disconnected the call. I couldn't believe how beautiful my day started to dealing with this. I took a deep breath and went through her phone, which didn't have a security code, so it was easy to go through her contacts and call Mom.

"Hey, baby, are you feeling better?" A woman answered with a soft voice.

"Hi. Your daughter is on her way to Cedars-Sinai. Unfortunately, she fainted just a bit ago."

"Oh my goodness." She cried out. "I'm on the way." As we made our way to the hospital, the EMT's worker made sure they tracked Lynn's vitals while I sat there in silence. As I held her hand in my phone, I couldn't help but be curious about the relationship she shared with my husband. Before I could stop myself, I went through their text, emails, and photos before we made it to the hospital. It hurt, but I needed to see so that I could move forward and decide what I would do.

"Hello?" Jason answered, sounding weary.

"Come to Cedars-Sinai," I said dryly as we got out of the ambulance.

"Tamera?"

"Yep." I disconnected the call and followed the EMT into the hospital, where I was advised to wait in the waiting room. I nodded and sat down just now, realizing I had left my phone and purse in my car back at Lynn’s house. I don’t know how much time had passed before I heard that same soft voice from over the phone now at the nurse’s station asking for information about her daughter. I sighed and made my way over to the petite woman who was the spitting image of Lynn, just a complexion lighter.

“Hi,” I said with my hand out. She looked over at me with a small smile before realizing that I must have been the one who called her.

“Thank you so much for the call.” She shook my hand.

“No problem. I hope everything is ok with your daughter. Here’s her phone.”

“Thank you. I didn’t catch your name.”

“I’m Tamera.”

"Oh, ok. Do you work with Lynn?"

"No, my ...she…." I shook my head. "Jayla is my husband's daughter."

"Huh?" She asked wide-eyed and confused. "No…."

"Yes. I just found out today. My husband of nine years has not one but almost two kids with another woman." I said, voice cracking.

"My lord. I had no clue." She pulled me into a hug, where I broke down sobbing again. We sat in awkward silence until a handsome man walked up to her introducing himself as Davis.

"I've heard so much about you." Lynn's mother smiled.

"As I have you, Mrs. Williams." he looked over at me and raised his brow. "Davis, I spoke with you over the phone."

"I'm Ta-"

"Tamera!" Jason yelled as he came through the emergency room doors. I didn't answer him. Instead, I just sat in my chair with a stoic expression.

"What's going on?" he questioned, coming over to me and bending down so that we were at eye level.

I shook my head and rolled my eyes. "I'm fine, Lynn, and your unborn are not. It would be best if you waited here with her family to make sure they are alright. I need to use your car since I left mine at her house."

"Unborn?" He asked, confused.

"Is that all you heard? Keys, please."

"I-I I'll just drive you." He said before running his hand down his face. I turned towards Lynn's mother and Davis and nodded my head as politely as I could before damn near running off towards the elevators. We stood there in silence, waiting for the elevator to come.

"I parked in the garage." He said once we got on. I pressed the button for the parking garage and stood there with my thoughts all over the place.

"Baby I-"

"No. Not right now." I put my hand up, cutting him off. He nodded his head and leaned against the wall until we reached the parking level. I followed behind him until we reached his truck. He opened my door and walked around so that he could get in. I sat my purse in the back seat and took a deep breath feeling like I was exploding.

"Tamera, I know-" His sentence was cut off by my barrage of fists. I don't condone domestic violence. Lord knows I don't, but I couldn't help myself. I felt like I was standing outside of the car looking at myself. I had climbed over in his seat on top of him and beat him like I was fighting for my life. The only thing that snapped me out of my rampage was me accidentally hitting the horn. I gasped when I looked down and saw Jason's face was bloody, and he was staring at me wildly. I sat back in my seat, and I was shaking so badly I could barely put my seatbelt on. I couldn't even cry like I wanted to. I just felt there physically, but mentally I was checked out.

"Take me to get my things," I said lowly before staring out of the window. Jason didn't say anything as he pulled out of the parking garage. I could hear him hiss now and again, and I'm sure he was in pain somewhere, but at this moment, I didn't give a damn. Let him hurt like I was. His physical wounds would heal. But, unfortunately, my emotional and mental may never.

CHAPTER 29
JASON

We rolled in silence as I drove to Lynn's house. I was damn near terrified to say anything to my wife right now. I have never in life seen her as she was in this moment. I know I deserved it. I deserved it all, but I needed her to hear me out so that we could work it out.

"Tamera, please hear me out," I said as I turned onto Lynn's street. Tamera shook her head and closed her eyes as tears fell down her face.

"Jason, I saw it all. The text, the photos, the emails. I saw it. I don't need to hear anything else, not from you or anybody else. Hear me, I'm going home, grabbing me and my son's shit, and I'm leaving your ass. Tomorrow, I'll see a lawyer, and I'll get you your divorce. When the papers come, just make sure you sign them."

"Baby, please. Can we go to therapy, something?" I whimpered.

"Therapy? For YOUR infidelity? No! That's a YOU problem!"

"Can we please just talk about this?" I parked the car and asked, looking over at her. "Please, let's just go home and talk, and I'll tell you everything."

"Everything?" She asked, looking over at me.

"Everything!" I said, nodding my head.

"Ok. We can talk." She grabbed her purse and got out of my truck. "I'll meet you at the house."

I nodded and waited for her to go to her car and get in before I pulled off. As I made my way home, my phone rang out, causing me to remember that my mother had been blowing my phone up for hours now.

"Yeah?" I answered, feeling a dull ache in my head.

"I've been calling you for hours." She yelled. "Tamera came by my bakery while Jayla is here. She knows!"

"I know, ma. I know." I groaned.

"Well, what's going on?"

"She went to Lynn's house. Something happened, and she knows everything. Also, Lynn is pregnant again."

"Noooo…." She whimpered. "This is all bad, baby."

"I know, mama."

"So, what are you going to do?"

"I don't know. Right now, I'm just working on getting her to talk to me. She said we can talk when she gets home."

"Well, that's good if she's willing to hear you out at least."

"I hope so." I sighed heavily.

"Well, baby, I'm praying for you. Let me know if there is anything that I can do for you."

"Thanks, mama."

"You're welcome. I love you."

"Love you too, mama," I said before disconnecting the call. Lynn's house was less than fifteen minutes away, and since I was driving with my head all over the place, I had arrived quicker than usual. But, unfortunately, Tamera hadn't made it yet, so I made my way inside and decided to take a shower to rinse all this blood off of me so I could look decent by the time she got there.

In less than thirty minutes, I was out of the shower and noticed that Tamera still wasn't home. She must've stopped and grabbed the boys, I figured. So I dialed her number to see where she was and if she wanted me to place an order for take-out because I knew she wouldn't feel like cooking today with everything going on. I got no answer and decided just to place a pizza order for delivery online. Going out was a no-go right now since my lip was busted, and my face housed a few scratches.

A few hours later

"Hey babe, it's me. You and the boys still haven't made it here yet, just making sure everything is ok. Please call me back." I called Tamera for the tenth time, leaving my fourth message. I had eaten half the pizza and had been sitting in the dark, waiting for her to pull up. I jumped from the buzzing of my phone and saw that my mother was calling me back.

"Yeah?"

"How are you?" My mother asked in her voice that always had the power to break me down, and I did.

"She left me." I sobbed, choking on my words as it hit me all at once what was happening. I knew Tamera wasn't on her way. She just wasn't coming. She had left me just as she said she would. I had to accept that I had caused all of this and figure out how to get my wife back.

CHAPTER 30
AERCA

"Uh Uh, that's enough! I'm not watching another Ted Bundy documentary!" I yelled playfully, trying to grab the remote from Ben Lee.

"Nah, my house, my rules. Ain't that what you said when you had me watching that damn Real Housewives of Pussyville." Ben Lee laughing smacking my hand away. I burst out laughing and swung at him.

"It's Potomac, you chink eyed fool." He gasped and pretended to grab his fake pearls.

"Well, I've NEVER." We both cackled loudly. "Now you really gonna watch some more Ted Bundy just for being racist."

"I am not racist. I love your disappearing eyes, boo." I teased, sticking my tongue out. Ben Lee and I had started seeing each other on a deep level two weeks ago. Before then, we had gone on dates weekly, and now we just can't seem to spend enough time with one another. So I'm either always at his place, or he's always at one of mine. Either way, I loved it.

"I got your disappearing eyes." He snickered, pulling me onto his lap and kissing me. Ben Lee and I still had not gone all the way, but I put those lessons to use that Nadia had given me. Ben Lee was no slouch when it came to kissing, and his slow kisses had a way of bringing my essence to a pool in my panties. Our kissing got so heavy that I started grinding on him and could feel him harden underneath me.

"Alright now." He taunted, pulling back from the kiss. "Don't get me started."

"Maybe I want to," I said, leaning back in for another kiss.

"You sure?" He asked with his brows up in question. I nodded my head and leaned in for a kiss in which he dodged. "What happened to waiting for marriage?"

"That's my parents' goals, not mine." I sighed heavily. "Now kiss me, Ben Lee."

Ben Lee stared at me without moving as if he was trying to read me through my eyes. I playfully rolled my eyes and pulled his face towards me with my hands, and began kissing him again. He gripped my ass with both hands as I ground into him and moaned into my mouth. "Aerca, shit girl." He huffed as I kissed his neck. I shook my head as I heard my phone rang out playing "An Ode to Hip Hop" by Erykah Badu, letting me know it was Tamera calling. Girl, I'll call you later. I said in my head as if she could hear me. Soon as my phone stopped ringing, it started back up again.

"Get your phone love, sounds like an emergency." Ben Lee said, nodding his head towards my phone that sat on his coffee table.

"I don't wanna." I pouted, crossing my arms.

"Cut it out." He smiled, leaning forward with me still on his lap and grabbing my ringing phone. "Here."

"Girl, this better be good. I was about to get this cherry popped like a bad kid finally." I joked, answering the phone.

"You crazy." Tamera snickered. "I'll call you tomorrow."

"What's wrong?" I asked, moving off of Ben Lee's lap.

"Nothing, just call me in the morning."

"Tamera, stop playing with me. I know you like the back of my hand. What's going on?" I asked as I walked out of the living area and into the hallway bathroom for privacy.

"He…he.." Tamera burst out sobbing. "Aerca, he's...he got a daughter."

"Huh?" I was confused. "Who?"

"Jason!" She screeched. "She's four."

"What? How? Where are you?" I asked as I burst out of the bathroom looking for my shoes.

"No, stay. I'm ok." She sniffled.

"Tamera, where are you?" I asked more sternly as I got Ben Lee's attention.

"I'm at the Beverly Hills Hotel."

"Room number?"

"Two oh nine."

"I'm on my way." I disconnected the call before she could protest. Tamera was that friend who never asked for anything and would be strong for everyone else until she caved.

"Babe, I gotta go. I'm sorry." I said to Ben Lee as I grabbed my purse.

"Nah, it's alright, baby, I get it. Go see about your girl." He walked me to the door and kissed my forehead, nose, and lips. "Let me know when you make it to her, ok?"

"I will, baby." I hurried to my car and made my way to the hotel, which was about thirty minutes from where Ben Lee lived. Once I got to the hotel, I valet my car and made my way to room two oh nine to see what was going on. I texted Tamera I was here instead of knocking in case my babies were sleeping. I pulled Tamera into a hug as soon as she opened the door, and she broke down into my arms sobbing again. My eyes pooled with tears because I hadn't seen my friend like this in over ten years, and I'd be damned if I let her go back down that path. We sat on the couch where I let her get herself together before telling me everything that transpired that day. I swear I wanted to find Jason and beat him more than she had. I never liked that orange-headed mothafucka.

"So what are you going to do? You and the boys can't live out of this hotel, love." I asked as I rubbed her back.

"I don't know." She shrugged. "I'll have to find somewhere to rent that has something available like now."

"Hmm, how many bedrooms do you think you'll need?" I asked as I pulled out my phone, going through my emails.

"At least three." She said lowly, shaking her head. "I can't believe this, Aerca."

"I know, baby." I sighed heavily. "Now, don't think I'm trying to sell to you in your time of sorrow, but we just picked up a house today that's four bedrooms. The owners are trying to have a short sale too. But, unfortunately, the husband is in the military, and they need to move like pronto."

"Four is a bit much, but let me see it." She reached for my phone and began swiping. "Oh, this is beautiful."

"Yes, I agree. Also, if you make a cash sale, they'll most likely lower the price too. I can also have them pay for the inspector, appraiser, and attorney fees."

"How soon do you think we can do this?"

"I can check in the morning. However, in the meantime, you need to get out of here. You and the boys can stay at my condo downtown."

"No.." She shook her head. "He knows about that condo. I don't need him popping up at your place."

"Girl, bye." I rolled my eyes. "He can pop up all he wants to, and I'll pop his ass like the fourth of July. You know I carry my twin on me at all times."

"I know you do, crazy." She smirked. "You and Jackie Chan over there be on go."

"Not you being racist!" I squealed in laughter.

"Girl, bye. You stay calling that man some Asian character." Tamera laughed, rolling her eyes playfully.

"I know. I'ma stop, though. I think it bothers him low-key."

"Aww yeah, if he doesn't like it, definitely stop. Don't want to create that type of atmosphere for you both."

"Right…" I nodded my head. "Where are the boys?" I asked, looking around.

"They're in the bedroom back there. They played their little hearts out. I told them we were on a staycation."

"Wow, so what will you tell them? Are you sure you want a divorce?"

"I do." She nodded her head. "I've told myself I would never accept anybody treating me less than I deserve. He didn't just cheat, but he had two babies with her. I can't forgive that. I wouldn't even be able to look at those kids without feeling some kind of way, you know? And those babies didn't do a thing to me."

"I understand. You done slapped a bitch unconscious. We don't need you doing anything else, Laila." I teased her by throwing my fist around playfully.

"Uh, Uh, don't put that on me." Tamera fake frowned. "She was already sick. Had I known, I would've waited until she was better and then slapped her ass...unconscious."

"Oh hell," I said as we cackled loudly. "But seriously, how are you feeling?"

"I'm better than I thought I could be. It hurts...like hell. But I've felt pain ten times worse. It just sucks to be made a fool of. All of them knew about this and just let me look like a fool." She shook her head. I nodded my head, understanding, and we fell into a comfortable silence until her phone began buzzing like crazy on the table.

"Jason?" I asked.

"You already know. There is nothing for us to even talk about."

"Does he know you all are here?"

"Nope." She said, popping the p in the word.

"You plan on telling him?"

"Eventually, but right now, I just need some space." She sighed heavily.

"I get it, boo, I get it. Get all the space you need."

"I will." She said, wiping at her eyes. "But anyway, what was going on with you and Mr. Ben Lee. Don't think I didn't catch you saying you were about to get that cooch broke in."

"Chile." I fanned myself replaying the evening before she called. "I was about to risk it all."

"Damn, you feeling him like that? What about waiting until you're married?"

"The marriage thing is my parent's thing. My thing was I was just waiting for the right person." I shrugged.

"I get that. So you think he's the one?"

"I do." I nodded my head smiling. Ben Lee is a great man. He listens, takes care of me, and makes sure I have everything I need at all times. "I see myself with him for a long time."

"Ok, that's good. Do you like his family?"

I scratched my head and looked away, refusing to answer.

"I know you fucking lying!" Tamera groaned. "You over there trying to give him your virginity, and you haven't even met his family?"

"I mean, I will eventually!" I threw my hands up in surrender.

"If you say so!"

"I'll be ok, sis, I promise," I said as I laid my head on her lap, yawning. "I haven't waited this long to mess it up."

"I hope not," Tamera said as she rubbed my scalp. Back in college, this was our routine when we lived together. We would come into one another's room, have a girl talk all night, and I would fall asleep in her lap with her rubbing my head. She wasn't just my best friend; she was my sister, and I would do anything to make sure she was happy.

CHAPTER 31
LYNN

"In Jesus name amen…." I struggled to open my eyes as I heard my mother and Davis praying over me. I desperately wanted to swat them away from me for worrying so damn much.

"Thank God." My mother squealed, kissing my forehead as I opened my eyes. I smiled faintly and nodded my head at her and Davis before lifting my hand. Then, almost instinctively, my hand went to my stomach and sighed a breath of relief when I felt my stomach was still full. "Do you remember what happened?"

I nodded my head yes and reached for the cup on the tray next to the bed. Davis reached for it, and I shook my head no, letting him know I had it.

"You have to take better-"

"Ah, Mrs. Charleston, glad to see you're up." A nurse said as she walked into the room. "I'm going to take your vitals and then have the doctor come and speak with you, ok?"

I nodded my head and sat up in the bed so that she could do whatever it was that she needed to do so that I could get out of here.

"Is Jayla still with Mrs. Walsh?" I asked my mother. She nodded her head and sat down on the couch in the room.

"Alright, and the doctor will be right with you." The nurse said after she finished her task walking out of the room.

"How are you feeling?" Davis asked with a small smile.

"I feel ok, just tired." I shrugged. I didn't want to be rude, and as much as I enjoyed Davis's company right now, I just wanted to be alone. I knew it was only a matter of time before my mother started preaching to me about whatever it was that she found out in regards to Jason and me. "Did you leave work?"

"Yeah, I was on the phone when everything happened, so I just told them I had an emerge-"

KNOCK. KNOCK.

"Hi Lynn, I'm Doctor Glover. How are you feeling?" The doctor asked as he came into the room wearing a face mask and washing his hands in the room sink.

"I'm ok," I said, giving a small smile.

"Ok.. so we have a few things here." He said as he looked down at his computer that he lugged into the room after washing his hands. "First off, you passed out because your blood pressure was through the roof. We were able to get your blood pressure down, but that leads to my next set of news."

"Ok." I nodded my head for him to continue.

"Well..." He took a deep sigh. "I'm sorry to inform you of this, but your baby didn't survive. The high blood pressure didn't allow enough blood to flow to the placenta. As a result, the baby didn't have enough oxygen or nutrients to survive. When we did the ultrasound, it looked as if the baby wasn't growing at its proper weight and had prolonged growth. Have you had issues with your blood pressure previously?"

"No!" I screamed out. "No! No! No! Not my baby!"

"Lynn, calm down." My mother cried as she reached for me. I slapped her hand away from me and continued screaming no over and over again as I knocked everything off of the side tray and anything that I could get my hands on.

"You're lying," I yelled at the doctor as I tried to get out of the bed. "I'm getting out of here. I'll get a second opinion." I threw my legs over the bed in a hurry, and Davis reached for me, stopping when I gave him a look of death. I stood up and fell back as everything turned black again.

CHAPTER 32
KYLAN

Here I was again up early as hell, making my way into the office. Only this time, it was my own office. Today was move-in day, and I was excited as hell. I had worked my ass off to be here, and nothing was going to fuck up my day. I had boxed up my old office Friday and had everything in my backseat ready for my new office this morning. I told Zelan she didn't have to come in today, and she could just start her week tomorrow.

I pulled into my parking space and turned my car off, smiling like the happiest man on earth.

Nigga we made it. I unlocked my suite door and smiled. There was a receptionist desk out front, and once you walked a bit further, there was a hallway that housed the bathrooms and a kitchenette for staff. On the far left, there was another hall that led to the offices. I had four offices total and wanted to keep my practice small and family-oriented. I had yet to hire a receptionist and told myself that I would reach out to a staffing agency so that I could get one pronto. My office was the biggest and was the last office in the hallway near the backdoor exit. I was out the streets, but the streets would never be out of me. Being back here helped me to be able to observe everything and get prepared and also make an exit if necessary. The local security company had already set up the alarms and cameras last week, so I could look at what was going on outside and inside of the building from my office monitors.

Three hours had passed when I finished mounting my under desk holsters and setting up my office and the kitchenette area; I didn't even realize time had slipped by, and ten am was nearing until I looked at my ringing phone.

"What's going on, man," I answered for Jason.

"Hey. How's the new office coming along?"

"Just got everything set up, so it's as good as it gets," I said as I leaned on the receptionist desk where I had just sat and plugged the phone in.

"That's what's up, man. Proud of you."

"Thanks, I appreciate that. You at the office?"

"Ah..no. That's what I was calling you about. Shit finally hit the fan, and I got some personal shit to deal with. I had a few clients I was supposed to see this week. Can I send them your way?"

"Oh, I don't know about all that man. People will think this is a part of that same company, and I'm not trying to have that. This my shit."

"No, I get it, man. I respect that. I'll just have Denison reschedule everybody." He sighed.

"Yeah, that's your best bet. So you don't think you will be in none this week?"

"I don't know, man. Tamera got some good hits in." He chuckled lowly. I shook my head, not seeing the humor in his situation.

"Well, alright. Let me know if there is anything else I can do."

"Thanks, man! Talk to you later." Jason said before I disconnected the call. I had been told him all that shit was going to come back around and sink him. That's how the universe works. You get back what you put out.

I made my way out of the office and back to my car, so I could find something around here to eat for lunch. Unfortunately, there wasn't much around besides a bunch of fast food spots, and I wasn't in the mood for that heavy-ass food.

"Kylan?" I looked up and frowned, seeing Tamera had pulled up next to me as I stood by my car.

"What's up?"

"What you doing over here?" She asked, looking at the building.

"This my new office."

"Yours, yours? Or an extension of the other office?"

"Mines. Mine only. The sign gets put up later today," I said, pointing at the pole that held the suite names.

"That's amazing! I'm proud of you! My building is down the street! It's still being worked on, but you know!"

"Oh…you big money that got the street all blocked up." I teased, pointing at a construction truck as it rolled down the street.

"I'm sorry." She pouted. "I'm just trying to get it all done… you wanna come take a look?"

"I don't know about that. I was just trying to find a smoothie place around this mothafucka."

"Come on! Come just take a look with me, and then we can go to pulp or one of these nutrition places close by." She unlocked her doors.

"So me saying no is out the question, I see," I said as I reached for her door.

"And you would be seeing correctly." She laughed as I got in her car. "It's good to see you again. I haven't seen you in months."

"I know. It has been a minute, and we have both been busy. Obviously." I teased as we pulled into traffic.

"Don't remind me." She said, rolling her eyes as we pulled onto her construction site. There were so many trucks and people around that we could barely get through.

"I know it's a mess, but you will get to see the vision." She said as we both got out of her car. I followed her until she reached a guy who had on a hard hat and construction jacket.

"Hey, Ben Lee. How is everything coming along?"

"Everything is going good, Tamera. The boys are moving on schedule as planned." He said, handing her and I hard hats and goggles before sticking his hand out for me to shake. "How you doing, man I'm Ben Lee. Nice to finally meet you, Mr. Walsh."

"Oh. I'm so sorry, Ben Lee. This is not my soon-to-be ex-husband. This is my friend Kylan. He works down the street from here and is a criminal lawyer if you or anyone you know needs one."

"Good to meet you, man." I shook his hand. "You're the architect?"

"Yeah, I've done just about half of the new buildings in this town."

"Oh, that's what's up. I have a friend who is looking to get some work done for his girlfriend's spa salons. You got a card on you?" I asked.

"Not on me, but I have some in my truck if you want to walk with me." I nodded and followed him as he explained to me what was going on in Tamera's building and her vision. He was good at what he did because I didn't have a clue what the fuck he was talking about.

"Do you know how soon ya boy is looking to get things rolling?" he asked, handing me a card.

"I don't, but I'm a give him your information and knowing him he's going to call you as soon as I do."

"That's all good with me. Scared money don't make no money. You from around here?"

"Nah, I was raised in the projects, niggas could only wish they were raised here."

"It's all good, you here now. That's all that matters."

"You right about that." He and I talked a bit more before Tamera came over, asking him questions about things she saw while walking around. That quick stop turned into an hour before we knew it.

"Come on, let me get you out of here. I have taken up enough of your time and still haven't fed you yet." Tamera joked.

"Right, got me out here starving and shit."

"You are so dramatic. Cut it out. It's a place literally around the block."

"Man, whatever. But your shit is fire, Tamera. I can't wait to see the finished results."

"Thank you, at least I OFFERED you a tour, even if it's not done." She said as she pulled into traffic.

"My bad. I got you. When you drop me off, I'll give you a tour, ain't much to see, but it's mine."

"And that's all that matters." She smiled at me. We headed over to a smoothie shop that was around the corner. They had all types of smoothies and healthy wraps, definitely up my alley.

"I love coming here." She said as we got our items and sat at a booth nearby.

"Yeah, this a nice little joint." I nodded my head as I opened my BLT wrap.

"So, when did you move into your new office?"

"Today."

"Oh, ok, cool." We both got quiet and ate our food for a while as we people watched. Once we finished, we made our way back to my office, where I showed her everything I had going on.

"This is nice! I love this Ky! It's homey in here and doesn't have that stuffy office feeling if that makes sense."

"Yeah, yeah, I get it. That's the vibe I was going for."

"Well, you got it. So when does your receptionist start?"

"Uhhhh.." I shrugged. "I don't have one yet."

"Ky! That should've been the first thing you did!" She fussed as she sat in the receptionist's chair and swung around.

"I know. I said I was going to call some temp agencies or some shit today."

"Good. Just make sure they understand what they're here for, and you should be good."

"Right, right. Shid the way you swinging in that chair, I'm about to assign you to that job." I teased.

"I mean, I can do it for a few weeks. All I do is check on my building and properties. The boys get out of school around three, so I would need to leave and get them." She said with her chin in her hand, looking at me.

"Yo, you dead ass? I was just joking."

"I'm for real. How much are you paying, though? Cause I'm expensive." She said, holding up her Louis Vuitton bag.

"Man, bye, big money. I ain't no slouch. I got you."

"I know. But when do you want me to start?"

"Shid, you can start right now! What paperwork do I need?" I said, laughing as I grabbed some blank papers nearby. Today was going damn good, and I for sure wasn't about to pass up an opportunity to have somebody I know as the receptionist either. Hopefully, Tamera didn't let what she was going through affect her doing her job, or else I would be telling her I'm good and calling those temp agencies sooner than I needed.

CHAPTER 33
JASON

"Hello?" I grumbled while answering my ringing phone. I had finally got some sleep after being up all night and after the fifth time ignoring the call, it was apparent they were going to keep calling back.

"Jason! Get your ass up now!" My mother yelled into the phone. I sat up in my bed so fast that I got a charlie horse in my leg.

"Shit!" I yelled out in pain. I stood up and pressed down on my foot, helping the charlie horse to go away. "What's going on, ma?"

"Lynn is up at this hospital, and she is about to have to push out your dead child. You need to be here now!"

"Ma, I don't even know if that baby is mine! What are you talking about?"

"Jason Elijah Walsh! You can play those lying games with somebody else, but I know you better than anybody in this world! Get your ass up here now!" She snapped before disconnecting the call.

"Fuck!" I yelled out again, throwing my phone on my bed. I had spent enough days off of work these past few weeks due to personal shit and really could not afford to reschedule more clients. I shot Denison a text asking him what was all on my schedule and rushed into the bathroom to take a quick shower. Then, I threw on some khaki pants with a white button-down for a casual look so that I could go from the hospital to work. It took me only thirty minutes to get to Cedars-Sinai since the traffic wasn't so bad this morning.

"How can I help you?" The guard stationed at the front asked soon as I walked in. I assumed because it was early morning, there was a different protocol.

"I'm trying to get to labor and delivery."

"Down this hall to the right, and you should see a pool of elevators. Take one to the fourth floor, and once you get off, you will see the sign for it." He told me, pointing at a hall.

"Thanks, man." I walked down the hall, trying to get my thoughts together. I needed to get up here and have a clear head about this situation. It kind of shook me as odd for Lynn to be claiming I was the father when she denied that she was pregnant when I asked, but to know the baby didn't make it was devastating in itself. When I got off the elevator, I could see my mother sitting in the waiting room. She spotted me immediately and stalked towards me, still looking upset. Instead of saying anything, she just reached out and hugged me.

"I'm so sorry, baby." She whimpered, rubbing my back. I nodded my head and waited for her to pull apart before asking what room Lynn was in.

"She's in four oh nine."

"Ok. I'll be back."

"Call me later, baby. I have to get back to my house before

your daddy and Jayla wake up and destroy my kitchen.

"I didn't know you had her." I frowned.

"She's been with me since the day...everything happened."

"Oh, ok, I'll be by to get her once I get off work."

"You're still going to go to work?" My mother asked incredulously.

"It's the only thing keeping me sane right now." She nodded her head before standing on the tip of her toes and kissing my cheek.

I made my way to Lynn's room and took a deep breath before I knocked.

"Come in." I walked in and saw Lynn sitting up in the bed, wincing in pain as she held her stomach., an older version of her was standing next to the bed rubbing her head.

"Hi. And you are?" The older version asked, sticking her hand out for me to shake as I awkwardly stood on the other side of the bed.

"Jason, nice to meet you, Mrs?" I shook her hand.

"Charleston. Charleston-Williams, but you can just use my former." She gave a small smile.

"You ok, baby?" She asked Lynn. Lynn shook her head, no closing her eyes as she continued to rub her stomach.

"Would you uh...like for me to massage your back to help with the pain?" I suggested.

"No," Lynn said lowly shaking her head. "I just really want to get this over with. I don't know why they're making me push a dead baby out. OWW!" She screamed, clutching the railing on the bed.

"I know, baby. Take a deep breath." Her mother said, practicing breathing with her. "Those contractions are getting closer and closer. You should have dilated more by now. I'll ask the doctor to come to check."

"No. Mama, please don't leave," Lynn said, gripping her mother's hand.

"I'll go ask." I volunteered. I didn't get a response as her mother was trying to keep her calm. I made my way out of the room and to the nurse station, where they advised me they would page the doctor and have him come in there as soon as possible.

Thirty minutes later…

"Last push….I can see the head." The doctor yelled out as he sat in between Lynn's legs. This would typically be a joyous occasion, but everybody knew once the baby came out, it would not be taking its first breath nor screaming like a healthy baby would, so the room was solemn, quiet, even eerie would describe the mood. I felt myself going numb as this tiny baby was pushed out, with minimal slime, a body darkened in color, most likely from not having any oxygen, but I didn't care; I still wanted to hold him. When the nurse grabbed the baby and tried to wrap him up discreetly, I grabbed her arm, almost ripping it off, and held my hand out. She looked alarmed before she quickly looked at me with sympathy. She nodded her head and handed me the baby, and patted me on the arm, probably saying sorry, but I couldn't hear anything as I stared at my son's face. His features were barely there, but I still felt connected to him even though his soul was no longer present. I hurried and wiped his face as my tears fell onto him and jolted out of my daze as Lynn screamed at the top of her lungs.

"Get him out of here. You did this to him!" She yelled, pointing at me. I looked at her confused, still in shock, wondering how she could be blaming me at a time like this when we both just lost a child. Her yelling got so bad that security asked me to leave; still in a daze, I handed them my son and walked out of the hospital room after giving him one last kiss.

CHAPTER 34
TAMERA

I knocked on Kylans office door and waited for him to tell me to come in before I entered. He was sitting behind his desk with his suit jacket off, and his sleeves were up to his elbow as he stared at his computer intensely.

"Yo?" He asked, looking over at me briefly before putting his glasses on.

"Why have I never noticed you rocking glasses?" I asked with a smirk.

"Because I only need them for reading, and if you tell anybody about them, I'll be forced to kill you." He smiled at me. "Oh shit, my bad, you gotta go and get the guys, right?"

"Yes." I nodded my head. "Shouldn't take no more than forty-five minutes, and then I'll head right back. However, I did get to file all your cases in alphabetical order. Here's the key."

"Already? Damn. That would have taken me all day."

"Yeah, I'm a pro at that type of stuff."

"My ADHD won't allow it, and I would have given up within five minutes." He joked. "But if you're already finished, that's all I have for you for today. You can call it a day."

"You sure? I'm sure I can find something else to do or ask the others if they need anything."

"I'm sure. Spend the rest of the day with your sons." He waved me off.

"Thank you, Kylan. I won't give you a bad review when I leave now." I joked, sticking out my tongue. He guffawed and shooed me away after balling up a paper and throwing it at me.

I gathered my purse and other items and made my way into my car. I smiled as I looked down the street at the progress that I saw with my building. I turned on my Apple favorites playlist and jammed as I made my way to the boy's school. I thought about transferring them to a school closer to where we lived but didn't want to uproot them so abruptly. I got into the parent line and did a happy dance when I realized I was first in line.

I waited as all the children were disbursed to their cars and frowned, wondering where the boys were. I put my car in park and hopped out of my truck, jogging over to their teacher.

"Miss Holt," I said, catching her attention. She turned towards me and gave me a confused look. "Oh, Mrs. Walsh, hi! Jason came and got the boys this morning."

"Oh yeah? He didn't tell me." I shook my head, playing it off how pissed off I was.

"Yeah, they were so happy!"

"Thank you so much! I'll see you later." I smiled before making my way back over to my car. I couldn't grab my phone fast enough.

"Hello?"

"Why didn't you tell me you grabbed the boys?" I asked, trying not to start screaming as I pulled out of the parent line.

"Oh shit, my bad. I meant to do that. I have a lot on my-"

"I'm on my way," I said, hanging up the phone. I was fuming as I made my way to his house, and I couldn't get there fast enough. I pulled into the driveway, leaving the car running, and made my way into the house. I could hear the boys upstairs in the family room laughing as the tv played loudly. I froze in the doorway as I saw all of Jason's kids sitting on the couch cozied up, eating snacks, and having the time of their lives.

"Come on, boys, let's go get your shoes and things," I said, trying to stop my voice from cracking as tears pooled in my eyes. I couldn't tear my eyes away from Jayla. She was such a beautiful little girl; if I had a daughter with Jason, she is what I imagined she would look like.

"Can I talk to you?" Jason asked after telling the boys to sit still for a moment. I nodded my head, finally tearing my eyes from Jayla, and followed Jason into my old bedroom.

"What?" I snapped once he closed the door.

"I'm sorry, Tam-"

"I don't want to hear any more sorries. Please keep them. The only thing you're sorry about is getting caught." He sighed deeply, running his hand through his curls.

"What do I have to do?" He asked, exasperated.

"Sign the divorce papers when you get them," I said as a matter of factly. He shook his head.

"I can't just give up our marriage like that. That's ten years!"

"Five were a lie. You been gave up on this marriage. Be real!" I said, storming over to our walk-in closet with him close behind.

"IT WAS A MISTAKE!" He yelled, throwing his hands up.

"THEN YOU HAVE TO LIVE WITH YOUR MISTAKES!" I yelled back as I opened up my suitcase and throwing whatever of mine I could get my hands on.

"What will it take for you to forgive me?" He asked after a few minutes of silence. I shook my head and swiped fallen tears from my face.

"I can't." I sobbed. "You hurt me bad."

"I'm sorry. Tamera, please let me make this right." He said, choking up.

"You can't. I'll never accept the fact that you stepped out of our marriage and made not one but two babies." I zipped up my suitcase and reached for another so that I could grab more stuff.

"Only one…" He mumbled.

"Jason, I'm not in the mood for your lies."

"She lost my son today. She had to push out a dead baby…."

I looked up at him sympathetically as I watched a tear fall from his eye. I wanted to reach out and hug him and tell him it would be ok, but I knew I would be lying. It wouldn't be ok, and as bad as I felt about the loss, it changed nothing.

"Well, I'm sorry to hear that. But you let that bitch know that when I see her, she better be ready to throw them hands now that I know she's not pregnant." I left the other suitcase telling myself I would come back later, and grabbed the one I filled. Then, I trotted out of the closet and back into the family room, telling the boys it was time to put their shoes on.

"Oh, ma! Can we please stay with daddy and our sister today?" Josh asked, looking down at his sister, who lay on his lap asleep.

"Josh, come-"

"Please, ma. Please! Please!" Johan asked, looking over at me with his hands clasped begging. I stuck my tongue out at him and told them they could spend the night with their dad.

"Will you stay with us?" Josh asked.

"No, mama can't. But I'll be there to get you from school tomorrow, ok? Be good for your father." I kissed both boys on the forehead and made my way down the stairs and out of the door. Jason silently followed behind me, looking like the fool he was probably hoping I would change my mind. He would be waiting forever. I popped my trunk to throw my suitcase inside, and Jason grabbed it out of my mind. We went through a tug of war for a few seconds before I gave up and stormed over to the driver's side and got in, watching him out my side mirror. I started to put my car into reverse once he closed the trunk but changed my mind. He wasn't worth the jail sentence.

"You sure you don't want to stay?" He asked as he made his way to my window. I rolled my eyes and rolled my window up on his ass.

"I have an appointment with a divorce lawyer on Wednesday," I said, rolling my window back down as I backed up.

"I won't sign." He taunted me by waving his hand goodbye. I groaned and put my car in drive, and rammed my car towards him. He jumped out of the way just in time and tumbled in the grass.

"Don't fuck with me, you bastard," I yelled, sticking my middle finger up before I backed back out of the driveway. I shook my head, forcing myself not to cry, not believing that this was my life. My husband had an affair and created outside children, and I'm the one on my way to my own home, by myself. I turned on some Mary J Blige and screamed out about no more pain as loud as I could until I reached my cul-de-sac.

What in the hell? I know that's not who I think it is! I slowed my car and blew my horn, causing him to jump and hit his head on the rim of his car. I burst out laughing and rolled my window down.

"I'm so sorry!" I chuckled, covering my mouth. "I thought that was you. You live here?"

"Man, gone." He frowned. "Making me hit my head and shit."

"You the one all scared of a damn horn."

"I ain't scared of shit. I just got my mind on other shit." He said as he walked over to my truck. "What are you doing over here? Are you stalking me? It ain't payday yet."

"Shut up, Kylan. I just moved in a few days ago at the house at the end of the cul-de-sac."

"Really? I ain't see no moving truck or anything."

"I didn't have one. So I just went to the store and got us an airbed and some food. The furniture delivery is set for tomorrow evening."

Kylan nodded his head and stared at me with an unreadable look.

"What?" I asked with my brow raised.

"Are you sure this is something that you want to do? The house and moving the boys and everything?"

I nodded my head. "Would you have stayed? If your wife cheated, got pregnant twice by another man, she worked with?"

He sighed heavily before he nodded his head. "Touche."

"Loyalty means everything to me. If I can't trust the person lying beside me every night, then I don't need them laying there."

He nodded again but didn't say anything.

"Did you know?" I asked, looking in his eyes for any sign of deception.

"Wasn't my place to say anything. I've always been taught to stay out of people shit."

I nodded my head and sighed. "I get it. You didn't owe me any loyalty, the people that did proved to me where their loyalty lies, and I'm cool on all of their asses."

"I mean, I get it. But at the same time, you can't put people in the middle and expect them to choose, especially when both of you mean a lot to them."

"It's not about choosing. It's about right versus wrong. I'm a always choose what's right."

"Well, everybody don't have that same code of ethics and morals. Some people only know one way of living."

"Hmph." I scoffed. "You're right. It just sucks, though. They were all I had at this point."

"No, they weren't. You got your sons, and I'm sure you got friends. You're just looking at everything that went wrong right now, but if you take a step back and look at your life, you're blessed."

"I know. It just hurts. I want to pretend it doesn't, but it does."

"Why?"

"Why what?"

"Why are you pretending it doesn't hurt?"

"So I don't have to feel it."

"Nah, that's not how you heal. Pretending it doesn't exist

doesn't make it go away. You have to feel it, experience it, and get through it so you can be healthy."

"Listen to you!" I squealed, squeezing his arm. "You'd think you were the psych and not me."

"I have a bachelor's in psychology." He smirked.

"Really?" I asked, shocked.

"Yes, ma'am. I've got a few layers." He winked.

"I see." I nodded my head as a car pulled into the driveway behind his vehicle. "Looks like your boo is home. Let me go."

"My sister." He corrected me. I nodded my head and put my car back into drive.

"I'll see you at work in the morning."

He stared at me for a few seconds before he tapped the top of my car.

"Ok, be safe."

I nodded and made my way to my lonely house. I was surely going to door dash a bottle of wine and finish my 'NOT GON CRY' concert.

CHAPTER 35
AERCA

"Ben Lee, did you take my damn squash out the cart?" I asked, rummaging through the cart, knowing damn well I put it in there.

"Huh?" He squealed pitch, going up a few octaves.

"I'm a kick your ass!" I swung my purse at him. "I need it for my Tchaka. You better go grab me another one."

"You can't make it without it? That squash had me shitting all day."

"Don't blame the squash for you being full of shit. Go get my squash!" I grit my teeth, pointing my finger at him.

"Mannnnnn…" He drawled as he turned to walk away. I chuckled and continued going down the aisle, grabbing the items I needed for the week. Usually, I would use a grocery delivery service, but Ben Lee figured that since we were passing the grocery store on our way back from the movies, we could just stop and grab what we needed instead.

"Here, man...Funky ass squash." He threw two squashes in the basket.

"Mmmhmm, next time you touch my squash, you gon pull back a nub."

"Girl, I'll drop you where you stand." He joked, getting into a ninja fighting stance. I guffawed, throwing my head back.

"Boy, bye. You better hope them moves save you from my bullets." I said, patting my purse.

"Girl, please, by the time you reach in that damn Chanel bag, I'd be done kicking your knee cap off."

"Yeah, whatever. Your mother would be proud to know she raised a son who enjoys kicking women in the knee." I teased, rolling my eyes playfully.

"She would beat my ass. She don't play that. She might have her vices, but she raised me to be respectful to women."

"Well, good...speaking of…." I said as we walked towards self-checkout.

"... okay?" He asked with his brow raised as he began scanning items.

"When am I going to meet your parents?" He got quiet as he scanned a few items. I immediately took that as him not wanting me to. "Forget I asked."

"No, that's not it." He said as he stopped scanning and rubbed his hands down his face. "My mom is just a lot. I'm nervous, maybe even scared a little."

"You think she gon run me away or something?"

"She has in the past."

"Well, them bitches weren't meant to be with you no way." I stuck my tongue out, passing him more groceries to scan.

"Plus, I want you to meet my parents. Soooo…"

"Okay." He nodded his head, swiping his credit card on the card reader. "I'll get with my mom this week and see when a good time is for us all to have dinner."

"Yayyyyyyy.." I said, pushing the cart aside and kissing him all over his face. "I knew you loved me."

"Yeah, yeah."

"Oh, also, Tamera is having a housewarming party in a few weeks, and we are invited, so once she gives me the date, I'll let you know so that both aren't on the same day."

"What the hell is a housewarming?"

"It's when someone moves into a new place and invites people over so they can view the home and stuff. We bring gifts that she could use, and we all hang out."

"Interesting.." he said as we walked out of the store.

"You've never heard of that?"

"No. Nobody I know has ever had one."

"Oh goodness! Do you even know how to play spades?"

"Spades?" He asked with a frown.

"I know you lying, Ben Lee. I don't care how Asian you are. You still black! Your ass better not embarrass me when somebody whip out cards!" I yelled as he put the bags in the trunk.

"I was joking." He laughed. "I know how to play spades, woman!"

"Mmmhmmm. I was gon leave yo ass in this parking lot." I lied as I got into the passenger seat. Ben Lee ain't have to know how to play spades, goldfish, or even UNO. He was mine, and I was gon stick beside him.

CHAPTER 36
LYNN

I held my mother's hand as we walked slowly to the front of the church to my daddy's casket. Mama was holding my hand so tight I thought she was going to break it off. I looked up at her and noticed her bottom lip was quivering, and she was whimpering and crying so much that her tears were falling off her face and onto the ground. That's all Mama had been doing since daddy died. I prayed and asked God to please help my Mama stop feeling pain and give me my daddy back. But he didn't. God didn't listen to my prayers because he would have never done this to us if he did.

"Oh, Edwinnnn.." My mother sobbed as we reached daddy's casket. Daddy looked like he was sleeping, he was still so handsome, and all I wanted him to do was open his eyes and hug me and tell me he loved me. I wanted more time with my daddy. This wasn't fair. Mama told me it was a good idea to bring all the things Daddy loved and put them in the casket with him so that way they would be close to his spirit. I couldn't think of anything, so I wrote daddy a letter telling him I loved him and that he should come back to us. I sat the note on his hand and rubbed his face, I could hear Mama still crying and carrying on, but all I could think about is wanting my daddy to come back to me.

DING! DONG!

I jumped out of my sleep and wiped my face. I had been having the same dream for the past two weeks since I got out of the hospital. I had turned my phone off and refused to communicate with anyone on the outside. Giving birth to a dead baby is something I wouldn't wish on my worst enemy. To carry a child and feel them kick and move around just for you to give birth and not be able to do any of those things. I was devastated, depressed and I blamed God for it all. Everything I love he keeps taking away from me.

KNOCK! KNOCK! KNOCK!

"Lynn, I know you're in there. I'm not leaving. If you don't answer, I'll call the police and have them do a wellness check. So it's either me, the police, or even worse, your moth-" Davis halted in his sentence when I snatched the front door open and rolled my eyes at him. He didn't look shocked by appearance; his eyes were empathetic and nonjudgmental. He nodded his head and walked into my house, closing the door behind him as I made my way back to the couch I had been lying on since I got home.

"I'm glad you finally opened for me. Have you eaten?" He asked, grabbing my blanket off the couch and moving it to the loveseat nearby. I didn't answer him; I just put my head into my hands, shaking my head. I didn't feel like having the it's going to be alright sympathy talk.

"Let me get you something to eat then."

"No!" I screamed. "Just leave me alone. I don't want to eat. I don't want to talk. I don't want to pray. I want to sit here. I want to grieve for my dead baby! I pushed my dead son out of my body, and I held his cold, stiff, lifeless body. So I don't want to fucking eat Davis."

Davis nodded and leaned back on the couch. He grabbed me by my hand, gently pulling me over to him until my top half was lying across his lap.

"I'm here. Whatever you need me to do, I will. I'll sit here in silence with you if you need me to. If you need me to run up and down the street naked, I will." I snickered for the first time in weeks. "Whatever you need, I'll do."

"Thank you," I said with a small smile as tears pooled my eyes. No matter how much I tried not to think about my son, my hand went to my stomach out of habit every few minutes, reminding me that his presence was no longer with me. I tried to hurry and remove my hand, but Davis stopped me by putting his hand over mine and rubbing my stomach. I took a deep breath and tried to muffle my sob, but it came out louder and stronger than I wanted it to.

A few hours later...

I woke up out of my sleep confused, I didn't remember falling asleep, but I also noticed I didn't have *the dream* for once. I looked around, seeing I was now in my bed. I got up and stretched, feeling a bit better than I had in a while, smelling food. My stomach began rumbling, and I made my way out of my room, where I saw Davis in the kitchen putting chicken in a colander.

"It smells good in here."

"Woman!" He jumped. "You almost scared the hell out of me."

"I'm sorry," I smirked. "What all did you cook?"

"I made some corn muffins, fried chicken, collard greens, and mac and cheese. I can make you a plate if you want."

"You made all this by yourself?" I asked, amazed, looking at the spread.

"I did. My grandma ain't play no games about men knowing how to cook in the kitchen it was always I ain't raising no lazy men. So you gon get your behind in there and cook so your wife can rest on some days. God made a woman your partner, not your damn slave."

"And she was right!" I smiled. "How about since you cooked, I'll make our plates?"

"You sure? I don't mind."

"I'm sure, Davis. You have done enough."

"Ok." He nodded his head. He left out of the kitchen and went to sit down. After I made our plates, I met him at the table. "Would you like something to drink? I think I only have water and maybe some crystal light."

"The water is fine. I'll grab it, though. Have a seat." He said as he got up and walked into the kitchen before I could rebuttal. By the time he made it back, I had already started devouring my food; all you could hear was me smacking and grunting like I hadn't eaten in weeks, and I hadn't. I looked over at Davis, and he had his head down with his eyes closed, praying over his food. I shook my head and continued eating.

"Why do yall do that?" I asked after swallowing what I had in my mouth.

He raised his brow in question before taking a bite of his muffin.

"Pray over everything, about everything… it doesn't make any difference," I mumbled.

"You don't think so?"

I nodded my head no. "God hates us. He takes people, fathers, mothers, babies. Look at this fucked up world."

"Some things are acts of God, yes, and others are free will."

"Like him taking my daddy? Or my fucking baby! FUCK GOD!" I blurted out, pushing my plate away. Davis sat his fork down and stood up.

"I'll be back." He said, walking towards the bathroom. I sat there by myself for a few minutes in my thoughts before Davis came back into the eating area.

"Can I get you to come with me?" He asked, putting his hand out for mine. I stared at him for a few seconds before I gave him my hand. He helped me up, holding on to my waist as he walked me down the hall and into the bathroom on the first level.

"What's this?" I asked, looking over at him. There were rose petals all over the floor, candles lit, and it smelled like lavender, the tub was filled with bubbles, and all I wanted to do was sink into it.

"This is your peace. I know this won't make everything better, but I wanted to do something simple but nice that would allow you to relax for a moment. So go ahead and get on in, I'll grab your phone, and you can play your music and just relax, ok? Take a moment and try not to think of anything. Just be in this moment."

I nodded my head and walked further into the bathroom as he walked away. I took off my shorts and shirt and climbed into the awaiting bath gasping at how good it felt.

"Is the temperature good?" Davis asked as he walked back in holding my phone. I nodded my head and pointed at the shelf in the bathroom where he could put my phone. "Alright, I'm going to go and clean up out here while you take your bath. Let me know if you need anything."

"Wait!" I called out before he could rush out of the bathroom.

"Yes?"

"Please get in with me?"

"Uh, I don't think that's a good id-"

"Davis, please.." I held my hand out for him. He stood there for a moment staring at me before he started taking off his shirt. I leaned forward and looked away from him to give him some piece of privacy. Davis stepped in the tub behind me and got comfortable before pulling me back so that I was lying on his chest. We sat in comfortable silence, enjoying the warm water before Davis advised me my mother called to check on me a few times as I slept.

"I'm sure she did. I'm surprised she didn't pop up over here." I chuckled.

"She was on her way, but I told her you were sleeping and promised I would have you call her when you got up."

"I knew it!" I grinned. "If my mother don't do nothing, she gon pray and pop up at my house."

"She is a praying woman. When I met her in the hospital, she was indeed praying over you."

I nodded my head and sighed deeply. "Ask me why."

"Why what?"

"Ask me why I hate God." I looked up at him. He sat his chin on my shoulder and sighed.

"Why?"

I felt around in the water for his hand and intertwined ours before telling Davis about my childhood. I explained to him how my parents raised me to think God was the beginning, middle, and the end, and how as long as we stayed prayerful and put him first, we would be given his mercy and love for all things. I told him about God taking my daddy from me and now my baby.

“I can understand why you would feel that way,” Davis said after a few minutes of silence.

“You do?” I asked, astonished.

"Absolutely. Being that young and impressionable and experiencing something so traumatic and not knowing how to handle it would cause you to lash out and find some*thing* or some*one* to blame. Have you ever talked to a therapist?"

I shook my head no.

"Hmph. Would you ever?"

"I'm not against it."

"That's good. I see one weekly. I've been going for years."

"Really?" I was stunned. Davis seemed so well put together. I would never have thought he would see someone weekly for problems.

"Is that a shock?"

"Yes. You seem to have it all together. I would have never guessed you go to a shrink regularly."

"Are shrinks only for people who don't have it together?" He quizzed.

"That's what I always thought." I shrugged my shoulders.

"Well, babe, people go to a therapist for plenty of things, not just for issues but for mentorship or ways to effectively break things down. Not always for bad things."

"...maybe I should see one. Can't make shit worse than it is."

Davis didn't respond; he just kissed my shoulder and leaned back into the tub. I meant what I said about getting a therapist. It was time that I talked to someone about how I felt, the things I've been through, and figuring out how to move forward. It's going to be a journey, but I know it will all be worth it in the end; although I lost my son, I still had a beautiful daughter to live for.

Chapter 37
Tamera

"Yeah, alright. Just don't be late to court this time, or I'm a drop your ass." I lifted my head from the computer in front of me and caught the back of Kylan as he walked his young client to the door. They exchanged a few more words before he made his way to my desk.

"Can you put court on my schedule for Friday at nine am, please?" He asked, tapping the desk.

"You got it, dude." I mocked the twins from Full House.

"How's your day going?"

"It's going ok," I said as I input the court date and time with the client's case and name on his online calendar and syncing it. "Oh, for my lunch break, I have to run to go and see this lawyer, so I may be a bit late back depending on traffic."

"That's a five-dollar fine." he joked, mocking What's Love Got to Do With It.

"Well, I-I-I'm sorry, Ike. But this has to get done."

"What's it for? If you don't mind me asking."

"Divorce and you are all set for your calendar. It should sync right to your phone."

"Ok, bet, and you sure that's something you want to do? You don't want to give it some time? Hasn't it been like a decade?

I nodded my head. "I'm sure. For half of that decade, he cheated. So that's that."

"Wow." He shook his head. "That's the last thing I would want to do."

"What?"

"Get divorced."

"Well, if you don't cheat, then you don't have to worry about it."

"I don't cheat. But cheating isn't the only thing that could break up any relationship or marriage."

"You're right. I also feel like a lot of things can be worked through. Some can't. That's why we always have to be conscientious of what we are doing when we do it."

"I dig it. So who are you going to see? Did you check their reviews and shit?" He asked, reaching into the candy bowl I had on the desk laughing when I popped his hand from grabbing a handful.

"You tried it." I giggled. "But yes, I did check his reviews online. They say he's good. Hell, he better be, with how much his ass charges, his name is a -" I paused to dig into the purse that I had in the file cabinet under the desk. "Joe Pittleston."

"Word? I know him. Tell him Ky said what's up."

"Oh lord. Who don't you know?" I groaned, putting the card back in my purse.

"Aye, I'm that nigga. Google me." He winked and smiled

before waltzing back to his office.

At the lawyer's office...

"Alright, so Mrs. Walsh in California, we have what is called a no-fault divorce. Basically, this means that California does not take into account any acts of adultery or proof of it. So we would need to file under irreconcilable differences. In the decree, we can discuss what you expect to leave the marriage with, and since there are children involved, we need to discuss custody arrangements. Is any of this lost on you?" Mr. Pittleston asked.

"I'm following you."

"Good." He smiled. Mr. Pittleston was a handsome middle-aged white man that favored Leonardo DiCaprio in Django minus the accent. We went over what I wanted in the divorce, running this meeting an hour longer than expected.

"Alright, Mrs. Wals-"

"Please, let's call me Miss Knox by my maiden name."

"Understandable. So, Miss Knox, I do want to warn you that the state of California is about four months behind with cases due to Covid, so this may take longer than usual."

I groaned and sat back in my seat. "And there's nothing we can do to expedite this?"

"We just have to wait." He said as he stood up. I followed suit and stood up, shaking my head. I wanted this shit over with now. The more it prolonged, the more Jason felt we had a chance, and I needed him to know his chances were slim to fucking none.

"You have a great evening." He said as we reached his office door.

"You as well. I'm heading back to work, so that's that. Oh yeah, Kylan Boudreaux told me to tell you hi! I work for him."

"Yeah?" He asked, surprised. "Ky's my man! Tell him don't be late this weekend at the pool hall, or I'ma bust his ass."

"I'll let him know." I cackled at the code switch as I walked out of the office.

"And Miss Knox." He stopped me. I turned back around and looked at him. "I'm sure I can find a way to get this expedited, ok?"

"Thank you so much, Mr. Pittleston."

"Call me Joe." He winked before closing his office door. Well, alrighty then. I shrugged and made my way out of the suite and back to work to finish my day.

Chapter 38
Kylan

"Shit! You scared the hell out of me!" Tamera screamed as she came out of the women's bathroom.

"My bad, I'm normally the only one here this early."

"Yeah. I was up early as if I had to take the boys to school, but they're with Jason, so I was just up looking crazy, so I just decided to come in and get some stuff done."

"Like what? You do more than enough around here." I joked as I started the coffee pot.

"Oh, hush." She laughed. "You all work so hard around here, so I just try and pull my weight."

"You work equally as hard. Don't play yourself."

She smiled and nodded her head. "Thanks for that. I admire everybody around here. It makes me more excited to get my building open."

"I'm excited for you."

"Yeah, we have so many sponsors, thanks to Ben Lee. They have donated over a million dollars so far towards education and supplies."

"That's dope as hell. So you will be like a counselor there on top of being the owner?"

"That's the plan." She nodded as she reached into the fridge grabbed the creamer out. "I'm also looking to hire about three more. One that can live on-site with the girls and two others."

"Cool. Let me know what you need from me."

"Hell, if one of the girls gets in trouble, I'll be calling y'all for help." She giggled.

"We got you, pro bono."

"Noooo!" She squealed. "Really?"

"Really, really." I nodded as I poured coffee into our mugs. "You've been a huge help here, so I got you."

"Ky, you're such a good man." She smiled at me. "After all you've been through, you still made it."

"And so have you."

"Yeah, but...I can't believe I put my dreams on hold for a man. After that, I gave up on myself."

"That was a selfless sacrifice you made for your family."

"Yeah, but I don't think that we should put our dreams on hold for the sake of marriage. I would think that's the time when we hold each other down if it gets too hard, you know?"

"I get it." I nodded. "I don't think I would have ever asked my wife to step back. We would have figured it out together."

"Yeah, never again."

"The right man would never ask you to," I said, looking her in her eyes. She nodded and stared back at me, opening her mouth to say something and closing it back as my phone rang out. I put my finger up and walked towards my office, seeing that it was Doc.

"What's up, Doc?" I mimicked Bugs Bunny.

"Bro, your sister out here getting her fucking head bucked in by this clown ass nigga Crip. What you want me to do?"

"Are you fucking kidding me right now, man?" I growled, clenching my phone as I held it.

"If I'm lying, I'm fucking flying nigga."

"Where you at, bro?" I asked as I took off my suit jacket and shirt. I kept casual clothes in the closet in my office if I wanted to go to the gym straight after work.

"I'm where Rip was born."

"Bet," I said, disconnecting the call. I finished changing clothes and shoes, hurriedly grabbing my keys, wallet and exiting out of my office running into Tamera.

"Everything ok?" She asked, looking me over.

"It will be. I'll be back." I grumbled, moving past her.

"I'm coming with you." She said, walking close behind me.

"No, you're not."

"Yes, I am. I see that look in your eyes. I feel like if I don't come and something happens, it'll eat at my conscience."

I didn't respond. I just kept walking. I didn't have time for any of this right now. Tamera wasn't playing, and she was on my ass as we both walked out of the suite, her locking up behind us and catching up to me as I held the passenger door open for her to get in. Tamera didn't ask any questions as I sped to the hood, it was still dark out, and everybody was outside like it was broad daylight.

When I pulled up on Sal's street, there was a crowd in the middle of the street, and I could hear yelling. I didn't even bother parking. I just put the car in park and hopped out right where I was. I pushed through the crowd and saw Juju standing around screaming while Doc had her punk-ass boyfriend at gunpoint. Crip looked like he had been beaten to an inch of his life, while JoJo looked like she was a poster girl for a domestic violence campaign. Once again, both of her eyes were black, and her lip was so swollen they looked like two oranges on her face.

"Kylan, stop him!" She screamed at me.

"Have you seen your fucking face?" I yelled at her.

"You don't understand!" She screamed. "Why did you tell him to do this?"

"I didn't tell him shit! But you should be happy I didn't get to him first!"

"I wish y'all just stay out of my life!"

"Your life ain't shit but a big fuck up! Look at you!" I yelled, grabbing her by her arm pointing at her face. "You look fucking stupid!"

"So what! That's my business! You think because you turned your life around that you're big shit. Don't forget about all the skeletons in your closet nigga!" She snarled in my face.

"Yeah, ok. I'm done! Don't call me no more. You wanna kill yourself with this shit, then that's on you!"

"I didn't call you, to begin with! I need him. We are having a baby." She cried. That's when I finally looked down and saw that she had a small baby bump.

"Wow. So you telling me, this the shit you want your kid to

see? What we went through wasn't enough for you? You wanna expose a kid to THIS?" I yelled, pointing around. "What the fuck do you have even to give a kid Jedidiah?"

"Don't judge me like you ain't from this same block nigga!"

"It don't matter where I'm from. It's not where the fuck I'm at! I ain't doing the same shit that kept us here. What about you?"

"Fuck you, RIP!"

"Yeah, ok, you remember that." I spat, walking away from her. I walked over to Doc, holding Crip at gunpoint, and punched Crip dead in his mouth, knocking him back to the ground.

"If I find out you are touching my sister while she is pregnant, you ain't got to worry about nobody or nothing cause you gon see why they call me RIP. You hear me nigga!" I said, kneeling in his face. He nodded his head as best as he could, and I stood up and stormed away.

"Kylan…"

I kept walking until I reached my car, only glancing up when I heard my passenger door open where Tamera climbed inside. I had been so focused on getting to JoJo I forgot that Tamera was even with me.

"Kylan… I know you might not want to hear this, but you're going to have to let her figure this thing out on her own until she realizes it's not love."

I shook my head before peeling off and back into traffic.

"This right here ain't none of your business, and I don't even want to talk about the shit." I snapped before turning my music on. She nodded her head and looked out of the window, not saying another word as I made our way back to the office.

CHAPTER 39
AERCA

"Now, when we get in here, please just act normal," I said to Ben Lee as we pulled into my parent's driveway.

"So, no karate moves? Got it." He joked, smiling at me. I rolled my eyes playfully and shook my head.

"Play too damn much. Neither of them speak English too well, so if you don't understand something, ask me."

"Ok, babe." I smiled and pecked him on the lips before he got out and came around to open the door for me. Like the Haitian parents, they were waiting on the porch, being nosey as ever, waving us over.

"Manman, Papa, this is my boyfriend, Benjamin Lee. Benjamin Lee, this is my manmnan Roseline Peters, and my Papa Emanuel Peters." I introduced everyone after kissing and hugging my parents.

"Very nice to meet you, Mr. and Mrs. Peters. You can call me Ben Lee." He said, shaking my father's hand. My mother swatted his hand away and hugged him.

"Come right on in." My mother said, smiling and grabbing my arm. We made our way inside, where we all made small talk about old pictures on the wall and their backstories.

"Hellllooooo..." I smiled as I turned towards the doorway as my sister Nadia made her presence known. Nadia was the rebel of the two of us. If my parents told her to go left, you better believe she was going right.

"There she is!" My papa yelled, pulling Nadia into a big hug. Nadia barely came home from college even though her college was only forty-five minutes away. She said it was the only way she could keep her peace when it came to our parents and their Haitian traditions.

"She leaves home and never comes back." My manman fussed, throwing her arms up in the air before kissing Nadia on the cheek. Nadia stood five foot eight, only an inch or two under me. We had the same chocolate complexion, almost identical; the only difference was that Nadia wore a nose ring, brow ring, and a Monroe piercing. Her hair was always in a short curly fro that fit her slim face to perfection.

"Hi to you too, manman." Nadia playfully rolled her eyes before moving to hug me. "And who is this blasian?"

"Can you not?" I snickered. "Nadia, this is my boyfriend Benjamin Lee, Benjamin this is my little sister Nadia."

"I've heard so much about you." He shook her hand. "Call me Ben Lee."

"Ok, then, Mister Ben Lee! Sis, he is fine!" She laughed. I shoved her, telling her to hush as we followed our parents into the kitchen.

Papa and Ben Lee set the table as manman, Nadia and I brought the food into the dining area. After praying over the food, we all began digging in. Manman cooked Pate, diri aj djon djon, vegetable stew, pain de mais, and lambi. By the sounds of everybody quiet and smacking on their food, we were all enjoying our dinner.

"So, Aerca, tell me something. Are you still a virgin?" Manman asked. I gasped and started choking as some of my food went down the wrong pipe.

"Manman!" I shrieked, wiping my mouth. My mother shrugged and spewed out that she had the right to ask in Haitian.

"She is grown," Nadia said, coming to my defense.

"I just ask a question."

"Ummm…" Ben Lee said, clearing his throat. "We have not had sex."

My eyes ballooned as I looked at him as if he was crazy. He shrugged and smirked at me before finishing his food.

"Well...now that that is out of the way. Ben Lee, what do you do?" My papa asked, taking a sip of his cremas.

"Well, Mr. Peters, I am the CEO of Suttles Architecture."

"So you do a lot of building and contracts of the sort?" Manman asked, nodding her head.

"Correct. That's how I met your daughter." He smiled at me.

"I see." My papa said. "She's a hard worker. She tell you she owns a house on just about every block?"

"Papa.." I whined. "I do not."

"She's modest too." Ben Lee winked at me. "We have both shown each other the properties we have. Real estate is the best way to close the wealth gap in America."

"I heard that on CNN." My mother nodded her head.

"Oh geez, why are you watching that?" Nadia frowned. "All you do is let that mess scare you."

"It helps me to stay in touch with what's going on in Haiti."

"CNN only reports less than one percent of what's going on in Haiti. You have to know people there to understand what's going on there." Nadia said, shaking her head.

"I know, I know." Manman nodded her head.

"So, Ben Lee, do you want to get married?" Papa blurted out, changing the table conversation causing me to once again choke on my food.

"I do." Ben Lee said, smiling before patting my back.

"And children?" Manman asked.

"And children! I want it all." He smiled.

"Well, isn't that good!" Manman said with a big smile. "He is perfect for you, Aerca."

I blushed and continued picking over my food.

"Nadia, when are you going to find a husband?" Manman asked.

"I'm a lesbian," Nadia said casually as she continued eating her food. Manman and Papa began cursing Nadia in Haitian as Ben Lee, and I sat there chuckling.

"She always tries to raise my blood pressure!" Papa fussed. Nadia shrugged and winked at me before she continued eating her food. The rest of the dinner went great. My parents caught up on Nadia's life and continued asking Ben Lee all of the embarrassing questions that they could think of. Afterward, we had Gateau Au Beurre with creme cocoye before Papa came back into the living area with a slew of embarrassing homemade videos of Nadia and me singing and dancing around the house as kids.

"Did you know they sing?" Manman asked as she smiled at the video.

"No?" Ben Lee said, looking over at me with a shocked expression on his face.

"Every parent thinks their kids can sing." I waved him off.

"She's lying." Nadia butted in. "We both can hold a tune, but Aerca can sang. I'm talking about KeKe Wyatt, Jennifer Hudson singing. Don't let her fool you."

I blushed and shook my head. It was true. I loved to sing in my spare time. It wasn't something I wanted to make a career of, but I could outsing many of these singers today.

"She's been hiding that from me. I've never heard her even hum a song."

"Oh yeah, if she wasn't doing what she was doing now, I'm sure she could easily have a music career." Nadia hyped me.

"Well, well, well... I'm learning all about you." Ben Lee teased me with a gleam in his eye.

"Do you ladies mind if I have a private talk with your friend here?" Papa asked as he stood up. I looked at Ben Lee, and he nodded his head.

"It's fine." He said, kissing my cheek before standing.

"Papa, be nice," I whined.

"I'm no Boogey, man. Don't worry." Papa teased as he led Ben Lee to his office.

"I like him for you," Manman said as they disappeared out of our eyes view.

"Thank you, manman. I like him."

"Look at her. She's blushing." Nadia teased.

"Leave her be. Be happy. That's all I want for you both. That's why we were so tough on you, but you both are amazing, and we will never be disappointed by anything you do."

"Awww," Nadia joked, wiping fake tears. "We love you too."

"Silly girl." Manman smiled, rolling her eyes. "I'm going to bed now. I've been up before the birds. I'll tell Ben Lee it was good to see him. Don't be a stranger."

"I won't," Nadia said, throwing her hands up in surrender.

"Goodnight, manman." I hugged her before she made her way out of the living area.

"Tonight went well. He deserves that gawk gawk three thousand sis." Nadia said, sticking her tongue in her jaw as if she was giving head.

"Bitch!" I whisper screamed. "Go to hell."

"I'll go after you let him bust that cherry." She teased me by sticking her tongue out at me.

"You're annoying."

"Nah, you're annoying for not living life the way you want to. Manman and Papa didn't wait until they were married but yet throwing that shit on you."

"I mean, I haven't up until now found anyone I wanted to give it to anyways." I shrugged.

"Mmhmm.." She rolled her eyes. "Anyways, I'm about to get up out of here. I've been here too long, and I miss my boo."

"Oh, whatever, in here getting them up in arms talking about you're a lesbian." I laughed.

"Oh, I wasn't joking. My boo is a she, and she is outside." Nadia said as she stood up, grabbing her purse.

"Really?" I quizzed. I would have never suspected Nadia of being into girls. But, she has always been a do what I want type of person, so I wasn't shocked.

"Really, really." She mocked Kevin Gates. "Walk me out so you can meet her."

I nodded and followed Nadia outside, where we walked towards a money-green SRT that had dark tints. She waved at whoever was in the car, and they turned the car off before stepping out. To say I was shocked was an understatement. A woman got out of the car looking like a supermodel. I don't know why I was expecting a stud, but this took me by surprise.

"Baby, this is my sister Aerca, Aerca this is baby." Nadia introduced us before she pecked the woman on the lips. I stood there smiling, showing all thirty-two.

"Monica!" She said, introducing herself, reaching her hand out to me after slapping Nadia's arm.

"Nice to meet you!" I shook her hand. "You are gorgeous."

"No, that's yall." She said, pointing at Nadia and me. "I've never seen women as beautiful as you all. Every time I look at her, I'm like wow."

Nadia blushed and shook her head. "She's so dramatic."

"I'm so serious."

I watched them go back and forth for a minute before we all

said our goodbyes, promising that she would bring Monica to Tamera's housewarming party. Then, I made my way back into the house where Papa and Ben Lee were coming from his office.

"Thank you again for inviting me into your home." Ben Lee said to Papa, shaking his hand.

"No problem, son! You are welcome here anytime!" Papa said, smiling hard. "I like him for you, Aerca. He has a good head up top."

"Thank you, Papa. I appreciate that." I kissed his cheek and grabbed my purse. "Well, Papa, it's time for us to get out of here. I have to work early as Ben Lee has to do the same."

"Ok, I understand. But remember what I always say, don't overwork yourself. Take time and enjoy the fruits of your labor."

"I know, Papa." I nodded as Ben Lee held the door open for me. Papa and Ben Lee exchanged a few more pleasantries before he and I were able to leave and make our way back to his house, where I had been spending most of my time.

"See, that wasn't so bad," I said after getting out of the shower and meeting him back in his room.

"No, it wasn't. They are all very loving and proud of you." Ben Lee said, smiling as I laid on his chest.

"Yeah." I nodded.

"Your dad tells me how you take care of everyone in the family."

"He said that?" I asked, sitting up raising my brow,

"He did. He's worried that you're allowing them to all be a burden, and he wanted me to tell you that they are all ok and you don't have to give them any more money. He said you won't listen to him."

"And what else did he say?"

"That you are too damn nosey." Ben Lee snickered, teasing me.

"No, he did not!" I squealed, laughing. "I know he said something else. Tell me."

"No. It's guy talk, nothing for you to worry your pretty little head about." He said before pulling me close to him and kissing me. I moaned into his mouth and straddled him. Ben Lee and I did light kissing and cuddling on the regular, but nothing had gone as far as it had weeks ago, and the way my coochie was thumping, there was nothing that was going to stop us tonight.

"Ben Lee…" I said, pulling away from him.

"Yes, baby?" He said, smacking my ass.

"Make love to me," I said, pulling my pajama shirt over my head exposing my nude body.

"You sure?" He asked, reaching up and massaging my exposed breast.

"Yes, please." I moaned, grinding against him. Ben Lee nodded and leaned up, still massaging my breast sucking my bottom lip into his mouth.

"Shittt.." He hissed as he grew hard under me. "I can feel your wetness through my fucking boxers."

"It's because I want you that bad."

Ben Lee flipped us over so that I was on my back and he was on top.

"You know this will hurt your first few times, right?"

I nodded my head, remembering how Tamera told me it took a while for her to start enjoying sex after she lost her virginity. I was snapped out of my thoughts when I felt Ben Lee's warm lips on my lower ones. He took his thumb and began slowly rubbing my clitoris. I moaned out and started grinding against his working fingers. Shortly after, Ben Lee replaced his thumb with his mouth and began kissing my vagina like he was french kissing me. I could feel my essence dripping out of me.

"I'm going to stick my finger in here, ok?" He warned me before I felt a finger creep into my entrance. I tensed up just a bit and relaxed when Ben Lee kissed the inside of my thigh lovingly. After a few seconds, he added another finger, and I moaned out, feeling my ocean rumble.

"You're so wet." He groaned against my clit, which intensified the heat and good-ass feeling that was stirring below.

Ben Lee added another finger and continued licking on my clitoris, and I felt the intense build-up I got when I played with myself in the shower. "I'm about to cum." I panted, reaching down and rubbing the top of his head.

“Do that shit then.” He said as he moved his fingers in a come here motion while continuing to lick. My grinding sped up as my body began to shake. Ben Lee pulled his fingers out and stuck them in my mouth, forcing me to taste my juices before kissing me deeply.

“Are you ready?” He asked against my lips. I nodded my head and pulled him back into a kiss as I felt him line himself up with my opening. I tried not to think too hard about it and stay in the moment of love. The moment of feeling him kissing me with everything in him so that when he hurried and pushed through my barriers, I didn't feel like I was dying. What I thought would be the worse pain in the world only felt like it was just a quick pinch.

"You ok, love?" He asked, pausing and looking at me. "You in pain? We can stop."

"No, it hurt just a little. Am I bleeding?" I asked, trying to lift a bit to look in between us.

"Shiiittt…" He groaned, closing his eyes. "Don't move, you're so fucking tight...warm...and wet...and if you move, I'ma nut all up in your shit...let me get a second, and then I'll look ok?"

I threw my head back and chuckled. "Ok, baby."

"Don't laugh.." He said with a smirk on his face pulling back a bit. "No blood."

I nodded my head and laid back on the pillow as he made his way back downtown. Before I knew it, my body was succumbing to the pleasure he gave to me. As my body shook, he made us one again and began delivering slow, calculated strokes. Feeling him invade my walls while he kissed me so profoundly had me feeling like I was experiencing an out-of-body experience. But in this moment of completion, fragility and love were worth the wait.

CHAPTER 40
JASON

I sat at my desk going over my case notes for court at one fifteen this evening. I knew I could get this case thrown out with no issues and just wanted to make sure I crossed all my t's when it came to looking up case files. Comparing your case to a previous case with a good outcome always helps things go in my favor in court.

KNOCK KNOCK

"Come in," I called out, looking up from the documents I was reviewing.

"There's somebody here to serve you. Ok bye." Terry said, opening the door before he jetted off, leaving a white girl standing in my doorway with a yellow envelope looking uneasy.

"Um...that was weird." She shook her head. "Are you Mr. Jason Walsh?"

"I am," I said with my hand out as she began handing me the envelope. Servers came by here regularly, most likely just something from the courts telling me about a past case. Nothing new. I sat the envelope on top of a stack of papers that needed filing and thanked the server before she walked back out of my office, closing the door behind her.

I picked up my office phone and called Denison. “Yes, sir..”

“Hey man, when you get a chance, I have a few documents from a server that needs to be filed.”

“Thanks, boss man, coming now.”

“It’s no rush, man.”

“It’s all good. I was reviewing some notes here. So that’ll help keep me occupied until court.”

“That’s exactly what I was over here doing. Court will be a piece of cake today.”

“Always is. I’m coming now.”

"Alright, thanks, man."

I stood up and stretched and chuckled to myself when my stomach began rumbling loudly. I had been on the move all morning and forgot to eat breakfast. I grabbed up my suit jacket that housed my keys and wallet and decided to go across the street to a local deli for something quick.

DING!

My phone binged with a message as I stood in line waiting to order.

I got the flowers you sent. AGAIN! Roses really smell like shit. It would be best if you took a hint from Outkast.

I smirked and shook my head. I knew she would have something to say about me sending the flowers. But I would keep sending them until we made some progress. I missed having my wife and sons in the same house. I know I fucked it all up, but I'm willing to do whatever I have to do to get us back to where we were.

I love you too. I texted back, seconds later, she sent back a middle finger emoji. I put my phone back into my pocket and moved forward as the line moved.

"Vanessa!" They called out at the pick-up area as I stepped up to place my order.

"Yes, can I get a chicken caesar wrap-" My words caught in my throat as

"Vanessa" came to grab her order from the counter. We were older, but I would never forget her face.

22 years ago.

"Aye, you hungry?"

I looked over from the couch I was sitting on watching tv at the girl that sat at the dining room table eating on a plate of food. Of course, I couldn't see what it was from here, but my mama always taught me not to trust everybody's food, so I wasn't about to touch it.

"I'm good," I answered, shaking my head.

"Damn your voice deep." She shrieked as she stood up, grabbing her plate and walking over to where I was on the couch and sat down beside me. "How old are you?"

"Sixteen." I lied. I had just turned thirteen a few weeks ago, but she didn't need to know that. "How old are you?"

"Too old for your young ass. I'm nineteen."

I frowned my face up at her knowing she was too old for my REAL age.

"Nineteen ain't far from sixteen."

"Shiiiddd, y'all don't know what to do with no woman." She rolled her eyes.

"Yeah, ok," I said and turned my attention back to the tv.

"You know she's not his client. You know what they're back there doing?" She asked, nodding her head towards the back of the house where my dad was with another "client."

I shrugged and tried not to think too heavily about what my dad was doing behind my mother's back. I already felt like crap having to hide it from my mother; saying it aloud made it too real. So I opted not to say anything.

"You a virgin?"

"A chicken caesar wrap?" The cashier questioned, pulling me from my blast from the past. I looked around and saw Vanessa's back as she left out of the deli.

"Yes, a chicken caesar wrap, some fries, and a sweet tea, please."

"Ok, that'll be nine thirty-eight."

I handed the cashier my card before straining my neck to look out of the window only to see that Vanessa had disappeared.

“Here you go, you can wait over there for your name to be called.” The cashier said as she handed my card back to me. I nodded and sat at the booth near the area she pointed to.

“Are you?” I countered. “You all up in my business and stuff.”

“It’s just a question, and you must be one.” She chuckled, shaking her.

“Yeah, ok.”

"Yeah, ok." She mocked me. I waved her off and continued watching tv, hoping she was done with her line of questioning. She appeared to be done talking but wanted to do some touching as she moved closer to me and put her hands through my curly fro,

"Aye, what are you doing, bro." I swatted her hand away, moving my head.

"Chill." She said lowly as she leaned over, kissing my neck. I was scared as hell right now. I was a virgin. The only vagina I had seen was on pornhub, and I had yet to kiss anybody. I took a deep breath and closed my eyes because what she was doing felt great. It didn't hurt that it was also coming from somebody who looked as good as she did. She took me not pushing her away as a sign to do more because she straddled me and began kissing me and grinding in my lap. I was in shock. I didn't even know that my dick could get as hard as it was now. Every lesson my mother and father had taught me went out the window when she reached into my shorts and pulled my dick out and lifted her dress and sat on me. I thought I was about to burst right then and had to hurry up and think of something else before she clowned me.

"Your shit sooo big."She groaned into my ear as she moved up and down. I didn't say anything back; I just tried to do like the pornos and push up into her while grabbing her butt. I must've been doing something right because a few minutes later, we were both squealing with her clinging on to me, telling me she was cumming. Her vagina had gripped me so tight that I knew I had nutted all up in her. Unfortunately, the moment was short-lived when we heard a door open from the back of the house, and we hurried to make ourselves look decent. She busied herself in her phone quickly, and I continued pretending to watch tv as my dad finally made his appearance.

"Alright, son, let's get out of here."

"Ok," I said, getting up. "Nice meeting you all." I waved to the chick I had just lost my virginity to but neglected to get her name, and the woman my daddy claimed was a client. They both smiled and waved at me as I made my way out of the front door my dad was holding open.

"Jason," my name was called. With my thoughts all over, I grabbed my order and headed back to my office, thinking about the past.

Will you be home when I pick up Jayla? I sent a text to my dad as I pressed the number for my floor on the elevator.

I'll be here all day. Is everything ok?

I texted back yes and got off the elevator as it opened.

"Yoooo, bossman, I need to talk to you," Denison said, following behind me as I walked to my office.

"What's wrong?" I asked as I sat my bag of food on my desk.

"I was filing the documents you gave me, and this one.....is for you." He replied, sitting a file on my desk.

"What you mean?" I asked as I pulled my food out. "It can't be filed?"

"No... look at it when you get a second. If you need me, I'll be in my office." He said before walking out. I shrugged and took a bite of my wrap before reaching over and grabbing the file.

The defendant Tamera Walsh is filing for a dissolution of marriage on the grounds of irreconcilable differences. After nine years of marriage, Mrs. Tamera Walsh feels that the marriage is no longer working....

I dropped the paper like it was on fire and pushed my food right into the trash. I suddenly had no more appetite. I picked up my phone with a shaky hand and called Tamera. She sent my call to voicemail, and I repeatedly called back until she answered.

"Jason, I'm working." She huffed in a loud whisper.

"You *seriously* filed for a divorce?" I quizzed with my voice full of emotion.

"Hold on...hey, I'm going to step out for a second and take this call. Let me know if you need me." She said to someone in the background. I could hear her walking and a door open before she came back on the line.

"Jason, I told you that I would file. Why are you acting shocked?"

"After nine years, you just gonna throw it all away?"

"ME??" She squealed. "If there is anyone who threw this marriage away, it's you!"

"But I'm trying to make this right! We don't need a divorce. I'll give you some space, but this is not needed."

"Says who?"

"Me! I'll work to gain your trust back, and I'll do right." I pleaded.

"No, Jason.." She sighed deeply. "We can't be fixed."

"You didn't try.." I sniffed, leaning my head back closing my eyes to stop my eyes from watering.

"I tried...for nine years. While I was trying to keep us together, you were busy destroying us."

"Baby ple-"

"No. It's final...I have to go." She said before disconnecting the call.

"Fuck!" I yelled into my hands, trying not to lose my cool. This was quickly becoming the day from hell.

A few hours later

I pulled up to my mother's house and saw her and Jayla outside playing in the flower bushes. In the past few months, these two have built the cutest bond ever, and it makes me regret waiting so long to introduce the two.

My daughter yelled and ran to me, gripping my leg as I stepped out of the car.

"You must've missed me?" I laughed as I walked with her on my leg.

"Yes, daddy!" She giggled. "I always miss you."

"Daddy always misses you too!" I picked her up and kissed her cheek a few times before she swatted me away, laughing.

"Are you going to help grammy finish picking these weeds, or are you kicking me to the side for your daddy?"

"Yes! I help grammy," Jayla agreed, showing all her teeth and trying to hop out of my arms.

"Oh, whatever!" I laughed, putting her down. "Is dad inside?"

"Yep, he's back there in the den watching his sports."

I nodded and walked into the house, stopping to grab two beers before making my way to the den.

KNOCK KNOCK

"Hey, there, son!" My dad said as I opened the door to the den.

"Hey, pops," I said, handing him a beer. "What you in here watching?"

"ESPN as always. What's going on?"

"Not much, coming from work to get Jayla from mom."

"Yeah, that's her buddy there. She misses Tamera and the boys."

I nodded my head and sighed. "Yeah, I know."

"How is that situation coming along? I know it's not easy."

"At all," I said before I gulped the beer down. "She's not budging at all. I just got served with the divorce decree today."

"Yikes." My father said as he picked up the remote, muting the tv. "You and Tam have been together almost ten years. So you don't think she will want to make it work?"

"I hurt her too badly. If she does, it will be a miracle."

"Keep trying. Your mother gave me a second chance."

"Yeah, but they are not the same person. Tamera done lost so much that she doesn't care about losing me. I should have told her months ago about all this shit. I think it's more so how she found out that she can't get over."

"Yeah. Your mother told me about that. She won't even speak to her. Your mother is taking that hard."

"That's my fault." I shook my head. "I should have never put ma in the middle of my shit."

"Listen, all we have sometimes is the shoulda, coulda, woulda's, but we can't change what has already happened. We can only change going forward."

"Yeah, you're right," I murmured.

"Yeah. Now, what's going on with her mother?"

"Jayla?" He nodded. I ran my hands over my head and shook my head.

"I'm not sure. I reached out to her the other day and got no response back. Her mother said she's just taking time for herself since the stillbirth."

"Damn, I know that was tough. But I know she has to want to see her daughter. It's been almost a month or something close to that since she's seen her, right?"

"Yeah."

"Has Jayla been asking about her?"

"Yeah, I just told her she's sick right now. Having mom is making it easy for Jayla to adjust too."

"I see. So what are you going to do when she wants her back? You going to go from seeing her daily to barely seeing her again?"

"No. Hopefully, we can work out some type of agreement."

"Hopefully so. Custody agreements can get ugly."

"Yeah, I don't want to go through that. All the begging she used to do, we shouldn't have that issue."

"Good."

"Hey! Me and my baby gon to run down to the bakery and do some errands. Yall need anything before we go?" My mom asked, peeking her head in the door.

"No, baby, I'm good." My dad said as he stood up and walked over to the door to kiss her.

"You?" My mom asked, looking over at me.

"I'm good." I waved her off.

"Alright, Jayla, come tell your daddy you'll see him later." She called out to Jayla. Seconds later, I could hear Jayla's feet running full speed to the door.

"Bye, daddy!" She yelled.

"Hey, come give me a hug," I yelled out before she ran back off. She laughed and gave me a big hug before grabbing my mom's arm and pulling her away.

"Dad…" I said as we were watching ESPN in silence.

"Yeah, bud?"

"Do you remember that girl from when I was a kid?"

"What girl?"

"The one…who took my virginity, Vanessa." My dad turned up his beer bottle and drank the rest before responding to me.

"Yeah, what about her?"

"I saw her today."

"Really? Where?"

"The deli by my job, whatever happened with that situation?"

"What do you mean?"

Two Months later….

"Jason!" My dad said as he barged into my room and slamming the door behind him.

"Yeah?" I asked, pausing my game and taking my headphones off my head looking at him.

"You got her fucking pregnant?"

"Who?" I asked, confused. My dad huffed and sat down in my computer chair at my desk in my room and shook his head.

"Vanessa."

"Who?" I asked again, still confused.

"The last "place" I took you to. I asked you did something happen with her, and you told me no." My eyes widened as I remembered what he was referring to.

"Oh...what do you mean she pregnant tho?"

"It means, did you wear a condom?"

"No. I didn't know I was going to do that. She just climbed on me!" I mumbled.

"SO WHAT" He yelled before stopping and calming himself down. "Listen, you're a boy that will eventually be a man that a lot of women want. I don't care what happens; you stop and put on protection, son."

"Ok." I nodded my head.

"We have to handle this like now. Get dressed and meet me downstairs in ten minutes. We have to hurry up before your mama makes it home, so come on."

I got up and threw on a pair of lakers joggers with the matching jacket. Then, I slid my foot into my Nike slides and made my way downstairs, knowing my dad would not be giving me a ten-minute grace period as he claimed.

One hour later...

"See, I told you she didn't have to lie about being pregnant!

He's going to have to step up and do what he has to do." My dad's "client" fussed, pointing her finger at me.

"It doesn't matter if she's lying or not. My son is thirteen. She raped him." My dad said with a smirk on his face. The woman and girl both snapped their heads towards me, looking at my five-foot-eleven frame in shock.

"No... He told me he was sixteen." The girl shook her head.

"Doesn't matter. By the eyes of the law, he's a child. You don't even know his name, let alone his age. But I bet the courts will handle all that."

"No. No!" My dad's "client" shook her head. "That's not necessary. She didn't know."

"Yeah, ok. It's her word against his. My son was a virgin." My face turned red, and I looked down in embarrassment as everybody got quiet.

"So, what am I supposed to do?" The girl asked.

"If you don't want to go to jail for rape, I suggest you get rid of the evidence." My father said as he walked towards the door. "That's the only option here."

After leaving there, we went to a gaming store, got the new games I wanted and went home. We never spoke about it again after that day. We just carried on as if the incident had never happened.

"Did she ever get the abortion?"

"Where is this coming from?" He asked, standing back up and going over to his bar.

"Seeing her made me think about it, and I just wanted to know." I shrugged.

"Yeah, well, you were a kid," he said, pouring some bourbon in a glass and taking a shot.

"And I'm thirty-six now."

"I handled that situation."

"So she got the abortion?"

"I handled that situation." He repeated, attempting to pass me a shot in which I declined.

"Ok, but why are you going around the question? It's a yes, or no." My voice raised.

"You better watch it, boy."

I pinched my eyes shut and took a deep breath. When I hid something, I did the same as my dad and ran around the question or just refused to answer it.

"Dad, please. I need to know."

My father didn't answer me. Instead, he took another shot and walked out of the room. I shook my head and stared blankly at the television, not paying attention to anything going on. A few minutes later, my father came back into the room with a manila folder, giving me a hard stare before he handed it to me.

"What's this?" I asked, opening the folder. A stack of papers and photos fell into my lap. Pictures of a boy who looked like my son's, the only difference was that his complexion was a deep brown, but he still had my red hair, freckles, and height. "Wow...how old is he now?"

"Twenty-two." My dad sighed.

"Does he know about me?" I asked.

"No." My dad shook his head. "As a part of the contract, she had to make up some story about who his dad was, and I would continue to send her money to take care of him."

"And she was ok with this?"

"She tried to hide the fact that he existed. For years she did, but something kept nagging me about the situation, and I looked her up and saw that she was living in a one-bedroom roach-infested apartment, so I did what I had to do."

"Why didn't you tell me?"

"You were still a kid. What could you have done?"

"I don't know, but what about when I was an adult? I deserved to know."

"You deserved to go to college and be who you are now!" My dad roared.

"What am I? I ain't shit but a nigga who lost his family, and now I got a son out there who doesn't even know I fucking exist." I yelled, pushing all the papers on the floor.

"I did what I felt was best!"

"For who! YOU?!" I shook my head and stood up, grabbing my keys. "I'm out of here, man." I walked out of my parent's house as fast as my feet would allow me.

CHAPTER 41
LYNN

"I see here on your intake form that you stated you just went through a miscarriage through stillborn?" Jeanie, my new therapist, asked as she looked down at her paper and back up at me. I nodded and sat back on the couch, moving my purse from my lap then next to me.

"Is this something you want to talk about?"

"Not right now, no." I shook my head. "Too fresh."

"I get that." She nodded her head. "So, what's on your mind?"

"Everything," I said, feeling exasperated. "Just too much going on, and I need to figure it all out so I can be better."

"Ok, well, tell me the first thing that comes to your mind, and we can talk about that," Jeanie said before taking a sip of her FIJI water.

I got quiet and thought about the first thing that came to mind: my sweet daughter. "Jayla."

"And is that your four-year-old daughter?" Jeanie asked. I nodded yes.

"Tell me about her." She smiled.

"She's so beautiful. She has this long curly hair that's the prettiest reddish-orange hue. She's so bright, the most amazing little girl ever. I miss her so much." I wiped my eyes. Thinking about her and realizing I had practically abandoned her hurt my heart. I needed to get well so that I could go and get my baby as soon as possible.

"You said you miss her, is she gone?"

"She's with her dad." I nodded my head.

"Oh, ok, and you two have a set schedule you follow?"

"No." I shook my head. "After everything happened, he stepped up to the plate and got her so that I could get better."

"That's great. It's important to have a supportive co-parent."

"Tuh. His hand was forced. He didn't have a choice." I rolled my eyes.

"What do you mean?"

"Jason hasn't been there for Jayla like he should have."

"Is that what you perceive, or is that a reality?"

"It's a reality. His wife found out about our daughter, and that's why he stepped up."

"Ok. So he was hiding your daughter? If I'm wrong, please feel free to correct me."

"You're right. He was. We had an affair years ago and created Jayla."

"Do you two get along?"

"Depends on the day. Part of me blames him for what recently happened."

"Hmm, what made you come to that conclusion?"

"I just feel like if I didn't have to keep hiding everything and could live freely, I wouldn't have been so stressed out, and my bab-" I stopped myself and started shaking my head.

"I understand. How did you two meet?"

"We are both attorneys. He was hiring, and I applied. Working together, we got close, and things just happened."

"It happens, sometimes we tend to blur the line in the sand. Did you know he was married?" I nodded my head and sighed. "But that didn't stop him."

"If he's not a man who knows how to fight temptation, it would not have stopped him."

"I don't think most men know how to."

"Fight temptation?"

“Yes. It seems like they all cheat.”

“I respectfully disagree. There are a lot of faithful men out there. It’s just all about where we are looking.”

“Hmm… I don’t know about that, but you’re the doc, so you know the statistics better than me.” She smiled and nodded.

“What would you say you look for in a man?” I got quiet and thought about it for a few seconds before shrugging my shoulders.

“I don’t know. Dependable, strong, good job, handsome, family-oriented, educated, tall..all of that.”

“What about religion? Does his religious orientation matter to you?”

“Yes and no. He can be religious but don’t bring that shit to me.”

"Do you think it would work if he is religious and you aren't?"

"I don't know. We should be able to keep the two separate."

"You think so? I would think that someone serious about their religion would incorporate it in all parts of their lives. For example, someone who prays a lot probably prays over their food or during certain times before bed. They probably don't celebrate certain holidays or celebrate certain holidays that you may not."

"I guess I didn't think of all that," I said before Davis popped into my head. It was a massive part of who he was.

"You wrote that you don't do religion. Is this how you grew up? Or as you got older, you went down this lane?"

"After my dad died, I gave up on religion. God doesn't care about me."

"What do you mean by that?"

"How can we say that he is the creator of all things and that he loves us, but then we die? He takes our family members from us every chance he gets. Does God not think about all the lives he affects? I was just a kid." I said as my voice cracked.

"You feel like God took your dad away from you?

"He did. One minute he's praying over me, and the next minute he's in his bed dead. What kind of God would do that?"

"So to you, God is responsible for death?"

"He has to power to take and give, so I would say yes." I nodded my head.

"I understand and respect your perspective. Do you do regular bible readings?"

“No. I don’t identify with any religion. We used to be Christian.”

“When you say we, who are you referring to?”

“My mom, dad, me.”

“Ok, and after your dad died, you stopped being Christian?”

“Yes. I just felt like it was all in vain.”

“That’s very interesting.” She nodded and looked at her watch. “It looks like our time is ending, but I want to get you set up this same day and time next week, is that ok?”

“I suppose.” I shrugged.

“Ok, and do you mind if I leave you with some work to do?”

“Ok.”

"Ok, so, I know you're not into religion, but I would like for you to take a look at Psalms ninety in the King James Version Bible, take notes and let me know what you think this verse means, and then we discuss your interpretation of it. Sounds good?"

"Yep," I said dryly. Of course, the last thing I wanted to do was pick up a bible and read anything in it, but if this was needed for me to start healing, then so be it.

I made my way out of the building after scheduling my next appointment and sat in my car, taking a deep breath to halt the panic attack I felt lingering. Then, finally, I picked up my phone and smiled at my screensaver of Jayla, and decided to text Jason.

How is she?

I waited for the bubble to pop up, and it didn't, so I started my car and headed to my mother's house, she had been begging me to come by and see her, and I was finally up to doing so.

My notifications went off, and I connected my phone to my car to read the message aloud.

Message from Jason: She is excellent. I am sure that she misses you. My system readout. Would you like to respond?

"Yes!" I said out loud.

Begin message:

"I miss her more. I'm sorry I haven't been present, but I needed to get my mind right. If it's ok, I can get her this weekend. SEND"

Message sent to Jason.

My mother's house wasn't too far away from the therapist's office, so I made it there in no time. I grabbed my phone and purse and got out of the car, dreading the conversation that I knew was left to come. My mother was a woman who lived by the bible, and fornicating was something she despised with everything in her. But, before I could make it to my mother's front door, it was already opening, and she stood in the doorway with a small smile that never reached her eyes.

"I'm so happy to see you." She said, reaching out and pulling me in for a hug. No matter how much my mother got on my nerves with her bible-thumping, being in her arms had me feeling like a kid all over again. Breaking down in her arms, she rubbed my back and told me it would be ok over and over again.

"Breathe, baby." She said, leading me over to the couch where I was heaving, trying to catch my breath as I sobbed heavily. "It's ok...breathe."

I sat on the couch and continued breathing in slowly as I cried. I had panic attacks often as a teenager, so my mother knew how to handle me when I got this way, but it was still a shock because she hadn't had to comfort me in years.

After getting me a cold bottle of water, my mother and I sat in silence as I calmed down.

"I'm sorry," I said, putting my head back on the couch with my eyes closed. "Didn't mean to come and burden you with my issues."

"Child hush. Your issues have been mine since I pushed you out."

"I know, I know. I just...keep making one bad decision after the next and being punished for it."

"Who is punishing you, Lynn?" I opened my eyes and frowned, looking at my mother. "Your God."

"My God?" She asked incredulously.

"Yes...I slept with a married man, so he took my baby, just like he took daddy."

"Wow…" My mother said as she placed her hand over her mouth. "You honestly presume God is a God who punishes you every time you make a mistake?"

"Yes!" I screamed, throwing my arms in the air.

"Then you have no clue who God is. As swift as you make a mistake, he forgives you for that same mistake. He knows we are not perfect people, baby."

"Yeah, ok, mom. You've made excuses for your God since I was a kid."

"It's not an excuse. It's the word. Yes, your daddy died, but that was just his expiration date. We all have one. We die, we resurrect and live again, and it repeats. Your daddy did everything that he was set to do when he came into this world. He changed so many lives for the better, including mine. He left me with a beautiful gift.

Would I have liked more time with him? Of course, but God is not to blame for his death. Your daddy died in his sleep peacefully."

"But what about my baby? My baby hadn't even made it into the world and had an expiration date." I cried.

"That baby may have come to you for a reason. Right now, we don't know it. But a week from now, we may. But God is not a God to sets out to bring you, pain baby."

"Ok, mama, whatever." I waved her off, picking up my phone that went off with another notification.

Of course. I would like to work out a schedule for us to have her equally.

I frowned and tapped away on my phone. *Are you trying to take her away from me?*

"Let me ask you something." My mother said, pulling my attention back to her. I looked at her questioningly so that she could continue. "How are you going to date Davis with how you feel about God? His ministry is to worship and live through God. You don't think it bothers him to hear you talk like this?"

"I don't know. I don't ask him anything about that. We just try and keep the two separate." I shrugged. My mother shook her head and sighed, saying nothing. Davis was a great man, I knew he was heavily into religion, but he didn't try and force the word on me and make me be somebody that I'm not. I don't see myself converting soon, so I hope it stays this way.

CHAPTER 42
TAMERA

"Ooooh, that is cute, diva!" I yelled out to Aerca as she came from the dressing room in a bomb ass SKIMS slip dress in camel.

"Right? It's gripping all the curves." She modeled for me turning in a circle.

"Yes, ma'am. If you think Ben Lee be on you now, honayyyyy!" I snapped in a circle. She blushed and waved me off, scurrying back into the dressing room. Aerca had been glowing ever since she lost her virginity to Ben Lee, don't get me wrong, my girl always had a sparkle, but she was luminous these days.

"I think I'm going to get this in all the colors they have here. It's so comfortable and cute." Aerca said as she walked back over to the rack that housed the dresses in Nordstrom.

“Nothing wrong with that shoot. You know me. I’ll buy one thing in multiple colors if it captivates me.” We both tried on a few more items before we took our pieces upfront to check out.

“Are these separate or together?” The cashier asked.

“Together.” We both said at the same time. Then, we looked at each other and burst out laughing.

"Oh no, ma'am. You paid last time." Aerca fussed, waving her diamond-studded nails at me.

"Who's counting?" I laughed, going through my purse, looking for my wallet.

"Nobody but I got it this time, boo. You can pay for lunch.... Ring my good sis up first so we can make sure our items are not placed in the same bag, please."

"Ok." The cashier smiled as she looked between the both of us. "I wish I had friends like yall."

"I wish that on you too." Aerca smiled, winking at her. "This woman has been my best friend since we were kids."

"True story!" I nodded, glancing down at my phone as it buzzed in my hand.

Can we talk tonight?

No. I sent the text back to Jason and put my phone back into my purse. I was not about to let him ruin my day out with Aerca going back and forth with him.

"Who was that?" Aerca asked as she handed the cashier her credit card.

"Uh, uh nosey!" I joked, grabbing my bags and turning my lip up at her.

"Girl, bye." She said as she grabbed her bags, and we made our way out of the store.

"That was my soon-to-be ex-husband." I rolled my eyes. "Where to next?"

"Let's go into the shoe store. I need to see if they got the Jordans Ben Lee was talking about."

"Ooop, you buying him shoes now? That dick must be the bomb!" I said, bumping her as we moseyed side to side.

"And is!" She laughed. I gave her a high five laughing along with her.

"I know that's right."

"But anyway, how's everything going with that situation? He still fussing about the divorce?"

"You know it." I shrugged. "Ain't nothing left to do but to sign when the time comes, he made his bed he got to lie in it."

"True, but are you sure this is what you want? He's all you know, sis." Aerca said, pausing to look over at me.

"Honestly? I'm not sure it's what I want. But it's what I need. I would never be able to forgive him."

"Never?" She asked, raising her brows. I shook my head and sat my bags on the bench next to us, and sighed.

"No. I went over there a few weeks ago, and his daughter was there, and I almost had a panic attack. My heart hurt so bad knowing that my husband really made another child and had an affair for over five years."

"She's innocent in all of this, though."

"Absolutely. But that doesn't make it any easier. It's embarrassing too. That woman sat in my face pretending to be cool with me, Aerca. Hell, I bought the little girl stuff so many times. I used to joke, saying she looked like my sons. The whole time the joke was on me." I sniffed, trying to hold back tears.

"Oh babe...don't cry," Aerca said as she skimmed through her clutch and handed me a small napkin.

"It just hurts." I cried, dabbing my tear ducts so that I didn't mess up my makeup.

"I know it does. I just want you to be sure this is what you want and not acting on emotions."

"How can I not act on emotion? I don't even want to be around him at all right now. Every time I see his face, I just want to spit in it." I mumbled.

"That's nasty." She quipped, fake gagging.

"So what!" I cackled. "He deserves it."

"Ok, so one last question, and then I'm done bringing it up. What if he and Lynn decide to be together, then what?"

"I don't know," I said before going quiet. I don't know if I was ready for Jason to move on, let alone be with the woman he had an affair with. I just knew that right now, I couldn't be with him.

At Lunch

"So, are you excited to meet his parents?" I asked Aerca. She would be meeting Ben Lee's parents in a few weeks.

"I'm scared, not excited." She said as she took a sip of her bloody mary.

"Why?" I asked, engrossed. "I think it'll be good for yall, especially since he got a chance to meet yours."

"Yeah, but my family is cool. I looked his people up on Facebook, and I don't know.." She shook her head.

"Aw hell, what's wrong?"

We paused in our conversation as our waitress came back with our food. I ordered cajun chicken alfredo, and she ordered a seafood platter.

"Ok, the sister seems cool. She's pretty as hell and has a gorgeous boyfriend." Aerca said once the waitress left. "But the mom? She's an all-lives matter, Trumper."

"Nooooo," I said with my eyes ballooned.

"Girl, yes!" She said, shaking her head. "And you know how those all lives matter people are."

"Damn...well, let's hope she's cool. I mean, she has black children, for god sake." I said before taking a bite of my pasta.

"True. I'ma try and stay positive about it. I'ma make sure I meditate heavily and smoke some weed before going." Aerca joked, putting her fingers to her mouth like she was smoking a joint.

"Shid, if that helps." I shrugged. "If his mom doesn't like you, is that a deal-breaker?"

"Nope." She said immediately. "She doesn't have to like me. I'm not fucking her. As long as she keeps it respectful, I'm good."

"I feel that. Just be careful." Aerca assured me she would, and we finished eating and talking about various subjects before we parted ways, agreeing to call one another that night.

CHAPTER 43
JASON

Can you talk?

No…

Please? I won't even bring up the divorce or us. I just need a friend right now.

Call your mistress… (middle finger emoji)

"Fuck!" I grumbled, slamming my phone down next to me. I needed somebody to talk to and get all this shit off of my mind, and I know Tamera hated me right now, but she's been my best friend for the past decade and has always been my go-to person.

It's important.

I saw the bubble appear on the text thread before it disappeared, and my phone rang.

"Hel-"

"Are the boys ok?" She asked.

"They're fine. They're sleeping."

"Ok…"

"It's not about them. It's about me and something I found out today."

"Does it involve my health?"

"What? No!"

"Ok, so what is it then?" She questioned, miffed.

"Today, I found out I have a son. He's about twenty-one or twenty-two."

"Excuse me?"

"Yeah…"

"Twenty-two means you were-"

"Thirteen, fourteen...yeah…." I sighed heavily.

"Wow. You are full of surprises."

"This was a surprise to me as well. I had no clue."

"Ok, Jason," She asked sarcastically.

"I swear.." I paused before telling her everything about my day and what happened to me as a kid. I even told her about my dad's affairs and how he took me along with him.

"Wow...I can't... I'm speechless." Tamera said once I finished.

"It's a lot...I just wish he had told me. I have a kid out there that I just don't know."

"That's a grown man, not a kid for sure."

"True."

"I wonder what story she has told him about his father."

"I thought about that too, like I wonder if he thinks I'm dead, or if I'm just some fucked up person who never cared about him."

"You didn't know, so that's not your fault."

"I know, I was just a kid, but still… I feel like I deserved to know."

"I know, I was just a kid, but still… I feel like I deserved to know."

"I agree. But then again, who knows what your life would have turned out as you know? You have a lot to offer him now, but who knows what you would have turned out like had you had to deal with the responsibility of having a kid so young. I'm not justifying what your father did, but I can see why he did it."

"Yeah…"

"This also explains a lot of your actions. You have a tremendous amount of childhood trauma that you haven't dealt with yet."

"I didn't have a bad childhood, though."

"I didn't say you did, but that doesn't negate the fact that you dealt with things that you should not have had to deal with as a kid. How many kids do you think have fathers that were taking them to their mistresses' house and then blackmailing them after with material items?"

"You got a point there."

"I know. Your dad was your role model and somebody you looked to for guidance, so it's easy for you to do as he did and not see anything wrong with it because to you, it was the norm."

"I mean, I knew it was wrong-"

"But that didn't stop you from making the same mistakes…."

"I don't know…."

"Jason, go to therapy. If not for you, go for your kids. You don't have to keep passing down generational trauma. One day you're already going to have to explain to them everything going on now. Is this all you want them to see you as?"

"No...I don't want to be like my dad."

"Then don't be, we can't change the past, but we damn sure can change the future."

"You're right, thanks for that."

"Mmmhmm, so does your mom know about your son?"

"No clue. I haven't gotten a chance to talk to her about it. She might flip out and leave dad again."

"Leave? When did she ever do that?"

"Apparently, she had found out about all that he was doing and left him without me even knowing. She said she would come in the mornings before I left out for school and stayed until it was time for bed, and once I was sleep or gone, she would leave and go back to where she was staying."

"Yeah, all the hiding and sneaking. They should have been open and honest with you. Transparency is so important in all relationships, whether it's parents, friends, work. There has to be transparency."

"So, what do you think I should do?"

"About?"

"My son...I want to know him. I can't just keep moving forward like I don't know he exists."

"I think you should speak with mom first. That way, you can figure out what she has told him. She might also feel some way still about the fact that she practically raped you since you were only thirteen. So do that first, reach out to her and see how you both feel you should proceed."

"Good idea. I don't want to scare him off."

"Right. Just ease into it, don't force yourself on him. He doesn't know you, so it will take time."

"You're right. Thanks for talking to me. I needed to get this off of my chest."

"Mmmhmmm, you just make sure you do what you're supposed to do in court next month."

The weight that had been lifted from my shoulders felt as if it fell right back on them once she said that.

"Tamera…." I said with dismal.

"What?"

"Maybe we can try couples therapy."

"No… no, thank you. I'm tired. Mentally. Physically. Spiritually. I'm tired. I just want to be done."

"Ok, I understand. Thanks again for helping me sort through all of this."

"Mmmhmm.."

"I'll have the boys call you in the morning."

"Goodnight." She said before disconnecting the call.

I sat back on my bed and went on Facebook and searched for my son's name: Ethan Washington, and none of the results that turned up looked like the pictures I had of him. Vanessa Washington I typed in, and her profile came up immediately. Her profile wasn't private, so I could go through all her photos and timeline to see what she had been up to. Vanessa was still a gorgeous woman, and by the pictures,

I could tell she took great care of Ethan. According to the most recent photos, Ethan had graduated magna cum laude and got accepted into medical school for orthopedics. I smiled widely, proud that he was my son and appeared to be doing good in life even without me being present.

I contemplated back and forth before sending Vanessa a message.

Hi Vanessa. My dad told me everything today, and I would like for us to meet and talk. Please call me as soon as possible at 310-408-9499. -Jason.

I sat my phone down and prayed this worked out. I couldn't take any more losses right now.

CHAPTER 44
KYLAN

"I don't take no shit from nobody. That's why it didn't work out with my ex. He knew he had to come correct or don't come at all. That's why I'm single. If I'm too much, then go and get less. Leave me the hell alone, you know?" My date Samantha, Samala, Sa something said. I nodded my head as if I agreed, as I had done for the last hour. She had been talking nonstop about herself, not once making sure she incorporated me into the conversation.

"How's the food?" The waiter asked, coming over to the table. I put my thumb up and continued eating.

"My food is not good at all. The meat is tough, and the salad was very old tasting." She said, pushing her almost empty plate away from her.

"Oh...ok. I'm sorry to hear that." The waiter said as he grabbed her plate.

"Is there something else on the menu that might be of interest?"

"No… I don't think I trust the food here anymore." She said, shaking her head before looking down at her phone.

"Sorry to hear that. Can I get you anything else, sir?" He asked me.

"Uh, no. Just the check. Thanks a lot." I said, trying to hide my irritation.

The whole time she talked, she tore that food down to the ground now. All of a sudden, she was complaining.

"They better comp that shit off the bill." She said once he walked away.

"It's all good. I can afford it." I said as I looked down at my watch. It was going on nine, and I could make it home and catch some highlights before bed if I got her out of my face quick enough.

"What are you doing after dinner?" She asked.

"Probably just go home and watch some highlights and go to bed," I said before yawning.

"Or...you could have a nightcap with me.."

"Oh really?" I asked with my brow raised. The chemistry over dinner was nonexistent, but I was open to testing out our chemistry during sex.

"Yep. I don't have to be up early, so I have a few hours to spare if you're down."

After paying and leaving a tip, we made our way outside. "You want to follow me to my house?" She asked.

"How about you follow me to the Marriott up the street?" I asked, pointing at the sign that was half a mile down the road. I didn't know her like that. For all I know, she could be setting me up.

"Hmm, ok. That works." She said, turning so that I could walk her to her car.

Fifteen minutes later...

"Oh fuckkk!" She screamed out as I stroked her from the back. She had been screaming bloody murder every since I slid into the pussy, and she was giving me a damn headache. I tried to drown her out and just focus on her pussy, but even that was annoying, she had a hard time staying wet, and this wasn't even worth what I paid for the hotel.

"I'm cumming." She yelled out as she bucked wildly against me. After she started shaking like Jell-O, I pulled out and made my way to the bathroom. I wrapped the dry condom up and flushed it down the toilet, not trusting her enough to put it in the trash. After using the bathroom and wiping myself clean as best as I could, I came out and found her lying in the same spot on the bed, fast asleep snoring. Leaving the hotel key on the nightstand, I left the room and headed to the valet to retrieve my car.

Eight am court for Martino Salone room two sixty-nine. A notification popped up on my screen. A few seconds later, a few other notices popped up, alerting me that my schedule for the week had been completed. I shook my head and smirked, knowing it wasn't anybody but Tamera. I don't know what I would do without her once her building was up and running. She had been a god-send for me.

Go to bed, woman. I sent to her. She told me how she had a hard time falling asleep these days and would spend hours in the night doing work or finding something to do until she exhausted herself out. It was going on eleven pm, and she usually had to get up around seven am to get the boys to school and then make her way into the office.

I'm not sleepy. (sad emoji)

Valet brought my car around, and I tipped him before hopping in my car and connecting the phone to the car. Instead of texting Tamera back, I called.

"The real question is, what are YOU doing up?" She asked with amusement.

"You don't even want to know." I groaned.

"Oh, but do tell."

"I had a date."

"Oooo, dates are good!"

"Not this one," I said, shaking my head.

"Awe, why? Catfish?"

"Fuck no. I knew what she looked like before this date. How do you think she got the date?"

Tamera burst out laughing. "I mean, I don't know how people are dating these days. I've been out of the dating scene for over a decade."

"Damn! It's been that long?"

"Yes. Jason and I were married for nine years. Before that, we had dated for a year before getting engaged."

"Sheesh."

"Yep. He's the only man I've ever been with."

"Deadass?" I asked, appalled.

"Yep. So I'm all out of the loop."

"I see. But no, I had met her coming from court. She was there as a support person for someone."

"Ah, I see. So what went wrong?"

"Everything. There was just no chemistry in no kind of way."

"None?"

"None. Not even sexual chemistry. That shit made it worse."

"You gave up the penis on the first date, Kylan?"

"We grown man." I laughed. "Don't nobody wait no more."

"Aw hell. I'm a just get some cats then." She chuckled.

"Cats are little fuckers." I said, shaking my head thinking about the neighborhood cat that used to scratch the fuck out of my leg every time I walked past him.

"Yeah, whatever. Now back to your story. So what went wrong with the sexual chemistry?"

"She just was making unnecessary ass noises."

"Wait." She burst out laughing. "You're mad because she was making noise? Maybe it was that good to her."

"Nah, I'm confident in me, but it was just not hitting like that for her to be making all that noise. She was barely wet."

"Oh noooo…" Tamera groaned. "That's embarrassing. So I take it there won't be a second date?'

"It might be a second date... Just not with me."

"Dirty," Tamera said before she burst out laughing.

"If she asks why I'll politely let her know how I feel, but she's not my type."

"Do men have types?"

"This one does. I don't know about other men."

"Well, that's good to know."

"You sure you want to get a divorce? It's rough out in these streets." I joked.

Tamera let out a hearty laugh. "I see! But this shit is just as rough. So I'll be alright."

"You heavy on the loyalty, huh?" I asked as I pulled onto our street. "I can see your lights on way down here."

"I know. I was just saying that yesterday that my house sticks right out and puts everybody in my business."

"I mean, I can't see in it, but I can see your lights on," I said as I pulled into my driveway.

"Oh, ok, well, good. You're coming to my house warming next week, right?"

"What day next week?"

"Friday."

"After work?"

"Yes, about six. Jason gets the boys around five-thirty, so that works just right for me."

"Oh, ok. And what is a damn housewarming?" I asked as I walked into the house, which was quiet. I'm sure Nelly passed out since she was an early bird.

"Ugh, men." She groaned. "So just none of yall know what the hell a house warming is, huh?"

"Shid, we ain't have whatever that was growing up."

"It's when someone moves into a new place, and they invite close family and friends over who bring them things they would think they need in their homes."

"Word?" I asked as I walked into my room, stripping out of my shirt.

"Yeah, it's fun."

"I wish I did know about that. I would've had muthafuckas bringing me a damn washing machine. That motherfucka alone cost me seventeen hundred." I groaned.

"See, you are going too far. Ain't nobody buying you no damn washing machine now." She laughed.

"You said they buy you shit you need. So it's rules to it now?" I joked as I sat on my bed, crossing my legs at the ankle.

"Yes, its levels. You might get a microwave or a gift card but not no washing machine."

"That's some bullshit."

"Nah, you just got expensive taste."

"Says the woman with nine hundred dollar tennis shoes."

"Uh. uh, don't do me." She laughed.

"I'm just saying. I ain't the only one with expensive taste."

"How do you know how much those shoes cost anyway? You bought one of your little girlfriends some?"

"Nah, I ain't tricking. I got some for my sister."

"It ain't tricking if you got it." She teased.

"Well shit, you got it, you tricking?"

"Been there, done that." She snickered before I knew it. It was almost three in the morning we had talked about so much that the conversation flew, we might have been tipping on a tight rope and crossing boundaries, but as long as it didn't go any further, we were good...or not.

CHAPTER 45
LYNN

I pulled up to Jason's house, excited to get Jayla. I hadn't seen her physically in weeks, and my heart was beating with joy. I stepped out of my car and shook my head, looking at the size of this house. I had seen pictures of it, but they did this place no justice. It was like a mansion. I could fit two of my home in this one. Before I could knock, Jason was meeting me at the door.

"Jayla's not back from the church event with my mom yet, but it should be over shortly. So you can wait or come back."

I nodded my head and looked him over. "I'll just wait if that's ok."

"It's fine." He said as he moved to the side to let me in. My mouth dropped in amazement. The inside of the house was better than the outside, and the color scheme was just beautiful.

"Your house is beautiful."

"This is all Tamera's doing." He said with a small smile. "I'll be downsizing in a few weeks. Just have to find me something."

"Really, why?"

"It's a part of our decree to sell the house and split the profit. But she paid for the house alone when I was in school struggling, so I'll most likely give it all to her. Can I get you anything to drink? I've got some water, some lemonade, and some orange juice."

"No, I'm ok."

"Ok, you can follow me up to the entertainment room." I nodded and followed behind him, impressed by his home. No wonder Jayla hadn't been too worried about coming home. This place was like a castle.

"So, how are you doing?" Jason asked, sitting across from me on the couch.

"I'm better," I said with a shrug. "It's going to take some time, but I will get there."

He nodded before sighing. "I get that. You went through a lot. I wish I knew-"

"What would it have changed? We already had Jayla, and you pretended she didn't exist most days." I spat. He threw his hands up in mock surrender.

"Alright, my bad, I didn't mean to trigger you. I'm sorry."

I rolled my eyes and shooed him away. "Ok, Jason."

"I uh...I got something made from our son."

I raised my brows and looked at him with a scowl on my face.

"I'll be right back." He said, shuffling out of the room. I busied myself checking my phone and confirming with Davis our dinner date in a little over an hour.

"Here you go," Jason said, offering me a gift bag. I hesitantly grabbed the bag and reached inside of it. Inside was our son's death certificate, along with his tiny hand impression and foot. My eyes watered as I looked up at Jason feeling all of the emotions fill my body as if I was drowning.

"How did yo-"

"I went out and bought it and begged them to let me have this memory of him before I said my last goodbye. I knew you would appreciate this as much as I do. I have the other hand and foot that way, we both have something of him." He said, wiping a tear that slid down his face.

I nodded my head as my tears fell and laughed lightly at the death certificate. "You named him Jason? Really."

"What?" he smirked. "I didn't know what to put when they asked me, and you were acting crazy, so I just named him JJ."

"It's fine." I nodded. "Thank you for this. This means a lot to me."

"No problem. I'm sorry about everything. I know it's too late to do the shoulda coulda wouldas, but I wish I did some things differently." He said as he flopped next to me on the couch.

"I'm sure we both do," I said, looking at him. Jason reached over and wiped a tear that fell down my cheek, his hand lingering. I know I should hate him, but I can't bring myself to do so. I know I shouldn't be lusting after him, especially after everything we have been through, but I can't stop the fact that I loved everything about him. From his freckles to his thick pink lips and the way he bit his lip when he was deep in thought. Before I could stop myself, I had leaned over and kissed Jason as my life depended on it. He grabbed my arms and tried to push me back, but I continued. he finally relaxed and kissed me back. I don't know how he got out of his pants so fast, but my dress was above my waist, and I was bouncing on his dick as if this would be the last fuck I would ever have. This dick was why I stayed in so much bullshit. Jasons dick felt like it belonged in my pussy, and he was pushing up under me, assuring he hit every crevice too.

"Oooo, Jason." I moaned out, and I leaned forward, kissing him again. Jason moaned into my mouth and then began attacking my neck, breast, and anything else he could get his mouth on. I had my head thrown back in ecstasy, feeling like I was on cloud nine.

CRASH

I opened my eyes and screamed as Jason's body went limp under me. All I saw was glass, and his face bloodied as I saw Tamera standing above him with a crazed look on her face.

"Give me one fucking reason why I shouldn't blow your fucking heads off," Tamera asked with her hand in her purse.

"Tam-I-I-I"

"Shut the fuck up!" She screamed at him before smacking the side of his head with a medium decor object that sat on the coffee table next to us. Jason instantly dropped, and I screamed before hopping off of his lap.

I shut my mouth and put my hands up in surrender as Tamera looked at me like I was her next victim. "Tamera, please."

"Tamera, please, what whore? You shouldn't even be talking to me. Let alone in my fucking house fucking my husband. You have no boundaries, huh bitch?" She yelled as I stood up, hurrying to fix my dress.

"I told Jason when you dropped that baby bitch we were going to throw the ones, so I hope you came prepared bitch."

I looked back at her, confused, knowing damn well she wasn't challenging me to a fight. I ain't saying I'm the toughest bitch alive, but I had at least five inches in height on Tamera. Tamera smirked and threw her purse on the couch, but before she could get back turned towards me, I grabbed her by her hair and punched her wherever I could to gain some leverage. I slung her left to right before I keeled over from being kicked in my stomach with force. Tamera punched me so hard in my face that my head flew to the side. I continued swinging, trying to make sure we both looked like we had been in a fight, but that was short lived when Tamera flipped me on my back and pinned me down by my arms, punching me in my face like she was trying to win a championship belt for women's boxing.

"Bitch!" *PUNCH*

"Fuck you thought!" *PUNCH*. With each punch, she hurled an insult at me, telling me how I helped ruin her marriage and how karma was going to whoop my ass. At this point, I'd rather wait for karma than keep being hit by her.

"Get off of me!" I screamed, trying to get her off of my arms. She knocked me in my head again, and I screeched before I was able to lift my legs enough to flip her off of me. I hurried and ran out of the room instead of attempting to fight her crazy ass again. I don't even remember how I got out of the front door so fast, but I ran right into Mrs. Walsh, who was putting her key in the door,

"What the hell!" She was shocked, looking over my appearance. I'm sure I looked rough. I could feel my eye swelling, and I knew my hair was matted and messy. "What is going on? Did my son do that?"

"No." I whimpered.

"I did it. Get out of my house bitch!" I heard Tamera say from behind me.

"Where's Jayla?" I asked as I scurried out of the house and behind Mrs. Walsh.

"They're all asleep in the car. I was going to ask Jason to help get them out. Where is he?"

"He's sleeping too! I'll grab my kids. Humpty Dumpty here can do what she wants." Tamera said as she stomped past us.

"I don't even want to know what happened." Mrs. Walsh said, shaking her head, eyes never leaving Tamera as she got both of her sons out of Mrs. Walsh's car and into her own. She didn't bother looking back before she got into her truck and zoomed off.

"I think you should leave Jayla here and go get yourself together."

I nodded my head and sighed. "Can I pick her up from your house? I need to go home and change."

"Yes. That's fine." She said, looking at me with sympathy. "Just call me when you're on the way, and I'll make sure she's up."

"Thank you," I said lowly as I walked to my car. Shaking my head, I closed my eyes as my head began to thump. I needed to get home and take some Motrin before I got to Jayla because I knew she would be a ball of energy, and right now, I just couldn't do it. My hands shook as I drove home, not believing that this shit just happened.

"Oh no…" I groaned, pulling up to my house and seeing Davis sitting on my porch. He had a massive smile on his face as he walked towards my car until he noticed my appearance.

"What in the hell?" He asked, snatching my driver's side door open. "Who did this?"

He looked at me for an answer as he held my face up with his hand looking over me. I shook my head and waved him off, moving my head and grabbing my purse out of the passenger seat.

"Long story." I got out of my car and attempted to brush past him, but he stepped in my way.

"Where's Jayla? Is she ok?"

"Yes," I said with a deep sigh. I just wanted to get inside and get myself together.

"Did her dad do this?"

"No…" I said distressingly as I moved towards my door. "He would never hit me."

"Ok, so what happened?" I shook my head as I opened my door, and he followed me in.

"Can we not talk about this right now? I need to get myself together, and my head is pounding." I said, walking into my kitchen and going into the refrigerator for a bottle of water.

"I'm just trying to make sure you're not in danger or something." He threw his hands up.

"I'm not. Just drop it." I yelled as I went into my cabinet, grabbing out a bottle of Motrin and taking two of them. He nodded his head and got quiet sitting on the stool at the island. I leaned against the counter with my eyes closed, hoping the thumping stopped. I felt terrible for yelling at Davis and knew he was only looking out for my wellbeing.

"I'm sorry for. All I wanted to do was have a good day today. I just wanted to get Jayla come back here, and we all go out to eat and then have a movie night where I was making cookies and laughing until we fell asleep, but as you can see, that didn't happen."

Davis nodded but didn't answer me, so I continued. "When I got there, Jayla wasn't there yet. She was with her grandmother at a church function, and they were on the way back, so he asked did

I want to come in and wait for her, me thinking it would just be a few minutes. So I'm like, ok, no big deal. So we were talking and ...stuff, and next thing I know, his wife is there attacking us."

"Oh wow. So she hit him too?"

"Yeah, knocked him out cold," I said, cringing, thinking about all of the blood.

"So she attacked both of you?"

"Mmmhmmm."

"I just don't understand why…."

"Yeah...me either." I lied. Davis got quiet again while staring at me. He then shook his head and scoffed.

"Wow."

"What?" I asked, frowning.

"So you're just not going, to be honest about it all?"

"What do you mean? She attacked me. Look at me!"

"I can see that, but you're not being honest about why. I can sit here and put two and two together, and you're acting like I'm blind."

"What the fuck is that suppose to mean?"

"Don't be disrespectful. If I don't talk to you like that, don't ever talk to me like that." He said sternly without raising his voice.

"It's disrespectful when you call me a liar!"

"I never called you a liar. I'm not saying you're lying but omitting yes."

"Ok, well, since you know so much, you tell me what happened then," I said, sitting on a stool across from him and folding my arms across my chest while staring at him.

Davis shook his head and stood up. "This isn't me. I don't do drama, and I don't do women who aren't over their ...baby daddies. I'm not a fool. You're sitting here ashamed with hickeys decorating your neck and breast and want me to believe she attacked you for no reason. The same woman who stayed with you when you passed out and came to the hospital. If she wanted to attack you for fun, she could have done it then. So I know how to read in between the lines. It's all good, though. I'm a praying man, not a begging one. Have a nice life, Miss Lynn. You will forever be in my prayers."

I sat there with my tongue cut out, shocked that he called me out on my lies. I couldn't say anything because I knew Davis was right. I was ashamed. I was disgusted with myself, and I couldn't do anything but watch him walk out of the door and out of my life.

I kicked my shoes off and made my way to the bathroom, gasping once I saw myself in the mirror; my lips were swollen, and my right eye was swollen, and my left eye looked as if a blood vessel had burst inside of it. I had a knot the size of a quarter on my forehead, and my hair was all over my head, and I had hickeys all over my chest and neck that I'm not surprised Davis saw. I held my tears in as I stripped off my clothes and turned on the shower. While that warmed up, I went into the bathroom cabinet and searched for my first aid kit so that once I was out, I could try and make myself look decent.

CHAPTER 46
TAMERA

"Alright! I'll see yall later, right?" I asked Kylan, Zelan, Michael, and Amber, the other paralegals and lawyers at the firm. They all gave me a few variations of yes before waving me off as I made my way out of the office. It was almost time to get the boys, but I needed to stop by my building to check on the progress first.

I made my way to my building, greeted by Joe, one of the overseers, when Ben Lee wasn't there; I was excited to see that they had all the frames up, and my vision was coming to life right before my eyes. After getting more updates and making small changes, I thanked everyone and made my way to the boy's school. After grabbing them up, I needed to get them home, changed, and fed before Jason's sorry ass picked them up. Thank God I hired a maid service to clean the house for the day, so that's one less thing I had to do to get ready for the house warming, but I know one thing I couldn't wait for was the drinks. After the week I had, I needed one badly. You wouldn't believe after seeing Jason fucking that bitch with my own two eyes. He tried to tell me it wasn't what it looked like. Chile, please.

"Mommy, when we leave, what do you do?" Josh asked from the back seat.

"Well, I just read and check on my building but other than that, not much.

Why?" I asked, looking at him in the rearview mirror.

"I'm just asking because I know you are lonely." He said with a shrug.

"Lonely?" I chuckled. "Alone, yes, but mommy is not lonely."

"What's the difference?" Johan asked.

"Alone means it's just me by myself. Lonely means I'm sad because I'm alone. I'm not sad because I'm alone."

"You don't miss us?" Josh asked.

"Of course, I always miss you guys when you're gone because you're my babies, but I'm not lonely."

"We can stay if you want us to," Johan said.

"No, mommy's ok, guys. Trust me. You go with your dad and enjoy yourself, ok?"

"Ok." They both said.

I turned on the boy's favorite playlist and continued driving home with my mind going haywire. I knew this split would affect them, but I didn't think they would be more worried about me than themselves. I could only keep praying for the strength for us to get through this whole ordeal unscathed. Finally, I pulled into my driveway and rushed the boys inside so that I could get everything set up before time snuck up on me.

"Alright, you guys know the deal. So go ahead and get changed, come back down, let's knock out your homework, and then snack."

"Ok." They both yelled, running off. I went into the kitchen, checking my email to verify what time the caterer was supposed to be dropping off the food, which would be in a little less than thirty minutes. The maid service did an excellent job and had everything sparkling and smelling like lemons.

"Hey, Diva!" I said, answering my ringing phone.

"You home? I just finished a sale on this house, and I'm in your area. It doesn't make sense to go back home and freshen up when I can just come there." Aerca said. I could hear her music playing lowly in her car in the background.

"Yes, we just got in. You can come on over, girl."

"Ok, boo! I'll be there in like ten minutes."

"Alright." I hung up the phone as the boys were coming down the stairs.

"Get that homework out. I'm going to run up to my room, and then I'll get your snacks out."

I went into my room and pulled out my yellow GG Jacquard jersey dress that I had been thinking of all day for the housewarming. Just as I sat it on the bed, my phone went off with a notification.

I should be there in forty-five minutes. Unfortunately, traffic is a bit backed up.

I rolled my eyes at Jason's text and made my way back downstairs.

"How's homework coming along?"

"Good, it's easy," Josh said, doing a happy dance.

"Well, let me know if you need any help. Your dad said he will be here in about forty minutes or so." I said, going into the kitchen. I grabbed them both a few crackers and a cup of milk and sat it on the counter. Just as I was doing that, the doorbell rang, and I could see from the kitchen that the catering company had pulled up, they were an exceptional black woman-owned soul food company, and I loved their food, so it only fitted that I hired them for my housewarming.

"Come and get your snacks, boys," I called out to them before making my way to the door. Just as I was opening the door, they were walking up.

"Hi, Tamera?" A woman with a company shirt on that said Porsha asked, looking down at a clipboard and back up at me.

"Yes, ma'am. How are you?"

"I'm great thanks so much for asking and having us. First, can you show us where you would like for us to set up, and then we can go over what the service entails and your purchase."

"Ok perfect. Come on in." I said, holding the door open for them to come in. "You can set up right in here," I said, walking into the kitchen and pointing at the countertops and island.

"Alright, will do. They will all go and grab the stuff while you and I go over everything and get this signed. Is that ok?" Porsha asked.

"Yep, that works. Have a seat." I said, pointing at the stool across from me as I sat down. After going over everything and noticing that her employees had set up everything swift and expertly, I tipped them and escorted them out of the house just as Aerca was pulling up.

"Girl, the traffic!" She squealed as she got out of her truck, looking bomb as usual. I waved at the caterers as they left and met Aerca at her truck, hugging her.

"That bad?" I asked, frowning.

"You already know! These mothafuckas get slower every day fucking up the damn flow of traffic!" She went into her backseat and grabbed a garment bag.

"What you got? I thought you needed something out of my closet." I said as she followed me inside.

"I had put this in my car this morning, I was going to go to my condo, but as you can see, that would have went all bad. How was your day?" She asked, closing the door behind us.

"I had a good day. The building is coming along so good. You have to see it soon."

"I know it is! Ben Lee showed me some pictures, but I know it looks even better in person."

"Yes! It does! Josh! Johan! Come say hi to your Auntie." I called out to the boys who came running full speed.

"Auntie." They yelled out as they hugged her. They loved their Auntie Aerca. She acted just like a big kid getting down and wrestling with them all the time.

"Alright, alright," I said, laughing as all three of them rolled around on the floor. "Let Auntie go get freshened up, and yall finish your snacks and get your shoes on."

A few hours later

Family emergency. I won't be able to make it. Sorry. (sad face emoji). I sulked, reading Kylans text for the second time, trying to figure out how to sound genuinely concerned instead of the disappointment I was feeling. I couldn't even explain why I was feeling disappointed, but I wanted him here. We spent a lot of time together since we worked together, and when we aren't working, we always find some way to end up on the phone all day. Kylan was like a male best friend and a fresh breath of air. He was very respectful and kept things platonic at all times.

Take care of your family, and I'm praying for you. Call me later. I text back before sliding my phone back into my pocket and laughing as Nadia and her girlfriend Monica sang their rendition of The Boy is Mine calling it The Girl is Mine. Nadia could sing, but lord Monica sounded like a cat in the alley, honey, but the switching of the words in the song is what really had all of us in tears.

CHAPTER 47
JASON

I smirked as I checked Jayla's bedroom and seeing her bed fully made, knowing that she had once again made her way into her brother's room and into a bed with one of them, my suspicions were confirmed when I opened their bedroom door and found her in bed with Josh who protected her all day from everybody under the sun. She was lying on top of the cover and had her leg draped over his body as he laid on his side. I kissed all of them on the foreheads and quietly left back out of the room, making my way into the guest bedroom. I couldn't bring myself to sleep in the master since Tamera left. It just didn't feel the same.

I grabbed the remote and sat on the bed, leaning back and cringed in pain, forgetting about the knot I had on my head. I couldn't even be mad. All I could do was shake my head, realizing I continued to fuck up and dig bigger holes for myself. After what happened, I knew I would never get Tamera back. All I could do now was work on myself and be the best father that I could be to my children.

I got up off my bed and grabbed my phone that lit up on the dresser, shocked to see that I had a Facebook message from Vanessa Washington, it's been almost two weeks since I messaged her, so I assumed she had no intent on speaking with me.

I don't know if I should be responding to you... her message said. I was confused by the response, so I sent back a few question marks. No sooner than I pressed send, she was calling me on Facebook audio.

"Hello?"

"Jason?"

"Yes."

"Your dad said he would kill us if we had any communication with you."

CHAPTER 48
DAVIS

"That sermon was great today Deacon Marshall." Senior Pastor Brown said as he shook my hand. "For a minute, I thought I saw your daddy up there. How is Pastor Marshall doing?"

"He's good. I talked to him this morning, and I'ma make my way over there to see him after I leave."

"You tell him I'm yet praying for him, and if he needs a ride tomorrow, to let me know."

"I sure will. I normally pick him up, but he complains about my driving the whole time, so he might take you up on that offer since he won't drive himself." I said before we were both filled with laughter.

"You tell my buddy I said to call me!"

"I will. I'm going to make my way to Sister Stephens and see if she needs any help before I leave."

"Alright, see you tomorrow for the fundraiser." Pastor Brown said before a group of members walked up talking. I said my hellos and turned to make my way to the kitchen where Sister Stephens was always cooking up something and was surprised to see Lynn's mother in my path.

"Sister Williams, how are you?" I asked, hugging her.

"I'm well, Deacon Marshall. How are you, honey?" She asked with a warm smile.

"I'm good. I'm good. It's so good to see you here. Are you visiting?" I had been in this church since a child have never seen her.

"I am. I came by to help Sister Stephens out for the day."

"Well, I was headed to Sister Stephens. You can walk with me."

"Sounds good. This is a beautiful church. I heard your sermon, and you have the gift. You gave me chills up there."

"Did I? That warms my heart. If I can reach one person with the word, that's enough for me." I said, showing all thirty-two.

"You've got the gift. Trust me. Not many people do, but you, it's in you."

"Thank you so much, Sister Williams." She nodded and cleared her throat before looking at me.

"You know, my daughter tells me you guys aren't on speaking terms right now." I opened my mouth and closed it when she put her hand up. "No need to explain yourself, I get it. She's a lot. It's tough as a Christian man to try and be with someone who is ...not. I pray for my daughter every night that one day she wakes up and follows in the steps of the Lord."

"I pray for her too, a lot," I said, nodding and not saying anything further as I opened the door to the kitchen leading her in, where Sister Stephens was.

"Sister Williams and Deacon! Amen!" Sister Stephens said, yelling. I loved me some Sister Stephens. She was a heavyset black woman who felt at home. She reminded me of the grandmother from the movie *Big Mamas House*, and she was always hugging and praying over you every time she saw you.

"Amen." We both said back with big smiles.

"I told you I would come by and help you out." Sister Williams said.

"I knew you would come. You always keep your word, Sister Williams. That's why the Lord highly favors you."

"Yes, Lord," I said, throwing my hands up. "I came back here to see if you needed any help from me."

"Thank you, Deacon Marshall. But Sister Williams is all I need. But that word today? Baby….you shook the church with that one Deacon. I'm a have to tell Senior to let you up there more." Sister Stephens said, winking at me. I thanked her and said my goodbyes before I finally made my way out of the church.

I pulled up to Sunny Days Assisted Living facility and parked at the parking spot nearest my dad's apartment. He insisted on living here, claiming that he didn't want to burden my life. No matter how many times I told him he wasn't, but he refused to listen. After mama died three years ago, he was adamant that I got out and lived life to the fullest.

As I walked up to my dad's apartment, I could see him sitting outside reading his bible.

"Hey, Old man!" I joked, grabbing his attention.

"Hey, there, son!" He said, closing his bible and standing up to hug me. "I ain't old yet now!"

"You right! We look like twins out here. I'll be grateful to look as good as you do when I'm your age."

"You will! You know what they say. Black don't crack." My dad joked, causing me to chuckle. "How are you, son?"

"I'm good. Just left the church Pastor Brown told me to tell you to call him later." I said before it slipped my mind. I pulled my vibrating phone out of my pocket, and pressing ignore on Lynns call.

"I sure will. He was on my mind today." My father nodded and looked back at me once my phone began vibrating again.

"Everything ok?" He asked.

"Yeah," I said with a deep sigh.

"You sure? Who calls are you screening?"

"It's a long story, pops."

"Well, I ain't got nothing but time. So what's going on?" He asked, crossing his legs at the ankle. I shook my head, ignoring another call and putting my phone on do not disturb before telling my dad about Lynn from start to finish. When I was done, my dad stood up while looking at me.

"Come on in and get a bottle of water with me." I nodded and followed behind him.

"So, do you like this woman?" My dad asked as he handed me a bottle.

"I do," I said, nodding.

"How much?"

"A lot."

"Hmph." He said as he took a sip of water. "Do you think she's marriage material?"

"She could be." I shrugged. "But it's hard to know right now."

"Nothing in life is easy. You pray for her?"

"All the time, pops."

"Good, keep praying for her. She will come around. Her issues aren't with God. Her issue is that she doesn't understand God and his word. She was young when she had all that stuff happen to her, but you said she's in therapy, right?"

"Yes."

"Good. When she heals her inner child, she will be able to see everything in a different light. When you're in a state of hurt, everything is unclear and foggy. But that light will soon shine on her."

"I sure hope so."

As much as I wanted to hold Lynn's hand through the process, I knew I couldn't. If she wished to change, she would have to initiate the process and be the change she needed. I prayed that she found her way before it was too late.

CHAPTER 49
KYLAN

9:00 am Saturday

"Ky...Ky," I heard as my eyes jolted open. I looked around, confused for a second, before realizing that I was in Nelly's room.

"Morning," I said, stretching my legs that had cramped up from sitting in this small-ass computer chair all night.

"I know dang ol well you didn't sleep in that chair all night," Nelly asked, shaking her head as I stood up.

"Yep. How are you feeling?"

"I'm ok." She shrugged, sighing. "I'm sorry I had you worried about me."

"You don't have to apologize for that, Nelly."

16 hours earlier... 5:00 pm

I pulled up to my house and hopped out of the car, checking my watch, seeing that I had thirty minutes to get ready before heading down the street to Tamera's for her housewarming. I still needed to get in the shower and find something to put on. I put my key in the door and froze as I heard sobbing nearby. I hurried and locked the door and rushed into the living room, where I saw Nelly in the dark sitting on the couch with a bottle of wine sobbing.

"Neliah, what's wrong?" I asked, kneeling in front of her. She shook her head and continued sobbing. "Talk to me, Nelly." I removed the bottle from her hands and sat it on the coffee table.

"I'm tired, Ky...."

"Of?"

"Everything." She cried harder.

"I don't understand. Talk to me, Nelly. What's going on?"

"I don't wanna be here no more, Kylan. I'm tired of this life. Why me?"

"Why not you? What would I do without you, Neliah?" I asked with my voice cracking. "You're my best friend."

"I just wanna feel normal, Kylan. I'm tired of being this way. All these meds and shit." She screamed, knocking over the bottle of wine that crashed to the floor and broke.

"I get it, Nelly. I understand exactly how you feel, fuck them meds, fuck that depression, fuck all that shit." I said, grabbing her into a hug and wiping my tears that fell. Nelly fought against my hug for a few seconds before she finally stopped and went still. A few minutes later, I heard light snores coming from her. Carefully getting up, making sure I didn't step on any of the glass, I picked Neliah up bridal style and carried her up the stairs and into her room, where I tucked her in and then made myself comfortable in her computer chair where I dozed off.

"Wanna go get some breakfast? My treat." Nelly asked with an uneasy smile.

"I could eat." I nodded my head. "I'm a go shower and shit, gimme about forty-five minutes."

"You mean an hour and forty-five minutes? It takes you longer to get ready than any woman I know." She laughed.

"Oh, whatever!" I laughed as I walked out of her room. "If I'm not ready in forty-five minutes, breakfast is on me."

6:00pm

Come open the door. I text Tamera before getting out of my car and grabbing the boatload of bags I had in the trunk.

"What is all of this." She laughed in a nighty short set with a wine glass in her hand, waving at the bags.

"It's your housewarming gifts," I said, sitting those bags down in the foyer and turning to go back to my trunk for the rest.

"Kyyyy.." She whined as I came back in with more gifts. "You didn't have to do all of this."

"I know," I said, closing the door behind me. "But you do more than enough for me."

"Awwww…" She said, wiping a fake tear. "You're so sweet! Let me see what you got!" She said as she picked up the bags, taking them into the living room.

"Ooooo, this is NOICEEEE!" She yelled out, mocking Tiffany Haddish in Girl's Trip.

"Yo ass is crazy." I laughed as she continued going through her gifts.

"What have you been sipping on cause your ass is lifted."

"Little bit of wine, little bit of hennnnnn…." She said in a sing-song voice.

"Aw hell Nah." I shook my head. "You ain't suppose to mix the two."

"I'm at home. I'll be alright. I'm just a little tipsy, so I'm good."

"Yeah, alright. We will see."

"I promise I'm good. This ain't my first rodeo." She winked at me.

"Matter of fact, let me get you a cup!"

"Nah, I'm good. "I shook my head, and she pouted.

"Don't be a party pooper. You already missed my housewarming."

"Mannn...I told you why."

"Mmh hmmm…" She rolled her eyes playfully as she pushed her curly fro from her eyes.

"Ugh, go get me a damn cup," I said, waving her off.

"Yay!" She squealed as she hopped off of the couch and skipped into the kitchen, looking like a big kid.

This was my first time in her house, and it was very nice. The oversized furniture and decor all looked great together.

"Here you go." She said, passing me a cup.

"Thanks. You hooked it up in here. It's nice as shit."

"Yeah? Come on, let me give you a tour."

I got up off the couch and followed her around her house, nodding at how tight everything was set up. Tameras house had a homely feel that made you feel welcomed. It smelled like apples and cinnamon and was clean as hell, even in the kid's rooms. Finally, we made it back into the living room and chilled out on the couch, sipping on our drinks.

"Have you eaten?" She asked, looking over at me.

"Not since this morning. You cooked?"

"Yeah, I always make too much even when I'm home alone. I've gotten accustomed to cooking for four people."

"Wasting food and shit, what you cook?"

"Uh, some chicken parmesan, mashed potatoes, a side salad, and some garlic bread. Is that cool?"

"Shid, that's better than cool," I said, rubbing my stomach. She laughed and stood up, going into the kitchen, coming back a few minutes later with a plate that smelled good as hell.

"I have water, some juice, and some flavored water if you want."

"A bottle of water is cool," I said before digging in. I had to close my eyes and groan. The damn chicken parmesan was so crispy and juicy that it made my damn mouth water.

"Here you go, how is it?" She asked as she sat the bottle of water next to my plate on the table. I rolled my eyes and did a cross over my heart as I chewed and swallowed.

"Damn, I ain't know you can burn like this, oooo weeee," I said before taking a forkful of the mashed potatoes and falling back on the couch.

"Mannnn."

She burst out laughing. "You a damn fool. It ain't that good."

"It is. I promise I'm a picky eater, and I don't eat everybody's food, but you gon have to fight me to stop me from coming to dinner every night." I wasn't playing either.

"That's cool. I'll have enough." I nodded and finished my food. Then, after Tamera offered seconds, I demolished that too.

"Damn...I ain't had food that good in a while." I said as I stretched out on her couch. "I got the itis now."

"That's when you know the food hit. Hand me your plate so I can get it cleaned." She said, reaching for my plate that I pulled further away from her.

"I got it. You cooked, so I'll clean."

"It's no big deal. It's just one plate."

"Exactly. Just one plate, so I got it." I said, getting up and going into the kitchen where I washed the plate off, dried it, and put it back in the cabinet. When I made my way back into the living room, Tamera had gotten comfortable on the couch and was sitting Indian-style as she scrolled through HBO Max.

"What's good on here?" I asked, sitting back down.

"Not much. You can find something." She said, tossing me the remote that I caught midair.

"I barely watch tv for real. I only catch shit when Neliah is watching something at the crib."

"That's the sister that stays with you, right?"

"Yeah, she's the reason I had to cancel yesterday."

"Everything ok?" She asked, turning towards me.

"Yeah, for now…." I nodded, turning back towards the tv.

"Wanna talk about it?"

"I mean, it's not much to say. She was having an episode. She suffers from depression and bipolar disorder and was just flipping out, so I had to make sure she was ok."

"I'm sorry," Tamera said apologetically.

"You ain't got nothing to be sorry for. It's only one person to blame for the shit me and my sisters go through, and it ain't you." I said, pointing at her with the remote.

"Who do you feel is to blame?"

June 2004

"Aye, I'ma head to the house. I got too much money on me and don't wanna get caught slipping." I told Doc as I pushed off the wall we were standing on.

"You got it nigga, need me to walk yo ass home?" He joked as he dapped me up.

"Fuck you, bitch!" I laughed, play swinging at him before I walked off towards my house. Ever since Doc put me on a year ago, I had been making more money than I ever thought I could see. I was able to keep the bills paid, so we didn't get put out. I made sure my sisters and I had clothes and shit that we needed. I quickly became the man of the house even though I was the youngest. My mother had long ago checked out, and she even stopped going to work. All she did was stay in her room and only came out to piss; most times, we had to go in there and spoon feed her just to make sure she ate. Her doctor swore that the meds he put her on should be helping her to get up more and be vivacious, but it seemed like all she did was just sleep. Jojo swore mama wasn't swallowing her pills and that she didn't want to get better.

"You.." I called out as I stepped into the house. Since I lived with all women, that was my way of letting them know there was a man in the house just in case they needed to get dressed or something.

"Hey, Ky!" Neliah said as she peeked her head out of the room she shared with Jedediah.

"What's good? You need anything?" I asked, kissing her forehead.

"No, I'm ok." She smiled as I walked into my room.

"Alright, bet. It's some food in there?" I asked out loud as I went into my closet to stash my money in another shoebox.

"Yes, Fran cooked before she left for work. It's good too." She laughed.

"Oh shit! I'ma have to sit down and eat for a minute. Who in the bathroom?" I asked, hearing the shower run.

"I don't know. I thought it was Micha, but I'm not sure." She shrugged before going back into her room.

"Nah, it ain't Micha. I saw her about thirty minutes ago before I came here." I said as I knocked on my mother's door before opening it. She wasn't in bed where she usually was, so it must've been her in the bathroom. I wouldn't have been so alarmed if this was normal for my mother, but it wasn't ever since Lake left Sidney, and Fran typically had to fight to get her cleaned up.

"Ma! You good?" I asked, beating on the bathroom door. I had my head to the door listening for an answer, and when I didn't get any, I jiggled the knob to the door to find that it was locked.

"Ma!" I yelled, beating on the door again. When I didn't get an answer, I stood back and brought my foot up, kicking the door.

"What's going on? Why are you kicking the door?" Neliah asked. I ignored her and kicked the door until it flew open. I almost fainted when I saw all of the blood on the shower floor and the bathroom rugs. My mother was balled up naked in the corner of the shower, not moving. I ran into the shower stall, cold water beating over me, and turned my mother over.

"Ma!" I yelled. Her lips moved, but I heard nothing from her. I grabbed her arm to see if I could feel a pulse.

"Kyyyyyy," Neliah screamed, crying. "What's wrong with mommy? Is she dead?"

"Call nine one one now!" I screamed as my tears blended in with the shower water that fell on my head.

"Mama, why you do this shit?" I asked, holding her hand. I felt her lightly grip my hand as her lips moved, but I couldn't make out anything she was saying.

"Why would you do this shit?" I asked over and over again. I could hear Nelly screaming in the background, but I couldn't take my eyes away from my mama. Finally, the paramedics came in what seemed like forever when in reality, it was only a few minutes, but even after they took her, I was stuck in the same position, crying, asking why.

"I'm so sorry you had to witness that," Tamera said, wiping her tears that fell.

"Why the hell are you crying?" I asked jokingly to lighten the mood.

"Because that made me emotional just thinking about it. How is your mom doing now?"

"She's cool, I guess. I don't deal with her like that." I shrugged.

"I understand." Tamera nodded her head. I picked the remote back up and settled on Why Did I Get Married. Twenty minutes in, Tamera was knocked out, and I fell asleep shortly after her.

"Mmmm…" I moaned out. I had a dream that I was being kissed all over my neck while my dick was being jacked. I hadn't had a wet dream since I was a little nigga, so I knew it had to be that damn Hennesey kicking in.

"Shit.." I groaned, tossing my head to the side, trying to wake myself up. When I did, I almost threw Tamera off me as she sat in my lap doing just what I dreamed about. "Yo! What are you doing?"

"What does it feel like I'm doing?" She asked, shrugging my hands off of her and leaning back in to kiss me again.

"Nah, man, you're drunk," I said with a frown turning my head.

"Kylan, I'm not fucking drunk." She rolled her eyes. "I didn't have that much to drink."

"Still." I smacked my teeth. "I'm not no rebound ass nigga shorty."

"Ok? Why would you be a rebound?"

"You just beat up your husband a few days ago, and now you trying to jump on my dick? Nah.." I said, picking her up and sitting here next to me.

"Ky…" She sighed. "That wasn't because I want him. It was the principle. That's the house I bought. That's it. Do you think you're rebound material?"

"I know I'm not," I said cockily.

"Then ok, don't blame it on me. Just say you don't want me in that way." She said with an attitude as she moved further away on the couch.

"It's not like that shorty, and you know it. I fucks with you, but I ain't tryna be in no shit."

Tamera didn't respond. She just nodded and turned her attention to the tv. I could tell that her ego was bruised, and that wasn't what I was trying to do. I just had to make sure she understood I wasn't no rebound to nobody.

“I’m not a rebound,” I said as I reached over and pulled her back towards me until she was back on my lap.

“I know, Kylan. I wouldn’t do that to you.” She said, looking at me in my eyes. I nodded and pushed her fro out of her face and leaned forward, kissing her. Tamera hesitated before she relaxed and kissed me back, sticking her tongue in my mouth. I received her fully and stuck my hand under her pajama top, squeezing her full ass titties, causing her to moan in my mouth.

“That feels good.” She said before she kissed me on my neck. I sighed as my dick grew harder than Chinese arithmetic in my jeans, feeling like my shit was about to break. Tamera ground against me, and I could feel how warm her pussy was getting. I pulled one hand from under her shirt and stuck it in the panty of her shorts, seeing that she ain’t have any panties on.

“Where your panties at, huh?” I asked, circling her clit.

“I..-oooooh...been in the house...mmmm..all day.” She moaned out as she threw her head back.

“Yeah, you better have been.” I pulled my other hand from under her shirt and grabbed her neck as my fingers attacked her pussy. I stuck two fingers in her and did the come here motion feeling her juices gush all over my head. “You hear that shit...sounds just like fucking mac and cheese.”

I moved my hand from her neck and grabbed her ass with my free hand.

“You better cum hard too.”

“I….am..” She said as she yelled out my name. “Kyyyyy, pleaseeeee..”

"Please, what?" I asked, pulling my fingers out and strumming her clit.

"You gonna make me cum so hard." She whimpered, leaning forward kissing my lips.

"Do that shit then," I said, sticking my tongue in her mouth as I pressed down on her nub right as her body began to shake. I pulled my hands out of her shorts and sucked my fingers before kissing her again. "You taste so fucking good."

"I bet you do too." She said, breathy, relaxing against my chest.

"You alright?" I asked in amusement, hearing her ragged breathing.

"I am…." She said before leaning up and kissing me again. "Take these off…." She spoke against my lips, tugging at my pants.

"You sure you want to go there? Once we cross that line ain't no turning back." I asked, looking at her once again.

She nodded. "I'm sure."

I tapped her butt, and she stood up, allowing me to get up. Once I was up,

I unbuckled my jeans, letting my jeans hit the ground. Tamera bit her lip and pulled her pajama top over her head, leaving just her shorts. "Sit down." She demanded of me, pushing me back onto the couch.

"You got it." I nodded as she stroked my dick that was sticking through the slit of my boxers. "Mmmm."

Tamera smiled and leaned forward, sticking her tongue out and teasing the head of my dick as she jerked me slowly.

"Shit.." I groaned. I looked at her, and she smirked before she opened her mouth and swallowed my dick. At that point, I couldn't do shit but throw my head back and grip Tameras fro. She had put my dick in the back of her throat and did some shit that felt amazing. Tamera had my dick soaked and had my toes curling in my fucking socks.

"Tamera, what the fuck.... You about to make me nut."

"Nut then, daddy." She said, popping my dick out of her mouth making a popping noise before putting it back in her throat.

"Fuck!" I yelled out. "I'm not trying to nut in your mouth. I wanna nut in that pussy."

Tamera slowly pulled my dick out of her mouth, letting spit hang from her lip before she stood up and pulled her pajama shorts down. I stared at her body in amazement for her to have had twin boys you wouldn't have known. The only thing that gave her away was the c-section scar on her abdomen. Tamera climbed over me and propped her feet on both sides of me before she lowered herself on my dick which was standing tall like the Burj Kalifa. Tamera only had the head in, and I almost came just from contact. Her pussy was so snug, warm, and wet that I had to bite my lip to stop myself from screaming out.

"Oh fuck, Kylan, it's so fucking thick and juicy." She said as she sank to the base of my dick and paused. I pulled Tamera by her neck and sucked on her lips and tongue as she slowly ground against me moving her lips back and forth in a slow motion. I don't know what you called that shit, but it felt so damn good.

"This pussy is so fucking good." I groaned, throwing my head back. Tamera moaned and started kissing and sucking on my neck as she began to bounce up and down on my dick slowly. I could hear her juices seeping out, and that shit was making me harder than I already was. I gripped Tameras ass with both of my hands and held her in place as I began fucking her from underneath.

"Ky…" She screamed out. "Oh my God."

"Mmmhmmm.." I said as I continued deep stroking her from underneath.

"Please…" She yelled against my neck.

"Please, what?"

"I'm about to cum." She yelled.

"I'm about to cum with you." I groaned out as she began to bounce wildly against me. All you could hear was her juices and our bodies slapping against one another before we both came hard.

"Uhhh Ky...my hair…." She said out of breath, chuckling.

"Oh shit, I'm sorry," I said as I let her hair go that I was gripping hard as hell.

"It's fine. I liked it." She said seductively against my neck before she started kissing me again.

"You trying to get round two started?" I asked, moaning.

"If you can hang." She said as she began bouncing on my dick again.

"You damn right I can," I said, smirking.

CHAPTER 50
BEN LEE

I pressed send again, dialing Tamera for what felt like the one-hundredth time that night. I needed her to answer the phone so that she could get to Aerca and make sure she was ok. I felt like I was about to have a panic attack and had to walk out on my balcony to get as much air in my lungs as I could.

"Hello?...Aerca?" Tamera quizzed, sounding as if I had woke her up. I cursed inwardly, looking down at my watch, realizing it was a quarter till one am.

"No, it's Ben Lee. Aerca needs you."

"What's going on? Is she ok?" I gulped and took a deep breath before telling Tamera why she needed to hurry up and get to Aerca.

Saturday Seven Pm

"Ohhhh fuck! You're so deep." Aerca cried out as I dug into her gushy tunnel from the back. This was our second session today, and I had discovered how to make her squirt, and I was quickly addicted to seeing her juices fly everywhere.

"Uh-huh...squirt for me," I said, pulling my dick out, smacking her ass, and going back in slowly.

"Ohhhhhhh shit!" She yelled out as she threw her ass back like she had a point to prove.

"Oh, you showing out, huh?" I asked, reaching around and rubbing her clit as I pounded her from the back.

"Ben...." She growled out before her body began shaking. I kept pounding, feeling her juices pour more and more just as my nut reached the tip. She squirted all over my hand, collapsing on the bed as she jerked.

"Shit, girl..." I laughed. "You almost snapped my shit off, falling forward like that."

"Shut up, Bennnn." She whined playfully, shooing me away as she lay still.

"Nah, get yo ass up. You know we got dinner at nine. It's seven sixteen now." I smacked her ass.

"Ok, ok. Let me nap for fifteen minutes. Then, I promise I will get ready at lightning speed. I'm not wearing make-up tonight." She mumbled, sounding like she was almost asleep.

"Ok, babe. You don't need that shit anyway, fine ass." I said, kissing the side of her face before she pushed me away, whining.

"Gone now..."

"Alright damn. I forget how grumpy your ass gets when you're sleepy." I laughed as I pushed off the bed. I set the alarm on my phone for thirty minutes and made my way into the shower, quickly washing and saying a quick prayer hoping that the talk I had with my mother a few weeks ago resonated with her. We had been going through this vicious cycle of her trying to control my sister and I's lives, and I wasn't dealing with it anymore.

I got out of the shower and checked on Aerca. She was sprawled across the bed butt naked with one arm above her head and the other on her side, and her mouth was wide open as her body fell and raised slowly. She was so fucking beautiful, her chocolate skin, perfect fucking features, and a body made just for me. I tip-toed into my walk-in closet and quietly got dressed in the camel muscle shirt and black pants that Aerca had purchased for me to match her dress. After spraying myself with her favorite "Sauvage by Dior" cologne, I walked out of the room and into my office to check emails and finish up a few drafts. I didn't get too far before my alarm went off, letting me know it was almost eight pm and time to get Aerca up.

"Hey, beautiful," I said, coming back into the room. She rolled over but didn't answer me. "Baby, it's time to get up."

Her eyes fluttered, and she looked around before her eyes landed on me, smiling. "Damn, I was knocked out."

"Yes, you were," I smirked. "It's almost eight. You gotta get up and get ready, baby."

"Ok." She said as she sat up, running her hands through her hair before her eyes got wide. "Ben, my fucking hair!"

"What about it?" I asked, confused. She had her hair blown out and flat ironed a few days prior, and it still looked good despite all the physical activity she had been doing.

"It probably looks a mess!" She squealed, hopping up out of bed.

"It's fine," I said, laughing as she fast-walked to the bathroom.

"You're lucky." She said, looking at me and winking. "I should be ready in less than twenty minutes. Is that enough time for us to make it to the restaurant and not be late?"

"Yes, it's only ten minutes from here, baby," I said before kissing her cheek.

"Good."

I made my way back to my office to get a bit more done. I was midway finished by the blueprint for a beauty salon when I heard light taps on my office door.

"Come on in, baby," I called out as I sat my iPad pen down. I whistled and hooted at Aerca as she stood in the doorway in a camel dress that hugged all of her curves. She looked like a beautiful sepia doll, and I wanted to bend her over and fuck her senseless right here on my desk.

"I don't know if we gon make it to this restaurant. Let me call my mama and tell her something came up." I joked, picking my phone up.

"Oh no, you don't!" Aerca laughed, snatching the phone out of my hand.

"I ain't wake up out of my nap for nothing. So bring your butt on."

"Okayyyy.." I pouted, kissing her lips a few times before letting her pull me out of my office. Once we were both in the car and on the way to the restaurant, I couldn't help but notice that Aerca was eerily quiet.

"What's wrong?" I asked, looking over at her. She was looking out of the window as if she was deep in thought.

"I don't know. What if she doesn't like me?"

"Doesn't matter." I shrugged.

"Why doesn't it?" She asked with a hint of attitude.

"Because I love the fuck out of you, so why would how she feels matter?"

"It doesn't, but it does complicate things." She said with a small smile.

"Not if we don't let it. Think positive, baby." I said, lifting her hand, bringing it to my mouth, kissing it.

She nodded her head and continued looking out of the window until we reached the restaurant. Once there, I parked in front of the valet and walked around to open Aercas door, who was shaking lightly.

"Baby, look at me," I said softly. She looked at me with her doe eyes that held a whirlpool of questions. "Everything will be fine. I promise."

"I know, baby." She said, giving me a small smile before kissing me lightly and then wiping her lipstick off of my lips.

I gave the valet my keys and led Aerca inside with my hand on the small of her back.

"Hi. Welcome to Providence. My name is Patina. May I have the name of your reservation?" The hostess asked with a bright smile.

"Yes, Benjamin Suttles," I said before kissing the side of Aercas mouth.

The hostess looked down at her tablet and back up at us with a smile.

"Right this way, your party has already arrived."

I knew my mother would be there before us. One thing about my mom is that she was never on time or late. She was always early. She had to make sure she could scope the scene out so that she was in control at all times. As the hostess led us to our table, I could see my mom smiling brightly at her phone; as we neared, she sat her phone down and looked up, scanning the hostess, me, and then Aerca where her face dropped, and she quickly stood up grabbing her purse.

"Here you are. Your waiter Joseph will be with you shortly." The hostess said before turning around and leaving.

"Hi Mother, you look beautiful," I said, kissing her cheek as she stood there stoically. "Mother, this is Aerca, Aerca this is my mother, Mrs-"

"Jesus, Benjamin! Another darkie?"

……...To be Continued...

About the Author

Reigning from Cleveland, Ohio, Martina M. Lanier is a 32-year-old mom of three daughters who have always had a passion for writing. Ever since a kid, she excelled in creative writing, even being in a statewide spelling bee. Martina has her hands in many genres and not just adult romance. She has written children's books that focus on social needs, safety, and emotions. You can find her books on Amazon, Barnes and Noble, and websites like Target.com, Walmart.com, and others.

You can find her on instagram **@JustwriteMartina**

www.ingramcontent.com/pod-product-compliance
Lightning Source LLC
LaVergne TN
LVHW010601100826
845148LV00014B/2798

* 9 7 8 1 7 3 7 2 2 5 7 2 0 *